Praise for Lamar Herrin's Writing

The Rio Loja Ringmaster
"There is throughout this fine and scrupulous book an irresistible pull toward the imaginary."
—Geoffrey Wolff, NY *Times Book Review*

"Herrin writes with authority, a promise both rare and important. Best of all, he reaches beyond his immediate subject to confront issues of significance: love and competition and savagery, the monomania of obsession, the possibility within each human being for healing change. *The Rio Loja Ringmaster* becomes at last a celebration, and that is the finest thing I know for a novel to do."
—Richard Rhodes, *Chicago Tribune Book World*

Fractures
"Here's an environmental novel that does just what you want it to do: Frame an important contemporary debate in profoundly human terms.... Plenty of readers will enjoy Herrin's book for its lustrous writing and poignant insight into the challenge of building a life worth living. But if you also want a novel that addresses a pressing political and environmental issue, *Fractures* is worth exploring."
—Ron Charles, *The Washington Post*

"Herrin's deeply contemplative examination of this contentious topic is less about the environmental fallout from an invasive destruction of the land and more about the emotional fragility of a family who feels all too deeply the loss of a way of life."
—*Booklist*, Starred Review

House of the Deaf
"Lamar Herrin redefines vengeance and innocence in *House of the Deaf*, a tale of political violence in which the life-blood of the spirit confronts the cold blood of the terrorist — a finely wrought novel of near-mystical dimension."
—William Kennedy

"The engrossing story, with its clipped, articulate style, lets us into the souls of a tormented family facing the loss of a child to violence, and it is done without sentimentality or mawkishness, building to a finale with grace and finely controlled tension."
—*St. Louis Post-Dispatch*

The Lies Boys Tell
"A work of unusual lyrical and moral beauty, of challenging metaphorical complexity."
—*The New York Times Book Review*

Romancing Spain
"[An] extraordinary love story…Herrin has plotted this book like a suspenseful novel. It succeeds as a unique love story and as an evocation of Spain: its sweeping plateaus and fragrant orange orchards, its great regional foods and attentive formalities."
—*The Louisville Courier-Journal*

The Unwritten Chronicles of Robert E. Lee
"A work of great imagination and care, unburdened by the usual conventions. Everything is here, the weather, the soil, the light— one can hear the tinny clatter of pots and pans as vanished men march into the legendary."
—James Salter

FATHER FIGURE

Father Figure

Lamar Herrin

Fomite

ISBN-13: 978-1-942515-53-1
Library of Congress Control Number: 2016943284

Fomite
58 Peru Street
Burlington, VT 05401
www.fomitepress.com

Cover art - #7, Acrylic on acid-free matboard, 33" H by 46" W
© Lavendier Myers

For my grandchildren,
Waira Catalina Herrin Manrique and Joaquin Herrin Marks.
And in memory of Hal Herrin.

"No god. Why take me for a god? No, no.
I am that father whom your boyhood lacked
And suffered pain for lack of. I am he."

The Odyssey
(trans. Robert Fitzgerald)

Part One

"Those Towns Down There"

I

THE STORY WAS TOLD that when my father was within days of being called up to the Big Leagues to play alongside his college teammate—and future Hall of Famer—Lou Appleton, my mother met with my grandmother and together they put a stop to it. My grandmother was a saintly, white-haired woman, who had a puffy little white-haired spitz, which sat like a ball of yarn in her lap, and my mother was a devoted and spirited young wife, and the story had it that they teamed up and informed my father that a baseball career was not for him. The culprit was Babe Ruth. My mother and grandmother sat out under the pecan trees in my grandparents' yard, and in the absence of my grandfather, a man of unalterable command, told my father he was not going to risk the shame that came from associating with a bunch of carousing and indiscriminately glad-handing ballplayers, led by the Babe. Ruth was a daily fixture in the news back then, and my mother and grandmother would have seen the beery shine in the Babe's eyes and the meaty glow in his lower lip and the bulge of a gut he carried in a swagger everywhere he went and said, No! Even if those were Depression days, there were better ways to make a living. There was a town of right-minded folk waiting to employ my father if only to repay the pleasure he had given them, not just on the baseball diamond but on every other field of play, and my father went along. He loved and honored his mother, and the town honored him for that. His marriage to my mother was a match the town had thrilled to, and perhaps he thought that together his wife and his mother voiced the town's will. He repressed, just enough, his irrepressible spirits and renounced all professional ambitions in the game.

Still, it is hard to imagine. He was said to have been so good. He played center field but was possessed of a genial range of movement, and a favorite play of his was to race into second to pick off an unsuspecting base runner while the shortstop and second baseman were otherwise occupied. He hit to all fields. He could throw to the bases with a sharper and more ringing authority than opposing batters could hit line drives. He ran the bases with a calculated abandon. He slid in and jumped up. A baseball field was something like a brightly lined and glowing green stage for who he'd become, and he took an exultant pleasure in the game. Yet the story was told that he'd put up no fight and allowed his mother and wife to take it away from him.

Told by whom?

I have an uncle-aged cousin, Hugh Langley, and it was he who told the story to me. But my sister Judy had heard it, too. Louise Langley, my father's maiden sister, who saw both her parents to the grave and assumed the role of family historian, gave it credibility. A story like that needed all the credibility it could get. It was not like my grandmother—so saintly—and not like my mother—so supportive—to make any unilateral demands of my father, so… gifted, so much the self-justifying natural in every activity he undertook. No more baseball. Time to step onto more respectable fields of play. As a young man my father had had curly fair hair, rounded cheekbones and ruddy cheeks, green eyes sprinkled with brown, a cleft chin—and a grin, which in towns like my father's went a long way. A grin was a young man's prize possession. The right sort of grin won you friends, admirers. "Disarming" is the word. But only one of the words. "Captivating" is another. The right sort of grin won you adherents, followers. My father sat there in a deep-slanted garden chair, under my grandparents' pecans—a sandy yard, with last season's husks scattered on the ground—and took his wife's and mother's demands grinningly. He wouldn't have put up a fight. He wouldn't have tried to argue his way out of the socially correct corner they'd backed him into. I have no doubt he could have. He could have crossed a leg, made himself at home, broadened the grin to include them, and led them to believe that the Babe and his cohorts were something like the rowdy preliminary act to a genuinely edifying main event, which awaited the right man to headline. What was "big" about the Big Leagues was that they gave you a bigger chance to make a fool of yourself, until—he could have easily convinced them, that man I never knew—some bountiful someone came along who brought the joy of it all back and allowed a stadium full of spectators to take their portion of that joy away with them.

My cousin Hugh, who'd lived through the hell of Okinawa, brought that joy-inspiring version of my father home from the War. By then my father had been shipped back from the Battle of the Bulge himself, minus his left leg. I had just been born. My sister was three. By the time I was old enough to consult memories of my own, my father had begun his own war, which required a daily sort of capitulation from the town. I remember the town obliging.

Hugh, who had a rosy but narrow-eyed face, as if he'd been squinting into the sun far too long, said, "Jaybird, your father was a four-letter man. Now, you don't hear much about that anymore, everyone wants to be a specialist nowadays, but his senior year in college your father captained the baseball, football, basketball and track teams. And you know what that means, don't you? It means that his teammates put him up there. It wasn't just some easily impressed folk in a small, sports-crazy town. Think about it. Bob Langley. He didn't campaign for the honor. On the contrary. They pleaded with him: Come be our captain, please! That's the man I want you to set your mind on. I close my eyes and see him drifting back and drifting back on a fly ball out there in center field. He was my hero. I couldn't imagine a fly ball falling until he'd settled under it. He could have given a whole country something to believe in, but chose to please his mother instead, and the woman of his dreams."

About the woman of Bob Langley's dreams, Hugh told another story, and this one my mother herself had hinted—on those rare occasions when something of the coyness of her girlhood found her and she let it show—might be true. Judy discounted it. Sick of beguiling tales from the other side of that great divide that had been the War, Judy married and moved away and advised me to do the same.

Hugh claimed—the last time when he'd given up money-making in the city and had gone to the mountains—that my mother seduced my father through the rearview mirror of a Model-A Ford with a rumble seat in back. "Seduced" was not the word he used. This was meant to be charming story, but when Hugh told it he conveyed that seductive moment so well it became a bit unnerving, too. Mother had been something of a tomboy. Her father was a college professor in an adjoining town, but she had two older brothers to keep up with, one of whom, Uncle Weldon, took a special pleasure in introducing his sister to the semi-forbidden. There were no such things as drivers' licenses back then, and although girls drove they did so only if properly attired and accompanied. Uncle Weldon taught his kid sister to drive so that she could chauffeur him and his dates around town. This might or might not include detours down lovers' lanes. Hugh didn't know how successfully that service Mother provided for her brother had turned out—after all, Uncle Weldon was no uncle of his—but word must have gotten around for it later transpired that an older friend of my mother's named Claire Goltz had a date with the most desirable boy in town, and this boy—my father—lacked a driver for the Langley family car. The friend with whom my father exchanged driving duties happened to have been sick. Hugh made it seem that driving around town on temperate summer evenings was the only way young people went on dates back then, and certainly Claire Goltz would have seen it that way, for she took it on herself to find a driver rather than risk losing this date of a lifetime with Bob Langley. She recruited my mother, three years her junior.

Hugh spent time describing Claire Goltz. She had round eyes, round cheeks, sparkling lashes, and curls strategically positioned around her face. Flapper-styled hair and a bow-lipped mouth. She was sophisticated and single-minded. In comparison, her younger lanky friend might have just climbed down from a tree. As Claire saw it, my mother was something of a protégé, and Claire was willing to give her a good lesson in how to hook and land a man. In exchange, all my mother had to do was drive and, as instructed, to take certain curves hard so that back in the rumble seat Claire might be thrown into Bob Langley's arms, and to take stretches down dark, honeysuckle-scented lanes as slowly as wheels could be made to turn. Claire drew a map of the town and its outlying roads that, if followed in the right order and at the right speed, should take the entire evening. Her younger friend should study it for it was as good as a seduction manual. For the detail in the flesh, she had only to keep her eyes on the rearview mirror.

Hugh paused at this point. We sat on the deck of a house he'd had built halfway up a mountainside at the northern end of the state. Inside, he had a bedroom with a glass ceiling and a waterbed to lie on as he floated with the stars. Hugh'd made money at everything he'd done, and made friends while he was doing it. At one time his and my father's professional paths had crossed since Hugh had been involved in designing the earliest shopping centers in our part of the state, and my father, calling in favors and playing his tips, had managed to acquire a large share of the land. Finally, Hugh had had enough and had taken what was left of a second family he'd raised and gone for a sort of spiritual regeneration to the mountains, where more money had found him. He became a realtor for other city-dwellers looking to restore their souls but held one piece of land apart for me. The day would come when I would need it. Jaybird, he called me. He spoke it with a rising inflection, a certain uplift to his voice as though he already pictured me in flight.

"Jaybird, how could poor Claire Goltz have known? Your mother probably had on an old torn shirt of her brother's. She probably had her hair combed straight back, if she'd bothered to comb it at all. Beauty marks? Little Claire Goltz-like touches up high on the cheeks, at the corner of the mouth? She didn't need them. She was only four-teen and a half. At the most fifteen. But she could drive a car and keep her eyes on the rearview mirror and either follow Claire Goltz's instructions to the tee, or, if she chose, with an opposite turn of the wheel, take Bob Langley out of Claire's arms at the decisive moment. I ask you: what was Claire Goltz thinking?"

Claire Goltz was thinking that rumble seats on balmy summer evenings were for one thing only and that that gawky creature a rear window and a car length away was about as much a threat to her as a mechanic would be were he to roll out, streaked with oil, from under the car.

Claire Goltz wasn't thinking.

The eyes in the rearview mirror—she certainly wasn't thinking about them. During the course of the evening, Bob Langley might be working to pin down the artfully elusive Claire Goltz in the rumble seat, and coming up for air would sooner or later make the mistake of looking back into the car. What would he see? It didn't make a lot of difference whether my mother swerved when she was supposed to or not, or whether Claire and Bob Langley had lovers' lane to themselves. Eyes were never gawky, never tomboyish, all elbows and knees, eyes were ageless, and according to Hugh the eyes my father saw looking back at him in the rearview mirror when he took a moment's relief from the squirming Claire were "silvery and serene, like two unblinking planetary orbs, suspended in space." From the spring-scented breezes back in that rumble seat, with maybe a little dust and gasoline mixed in, my father went to "the interstellar breezes blowing out of your mother's eyes and a coolness he could feel along the bone."

And that, according to Hugh, did it.

Hugh had done a bit of writing in his professional life, and he claimed that one of the ways he'd stayed sane in his foxhole in Okinawa, while ninety percent of his company was being destroyed, was by reciting poetry. Certainly it was poet in him who identified the closest of near misses of the Japanese machine gun fire by "the puckering sounds" the bullets made as they passed by. Many times, he claimed, he'd come close to that fatal kiss. He'd concentrated on my parents, held them before his mind's eye like some sort of devotional charm. If the world was worth going back to it was because Bob Langley and his wife were still in it. The Japanese machine gun fire puckered past his ears and he dug in.

In the green reaches of center field, Bob Langley continued to drift back and drift back, always in stride with that white ball arcing across the sky's blue. My mother's eyes hung suspended in that rear-view mirror, silvery, breeze-emitting, planetary orbs.

Mother's name was Frances Knowlton although for Hugh she was Bob Langley's lovely wife or my mother. Her friends called her Fran. Frannie I didn't often hear, perhaps only someone like Claire Goltz, puffing herself up before her big night, would have addressed my mother in that way. Frannie, keep your eyes on the rearview mirror and you'll learn a thing or two. Keep your eyes on the road but keep them on me, too. I'll dodge and I'll duck, and, as good as he is said to be, I won't let him catch me until he's given up hope. Then I'll give him a little, not much, just a little, a handful, let's say. But by that time you should be looking straight ahead.

According to Hugh I owed my existence, and Judy did, too, to Claire Goltz's presumption and to Bob Langley's unrewarded exertions and to Fran Knowlton's silvery and serene eyes in a rearview mirror. My mother didn't discount the story entirely (her eyes were a crackled china blue as the years wore on). She admitted to once driving a car that my father and a friend were passengers in. No mention of a rumble seat, or of honeysuckle-scented lanes. Aunt Louise emphatically discounted the story, perhaps not willing to picture her brother—pre-war, fully limbed, so happily sufficient unto himself—creating a public spectacle with a little tease named Claire Goltz in the rumble seat of the family car. My sister Judy said it was just another way that they—and she meant that red-clay nothing of a town devoted to its schoolboy heroes—chose to mythologize themselves, and, affecting a weariness, wondered when I was going to learn. Claire Goltz, of course, would have known the truth of the story, but the fact is I'd never heard of Claire Goltz until Hugh told me about her. There were no Goltzes in town when I was growing up. I came to believe she and her whole family had left town before the War, perhaps in disgrace, the disgrace of seeing her wiles undone by a schoolgirl of a driver with designs of her own.

Of course, there was my father. I could have asked him. I could have said, Dad, there's an old story making the rounds about how you and Mom met...but I would have gotten no further than that. When he returned from the War my father rarely used a prosthesis, almost always a crutch, and he could bring that crutch crashing down to the floor like a gavel. He was never Dad, she was never Mom, and the man in whose house I was raised would permit no reminiscences.

That left Hugh, who had a cause to defend. When he returned from the Pacific after the war, my wounded father had preceded him back in town by, perhaps, four months. But Hugh had come through before that. While a college student, with of all things a pre-theology deferment, he had enlisted in the Merchant Marines, a branch of service he could enter and leave at will. He was in the Indian Ocean, in the Suez Canal, and dodging icebergs and U-boats he was back and forth across the northern Atlantic, delivering armaments to England for the Normandy invasion. Once in a fog so dense he couldn't see the water, he was called on to steer the ship and given a single star to steer by. Back in port, he left the Merchant Marines and joined the Marine Corps itself, just in time for the last big push in the Pacific. He went from being a transporter to being a transportee, a living armament himself. But before that he'd had a week's leave and was back in his hometown. He saw his father, my Uncle Raymond, who ran the town's furniture store. Uncle Raymond had been in World War One and carried a wound like a little sunburst of scar tissue in his right shoulder. Looking up from the business he was transacting, Uncle Raymond asked coldly, Where have you been? And rather than trace his itinerary half way around the world, Hugh went in search of his father's younger brother, who would have known exactly where Hugh had been because he had sent my father the letters he had not sent Uncle Raymond, and my mother would have read those letters, too. From Australia up the Euphrates to Baghdad, through the Suez Canal to Alexandria. Along the Mediterranean to Gibraltar, Casablanca. Back and forth across the Atlantic to Old England. But my father wasn't at home. My father, who'd been a college graduate and sent to work as an expediter in a B-29 bomber plant, had, as the War entered its decisive stage, all but bolted and demanded he be allowed to fight in the last push against Hitler. Perhaps he wanted to avenge his brother Raymond's wounding. Perhaps the call to action was too strong to resist. It was not like him, but who behaved according to script back at that time? He left a wife and a two-year old daughter behind. Aware of none of this, Hugh had knocked on the door and the woman he referred to as my mother or his idolized uncle's wife appeared. The world was still at war. She would have shaken her head. Gone, she uttered. And Hugh, when he'd found his voice, would have told her, But he will come back.

The ages can be confusing here. My father was the youngest of six children. Uncle Raymond and his brother Edward were the oldest, and both had served in the Great War. Hugh was Raymond's oldest child, and shortly, a matter of months, after he was born his mother died, perhaps of lingering complications from the birth-giving itself, it was never clear. That Uncle Raymond would attribute his young wife's death to Hugh's arrival in the world was a hard blow, but Uncle Raymond was a grudge-bearing, taciturn man and his son Hugh was anything but. My grandmother, the saintly white-haired woman with the powder puff of a dog, gave birth to yet another child after my father named Millie, but at the age of four Millie died of diphtheria, which brought that generation of Langley children to an end. My father was only eight years older than his nephew Hugh, perhaps for hero-worshipping an ideal difference in ages. My mother, Fran, was only five years older. A five-year age difference would enable Fran Langley to mother Hugh when he needed it, while continuing to stand beside her husband as half of the most glamorous pairing that any town thereabouts could offer. Back in town, between theaters of war himself, Hugh knocked on Bob and Fran Langley's door and was told that his hero was gone and his hero's wife, judging by the stunned and bereft look Hugh saw on her face, felt herself to have been abandoned, and his first reaction was to protest: Why were they fighting this war if not to keep Bob and Fran Langley safe from harm?

As best I can determine, my father was completing his basic training when cousin Hugh came through town. My father would cross the Atlantic in October of 1944, landing in Cherbourg, France. Hugh would train to die on the beaches of Okinawa in the spring of '45, and if he survived that assault at any number of sites in mainland Japan. The big league baseball season that year was a sad semblance of what it once had been. It was deemed worth playing if only to offer an encouraging continuity to the folks left at home, but many of the sluggers and ace hurlers had gone off to serve. Teams were down to the dregs. It would reach the point that the Saint Louis Browns would play a one-armed man in the outfield. A one-armed man, an inspiration, surely, a hero in his own right, who, after ranging back on a fly ball, would have to retrieve the ball from his glove and tuck his glove under the stump of his amputated arm before making his throw into the infield. The world would come roaring back, but there was a time when everybody was putting on a brave face to face the dread of having nothing to come back to, which was about the time that Fran Langley had shaken her head and, as an act of commiseration, consolation, and as a balm for her own sinking spirits, invited her husband's nephew to step through the door.

II

M Y SISTER JUDY was fond of musing—although "musing" may be too contemplative a word: Once you cut the tether to the town where you were born, you can end up absolutely anywhere in the world, and you have no idea where that might be. Who would have thought I would be spending twenty-five years of my life here? No one. Isn't that wonderful and strange? No one. All it took was leaving that town, breaking clear of its gravitational field. You know what I mean, Jay, don't you? It's that first struggle, that first push. After that you can be anywhere. You can be in Hong Kong, you can be in Africa. I've seen islands in the Florida Keys, uninhabited, just the right size. The most insignificant point on the map. All it takes is cutting that tether and making that first big push. After that a case can be made for any place. If not here, somewhere else. That's what that river out there's for.

The river was a lovely glassy river that flowed by her kitchen window with one broad current, as though of one mind, and after snaking through a number of states, poured into the Atlantic at the

Chesapeake Bay. It had a long, snaking Indian name. Once, before railroads began to do the work, it had been a shipping artery, and perhaps farther downstream some town to town shipping still got done, but the river had silted in in too many spots, become scenic rather than serviceable, and now it was mostly fishing boats or weekend canoers I'd see drifting by. The kitchen window we looked out of belonged to a carriage house, which in turn belonged to a large turreted Italianate house my sister and her husband had once owned. A broad lawn sloped down to the river. They'd raised a daughter in this house. Then the daughter, with barely a tether-tug of her own, had gone, soon followed by the husband. The price of the husband's departure had been the house, which my sister sold but with the unusual condition that she be allowed to live in, if no longer own, the carriage house, down closer to the river. The carriage house's loft she made into her bedroom, with another smaller room for a guest, and when the river rose out of its banks, as it did every so often, she remained high and dry and perfectly positioned to enjoy the show. There was yet a third floor to the carriage house, which she might also have converted. That would have given her four windows worth of light, instead of two. In addition, there was a lovely fantail window at the peak of the front façade, whose light was going to waste. On the back half of the second floor, the only window was the one in the kitchen opening up onto the river, and when I asked her why she didn't cut out others and, while she was at it, enlarge the sitting room a bit and add at least another larger bedroom on that third floor, she said, One guest at a time, please. More rooms, more light and she might attract a family, and that wasn't why she was here. The river was lovely, in every season, but the loveliness of the river was not why my sister was here, either. The town, once wealthy, had been nicely preserved, especially the brick buildings along Front Street, but the historial awareness evident in the town was not a reason my sister was here either.

She walked down what was an extension of Front Street into the business district of the town almost every day, to make a purchase or two or just to pace off her space. She was tall. She'd gotten our father's height and maybe something of our mother's, too. And she was thin. And fit. She had an erect bearing. It made no difference what she wore, when she walked down the streets of the town it was as if she were staking a claim, which no one disputed. But she didn't belong to the town. She might have lived there twenty-five years and she might have even taken her turn on certain town boards, but she lived in the carriage house of a house that had once been hers because she didn't live somewhere else. She was in no way the town eccentric. She was clear-headed and well-spoken. After a prolonged period in an eastern city, she and her husband had discovered the town, the house, and the river and concluded it would be a perfect place to raise their daughter. Which they'd done. Husband and daughter had left, and Judy was where she was because she hadn't gone somewhere else. It was baffling talking to my sister, but she didn't utter an unclear word.

"Jay," she said, "you're a fool. You stayed there until the man died, and now you haven't got the strength or willpower to leave."

"Yet, here I am," I said.

"No, you're not."

I wasn't going to argue the point since when my sister talked about being in a place she meant something different from almost anybody else in the world. Instead, I said, "You'd be surprised how many people didn't come to the funeral."

"I'm his daughter, and I didn't go. Why should I be surprised?"

"They'd loved him and then feared him, and for a good half century they paid him a sort of ransom for having loved him too much. You'd also be surprised at who did come."

"Would I? Let's see... How about an old ballplayer buddy of his? Somebody who should have been dead twenty-five years ago, but wasn't. An old salt of the ballpark, one of the old all-time greats. Somebody like that?"

"You read about it."

"Sorry."

"Word came downriver."

"That river talks another language."

"Lou Appleton came."

"Greek to me."

"Hall of Famer. Two-time batting champ. Teammate of Dad's in college. Who somehow managed to outlive him. Bandy-legged and gnomish now, you've got to picture him come hobbling up between the gravestones."

"Who said, 'Ole Bob...Ole Bob...could have been one of the all time greats.'"

"Lou Appleton actually played in an old-timers' game a couple of years ago. Managed to get good wood on the ball."

"And probably peed in his diaper he was so happy. Jay... Jaybird..." my sister shook her head and released a long, mostly for show sigh.

"Which reminds me, Billy Langley and his family were there."

"Billy Langley?"

"Hugh's oldest son."

My sister shook her head again. "I don't see a face."

"No reason you should, even though Dad employed him for a while. He looked nothing like Hugh, so round and rosy. Had a sort of thin, sharp face, a little rodent-like. You do remember Hugh? He was there too."

Unless she performed a daily exercise to wipe her memory clean, scour and scrub, scrub and efface, until only the most stubborn of lineaments were left, she would not have forgotten Hugh. She said, "Anybody else?"

"Yes, a man named Wallace Keever, who lives downstate. Saw the notice of Dad's death in the state paper and drove two hundred miles up for the funeral. Actually, a nurse drove him up. He said he had no idea, couldn't believe it. He'd thought Bob Langley had died in the Ardennes. The snow had been up to their knees. They were crossing a cow pasture, with German snipers said to be in the surrounding forest. By the time they got to the forest themselves, Dad had disappeared, and Wallace Keever, the last man to have seen him, the last buddy, fellow platoon member, teammate, whatever you want to call him, had begun to grieve. Said he saw the obit in the paper and it was as if Dad had climbed out of the grave—only to fall back in."

Her defenses up, Judy did not respond. We sat out beneath the trees along the river in the deep slanted chairs they called Adirondack up here, but which could very well have been the same garden chairs—just otherwise named—that my grandmother and mother and father had sat in down there, out under the pecans, when Bob Langley's life had been directed away from the ball diamond down a more respectable path, and let the river flow by. A body of water flowing as one. No main thrusting current and little trailing currents off by the shore—just a broad, steady, glassy flow taking the green of the trees on the hills rising out of the opposite bank for its coloring. If you were so disposed, the water could have a mesmerizing effect. You'd have to be on guard. If you gazed out over water like this on a prolonged basis you might forget a lifetime, day by day. Fishermen and kayakers or canoers might break the spell, restore pieces of your life, but eventually a river like this, once a smoky shipping artery, with its heave and its ho, would carry it all downstream and leave you with a bright glassy morning. Of course, Judy didn't want to leave.

She said, "Karen and I have stayed in contact, you know."

For an instant the river had its effect on me. "Karen?"

"I know you knew she married. I don't know if you know she divorced."

"No, I didn't know."

"She asks about you and I tell her. She also heard about our father's death. Don't ask me how. She has other contacts, closer to home, I suppose. But I'm her contact closest to you."

"I don't have to ask you why we're talking about Karen now. But I'm going to. Why are we talking about Karen Ambrose right now?"

"You two were together for eight years, Jay."

"That sounds about right."

"She wanted to marry you. Lord knows why. But you wouldn't leave that town, not while…"

"Our father?"

"Not while Bob Langley was alive."

"That oversimplifies it, Judy."

"At the end, finally, things do get simple. You stayed there waiting for him to show you an ounce of humanity and treat you like a son. I'm guessing he never did."

"There were moments…"

"There are always moments. They don't amount to anything unless they add up to something that lasts. You know what my first memory is? It's of him. Actually, it's of the cardinals that flew around my bedroom window. They must have had a nest out there, or maybe there was more than one nest because there were a lot of them, and they were all bright red. The females aren't, you know, they're brown, but these cardinals were always bright red in the morning sun. They hung there, fluttering like hummingbirds, and I stood in my crib laughing and I'm sure crying, 'Burdie, burdie,' and never wanting it to end. Mother would come in, delighted she had such a happy baby, and she'd pick me up and probably sing along with me. And then my memory is of him. He would come into my baby's room very quietly and kneel down beside the crib, and before I saw him I smelled him, a smell like the sun in fall leaves, a woodsy smell, and then I'd hear the manly depth of his voice. I remember him talking to me. About the 'burdies' I suppose, and what a wonderful life we all had in store, but it's that great soothing depth in his voice I remember, and the glow he gave off. The cardinals were flashing red outside the window in the sun, and out past our yard they were making those B-29 bombers, of course, but I stood there in my crib basking in the fireside glow of my father. Do babies that age bask? I suppose they do if they have something memorable to bask in."

"This was before he went to war," I calculated. "Which means you couldn't have been more than two. I'm not sure I believe you."

"No?" she replied evenly.

"Two year olds don't have memories like that."

"I remember the birds and I remember a glow and I remember the depth in his voice."

"Like the voice of God?"

"One memory. One moment. That's all, Jay. God, if there is a God, would not have left me stranded like that."

"That's more than I had, Judy."

"Well...the 'burdies.' You can have them. I give them to you. But you have to take the B-29's with them. They're out there, too."

I heard sounds from back in the house where Judy had once lived, perhaps a hundred, a hundred and fifty feet from where we sat beside a riverside willow. The house was painted yellow, freshly painted and bright in the areas the morning sun caught. It had protruding eaves and carved brackets. There was a cupola, a widow's walk, whose panes of glass shone. From a house like this you expected a lawn or garden or some sort of cared-for extension sloping down to a river or a lake or the sea. You expected a gazebo, and there was one, perhaps a third of the distance up to the house. The carriage house was where you'd expect it to be, too, just where a river or the sea or some sort of water-borne breezes could carry the smell of horse manure and befouled hay away. The smell of the river itself was fresh but with an iron-like tinge and a trace of what had crawled or slithered or been washed up onto the muddy margin of the bank to die. All in all, a bracing odor, wind-dispersed and wind-renewed.

"I'll want to meet your neighbors before I leave," I said. "In case I need to get in contact with you and you won't come to the phone."

"I have email, Jay. A cell phone. We're not antebellum here."

"It does feel like it, you know. I assumed that was part of the place's charm. Or maybe we're not talking about the same war."

"Probably not."

"Still, I'd like to meet them. I want to picture you in somebody's vicinity."

"And in whose vicinity am I supposed to picture you?"

"Ahhh…" I conceded the point and ran through the people in town Judy might know. Finally, the Langleys in town were all dead or gone. Old family friends also gone, or permanently disaffected. There were Langleys in outlying towns, Billy Langley, for one, and Hugh Langley and other children of his were still in the mountains, and Langleys had migrated as far west as Texas, as California. A Langley, featuring himself an artist, had gone to Europe and never come back. And strictly by hearsay, I knew of one drug-offending Langley in jail. A Langley had intentionally or not set fire to herself in a house trailer, and occasionally rumors reached me of others, but a line of Langleys worthy of fighting a world war for… you'd have to go to the cemetery for that.

"Call her up, Jay, for Christ's sake."

"Why? To what purpose, Judy?"

"Just to be civil. I don't know, so you can console each other, with both of your lives in a shambles…"

"Shambles? Weren't you just telling me that I'm free now? That I finally outlasted him. That I'm alive and he's not and there's a brand new river out there you never step into twice..."

She waved the river comment off as fanciful nonsense. "Don't you have any feelings left for her?"

There was a sad plainspokenness to her voice now. She had come out of her chair and up on the armrest to face me, tensed against the chair's deep slant. These were chairs you didn't squirm around in, get up and down from. You settled in, as before a lake, a mountain range, a human destiny, and somewhere up in the Adirondacks told yourself to be content. I reached over and held her by the sinewy forearm. She looked like both of them, and neither of them. As a baby she'd been special, the darling of photographers, but there was a shadow in the set of the eyes that reminded me of mother's, and there was the hint of our father's dimpled chin, and the slow way she turned that chin toward you, as though redirecting the prow of a boat, was our father's, and she moved on the steady advancing keel our father might have if he'd not had his left tibia shattered by a German bullet and what remained of his leg amputated to above the knee. But you had to look hard and you had to catch her off guard if you hoped to see anything of that couple that had made a whole town rejoice in and then grieve its fate.

"You'll remember," I reminded her, "I said I knew why you brought the name of Karen Ambrose up. It was because I told you about a man named Wallace Keaver, the last man who knew the Bob Langley I never met and had his nurse drive him two hundred miles north to stand beside his war-buddy's grave. The father I never met,

Judy, but you did. You met him and he gave you the cardinals, and if you made that story up, who can blame you? Not me. But Karen Ambrose—"

"I'm not listening to you, Jay," my sister broke in. "Karen is not a pawn in some game."

"We were finally burying our father, Judy, and Wallace Keever—he asked me to call him 'Wally,' the way our father did—comes and just when we thought we could turn a new page digs him back up again. Tell me I'm wrong. Tell me Karen Ambrose wasn't your way to get me to walk away from that grave."

"Jay, for God's sake, stop this please!"

"Then tell me this. How can you stand it? All the stories we heard about them. Those were Depression days. Maybe that was what every town did to get by, but something tells me Bob and Fran Langley were more special than that. Maybe they were elected to uphold the town's hopes, but they carried their own special glow. Even a two-year old could remember that glow. You did. And they did no wrong. They excelled. The town survived. They were beautiful. It's not my imagination, Judy. You've seen the photographs and you've heard the stories. Even if half the stories were untrue, these were once in a lifetime people, and everybody knew it. Hugh…"

My sister groaned.

"Hugh," I repeated.

My sister groaned again, a sadder and more futile sound now, as if she knew I could wear her down, and as if she were genuinely beginning to regret having invited me north.

"What are you trying to tell me, Judy?"

"That Hugh was star struck."

"The whole town was."

"And he was in love with them."

"Who wasn't?"

"I wasn't. You weren't. Our mother became more matronly and aloof and picky in her pretensions and critical of everybody else, and our father became…there's one word and I'm not going to bother to look for another…a monster."

"You have to qualify that, Judy."

"Why? So he can thwart me in everything I try to do again? So he can shit on me again?"

"So that we can factor in all that happened to him."

"You mean his war experiences? His war wound? Other men lost legs and arms and worse than that."

For her sake I made the effort. I cleared out a space. I took a deep breath of river air. "We never saw them back then. We kept being told, but we never saw it ourselves. Is this what wars are supposed to do, go around looking for the most beautiful people on the planet and then give them two children who wake up when the war's over and can't make sense of it? A world war, of course, deserves a major disillusionment. No end to the stories, Judy. Everybody in town has one. If you stay on alert, you keep thinking you might catch flashes of the way they were, you might…" My throat closed up. I grimaced, shook my head, and breathed deeply again. "How can you stand it?"

"I got away, Jay. I came up here."

"That's the easy way out, Judy."

She turned back to the river, the valley hills across the way, took a deep breath of her own and then let it out, as if re-staking her claim. It wouldn't be long before she'd ask me to leave.

"Well, at least you had your 'burdies,'" I said.

"I made them up, Jay."

"No you didn't."

"You were right. No two-year old remembers stuff like that. I needed them so I made them up."

"You didn't."

"Make up your own burdies, Jay. Make up whatever you need and then bury the rest as deeply as the law allows. Call Karen."

"Karen?"

"Or don't."

I didn't leave that day. Those were not the last words we exchanged. And I did meet the people who had bought Judy's house and, in effect, had bought her, the curious woman in the carriage house out back, not yet an eccentric, or if an eccentric tolerably so, but who knew how long that would last? And who would buy a house on a condition like that? Wouldn't they have investigated Judy first? Run some sort of a check? Of course, they might have—it wouldn't have taken a detective, just a computer and the patience and faith that would allow one link to take you to another until a credible picture began to form. I could Google my father, I could Google Hugh. The words "monstrous" and "starstuck" would not appear. I'd get a plainer truth. Judy, I'd bet, would come out with all her sanity intact, at the high end of the sanity spectrum, my sister Judy nee Langley but now and forever more Judy Wilcox, all that she'd kept, in addition to the house, that had belonged to her ex-husband. She'd carry the name on in spite of him but, I believe, with no spite in her heart. She just preferred it to Langley.

The husband-half of the family she'd sold the house to was named Jeremy Segal. His wife's name was Rachel. Their little girl was Amy, and so on. Rachel Segal was pregnant again, and I got the impression if it went on long enough my sister would become like the aunt to them all, or the great-aunt, tall and strange and other-minded enough to take on a semi-fabulous stature. Judy had lost some of her accent, which I couldn't really hear anyway, but when I listened for it, with Jeremy Segal's ear, for instance, I could hear enough, which helped me to understand when Jeremy Segal asked about her, the curious lady back in the carriage house, where he was really coming from. It was wonderful that I had come to see her, he said, implying that not many others had. He hoped I would come back soon, implying, perhaps, a certain urgency and a certain apprehension. With no future visitors at all how long would it take before my sister's poise and civility and her measuredness took a lonely and defensive turn and she dug in against the world? Jeremy Segal worked ten miles down the road as a programmer in a manufacturing plant for military hardware, in aviation technology, I understood, and it would only be natural that he'd adopt a long and painstaking view toward an eventually explosive end and that he'd tend to see my sister, or any phenomenon that defied his immediate understanding, in that light. He wanted me to know he cared for her, and so did his family. He was young but sedentary and soft. I had already noticed he had a landscape gardening team come in to take care of the grounds and mow his lawn. He moved slowly, in a bit of a daze. He had a friendly but last-minute smile. Behind thick glasses, the definition in his brown eyes broke down. He told me he'd never mention it to my sister, whom he thought the world of, but if I ever learned that she was ready to give up the carriage house and…well… move back where she'd come from, would I let him know. The Segals would do everything they could for her then.

We exchanged phone numbers, which I was glad to get around to, but I did want him to know that while my sister hadn't exactly been the rebel in the family, she had been the one who'd struck out on her own, which for those of us who had stayed put made her… maybe just a bit "mysterious." The proof of which was that there she now sat. We glanced in her direction, back in her chair by the willow before the river but in close proximity to the carriage house. Far from mysterious, she seemed at home, but I suspected Jeremy Segal would not see her that way. She was the result of a curious programming of some sort. He was a deliberate man, not unkind, and he would puzzle her out, but at bottom, I suppose, that as father of a young daughter and a baby on the way, and with a river flowing right by their property, a river my sister showed a peculiar attachment to, it was only natural he would come to fear her.

But Judy genuinely did like it up here, and before I flew back she drove me around. Valleys, forested slopes, creeks, lush green bottom land, not a trace of a red clay bank, the remains of old mills, a covered bridge, brick houses with slate doorsteps, flaking porch railings, brick warehouses, high-steepled churches, all built right down on the margin of the country roads, all dulled with disuse; the little towns, half abandoned now, the roadhouses, almost nothing new. Glaciers had withdrawn up these valleys, my sister told me, and adventurous men and proto-entrepreneurs had claimed this land as the ice had given way. Before recorded history. Almost all the little towns had lettered iron plaques in recognition of original settlers or a skirmish of some sort in an Indian war. Recorded history. The shell of a mansion or two that every town possessed, no matter how small. The wintry look, even in spring, even in summer, these towns wore. Those weeks of blazing fall color before it all hunkered down again. The dwindling populations, the isolation, and the common fate of those who remained.

You drove from one little town to another, my sister said, and it was clear that nobody had the upper hand. The valleys narrowed, twisted this way and that. Hawks and buzzards and other birds of prey flew over them. She claimed she liked it. She'd spend days driving, in futile search of some novelty. Bright plastic ornaments in small front yards of a few elderly residents, nothing more. You could get lost again and again and always find your way home. There were schools and school buses you could get caught behind but no traffic jams as the rest of the world knew them. Just children, drably dressed, plodding back up lanes and rutted drives and trailer park entrances to living quarters that had nothing to recommend them except they gave shelter. No room for heroes here. A sane sort of sameness. "Desolation" was not a word she used, rather "a close of day," one for all, at which point she'd come back to her carriage house and the sound of water flowing by, which in no way resembled the sound of human voices gathering at night to tell old stories. Just water, dirt, occasionally the loose log, tree trunk, or a plank the river had finally worked loose from an old dock, although there couldn't have been many of those left. So far, so good, she said. I asked about friends, townspeople, fellow board members, perhaps a male friend, anybody, and she said she had them. When she needed them they appeared. I'd just have to believe her, and when my time there as her guest and, I suppose, as Jeremy and Rachel Segal's guest, too, came to an end, she slipped a piece of paper into my hand on which she had written a name and a number and told me again that I was a fool.

III

THERE WAS A PHOTOGRAPH of our parents when they were recently married. Both had winter coats on. My father wore a light-colored fedora with a dark band and my mother a cloche hat perched back on her head. They sat side by side on a low brick wall leaning into each other, the sun on their faces. My mother's playful and piquant smile showed the white of her teeth. My father was smiling, too, but with a confident, far-ranging look, as if as far as his vision extended he saw nothing to displease him. The remarkable thing about this photograph was that, in spite of what I knew to the contrary, my mother and my father looked so much alike they might have been twins. Hugh Langley had taken the picture, I had to believe, and Mother's smile was probably meant for him, while my father's far-ranging one would have included Hugh, too, as it swept out over the land. After all, it was all family. Husband and wife, uncle and cousin-aged nephew, the young wife and aunt-in-law, cousin-aged herself to the boyish young man whose camera had caught them and who under other circumstances might have been her beau. The times were bad, but there was such a generous well-being in the two people pictured there that it was not hard to believe that all trifling differences got brushed aside. It was winter but here was spring, and this was what people fortunate enough to live in that time and place in the presence of Bob and Fran Langley looked like. They looked the same. Essentially the same.

The collar to Bob Langley's overcoat was partially turned up. Fran Langley's hands rested lightly on her purse, which lay in her lap. The photograph was a bit grainy, but, if you were looking for it, you could make out the diamond ring. The last time I'd seen him, Hugh had given the photograph to me. Entering his eighties, he'd been going through his possessions and come to those he'd prized. Here was a snapshot he'd kept for all these years. In a way he'd forgotten he'd had it, but that was only because it had taken its place in the single huge edifice that was his memory of Bob and Fran Langley, as they had been back then, just as a single block of stone took its place in the enormity of a cathedral.

I recognized the low brick wall. It extended beside the porch stairs in front of my maternal grandparents' house. I knew it with a flower urn positioned out at the end, an urn which I remembered overflowing with petunias. Behind my parents was a large blurred rectangle, which, only because I'd been in the house, I knew to be the many-paned parlor window. The photograph could have been sharper, but the camera had probably been an inexpensive Brownie model and the photographer's hand might have trembled. At just the right hero-worshipping age, Hugh had happened on my parents, or he had followed them, stalked them. He wanted me to have the photograph. He did not say it was not to be shared, but he wanted me to know, to see, that even though a little blurred my mother and father back in those wintry depressed days before the War had essentially been the same. The playful and piquant smile and the far-ranging one were essentially the same. Without instructing me to do so, he expected me to study this photograph closely until I saw what he did and there would be no differences left between the two of us either. It was indeed all family. Then he'd tell me again to fly up to the mountains where a piece of land awaited me if I didn't wait too long.

Jaybird.

I studied the photograph, not until I knew the two people pictured there as parents of mine, but until I knew them as a ballplayer's ballplayer, Bob Langley, and his spirited bride, Fran Knowlton, recently converted into a Langley herself. Look at any photograph long enough, in just the right suggestible state of mind, and one day everything will turn around. You'll look from the photograph back out at the photographer. You'll see that Hugh Langley was in a hurry. He couldn't expect Bob and Fran Langley to hold their pose long. The sun was out and the season was about to turn. It was easy to picture Hugh Langley, the pink of his face bright with expectation, his black curls rippling up off his forehead as though in a wind he was continually plunging into. He'd stopped with the motion still on him and taken this picture, and as soon as Bob Langley had heard the camera's click he'd told his nephew to get his ball and glove. It would be like throwing a ball to a dog, who never failed to retrieve it and deposit it at his master's feet, except each throw would be a little longer and a little higher until Hugh could drift back too, drift back and drift back until on the right summer's day there would be no ball he could not outrun. But it was still a sunny, overcoated winter. And Hugh was short-legged and his eyes were narrowed in a squint even if the sun was not shining into them. Bob Langley factored all this in and measured his tosses accordingly. He gave Hugh one to catch over his head, one he had to race in for and catch off his shoe tops. He didn't have fingers on enough hands—and there weren't enough hands in town—to count the times that Hugh's own father had not played catch with him. Yet he was not consciously setting out to take his older brother Raymond's place. He was limbering up his arm. The ground was still bare. It did not smell of grass so much as of winter's mud. But measure his throws as he might, Bob Langley knew he was fighting nature. It was not in Hugh Langley's nature to range over the town's ball field (where circuses and religious revivals were also held) with the same sort of license that his uncle possessed, but Bob Langley made the effort that his brother Raymond wouldn't have, he took a boy out to play catch with, to snag fly balls with, thinking, of course, of the son he and the woman who was still, after all, his bride would have, watching his son range back, effortlessly pulling down balls over his head, not really outrunning a long fly but timing his speed to its flight, knowing the ball would come down and you would be there to receive it and that once you had it securely in the pocket of your glove, you could continue running, run out the speed of your momentum until you decided to come back, to cheers, always cheers, whether fans were in the stands or not, cheers from your father, from your uncle-aged cousin, until you reached the point where you had the arm for it and could throw the ball back to him, to your father's glove, and the sound the ball made as it hit the glove's pocket was clean, solid, and deep, an instant of absolute communication like little else.

Bob Langley played catch with Hugh Langley with his short churning legs as he would one day play catch with his son, as Fran Langley slipped down from that low brick wall herself and with the same assurance as her husband, and just as unrehearsed, went up to the photographer, who was this motherless young man in the family she'd married into, and did not mother him on the spot but asked to see his camera and got him to show her exactly how it worked and then took it and took a picture of Hugh Langley himself that would probably be lost except that Fran Langley clicked it and kept it in her mind. He was compact, his eyes were squinted, a deep-sea blue, his mouth was pursed, and his cheeks were bunched, he was narrow-shouldered, his short legs were slightly bowed. He was unathletic, yet she saw at once that on the strength of willpower alone he might be capable of some amazing physical feat. She took the picture. He was a Langley at the other end of the spectrum from her husband, who was weak and ill-proportioned nowhere that she had detected. Even his adoration of her seemed to have a combustible, self-renewing energy behind it as never-to-be-doubted as the sun's. Taking a snapshot of Hugh Langley put her in mind of her husband, and Bob Langley, with all his prowess and natural gifts, put her in mind of those in need, who made up for the lack of god-given abilities with the fervor of their desire. She saw how one grew out of the other—inescapably. She took the picture. She handed the camera back and whispered something in Hugh Langley's starstruck ear. It caused a rich reaction. Imagine two halves of a watermelon breaking apart on a natural fault to reveal just such a richness inside. But that was a summer's sight and this was still winter, the last few days. Bob and Fran Langley had married in the winter. Hugh Langley had followed them up the street (or had waited behind a tree or had materialized at the opportune moment) and had caught them as they were about to step out into spring. Those winter coats they were about to shed on this day that ushered the new season in. The newborn always looked enough alike in that transcendent moment that they might be considered twins.

That was when Hugh Langley had snapped his picture. Bob and Fran Langley. Depression days. Then Hugh, a boy in need but who was very smart, and who always looked ahead to determine the next day's needs, too, ran on.

⸺◈⸺

Aunt Louise was hard of hearing, wore thick glasses, and spoke in a gushing, good-humored croak, happy to lay eyes on any Langley and for some reason especially happy to lay eyes on me. She had buried her strong-willed father and then the white-haired woman he adored and lived in the large wood-frame family home with the pecans out front until its size overwhelmed her (although not the memories, those she would have lived with room by room), at which point she had my father sell it for her and moved to a brick bungalow down the road, neutral ground and about to be engulfed by a wave of kudzu billowing up from in back unless she clipped each day's fresh growth. "Lord 'a mercy!" "Land sakes alive!" "Great day in the morning!" were some of the exclamatory expressions she used. For years she organized Langley summer reunions out on a farm a great uncle of mine, Uncle Chester, owned and badgered any Langley within driving distance to attend until Langleys finally outdistanced her. As a boy I came to those reunions, at which my father made an occasional brief appearance and stood on his crutch under a broad-leafed catalpa tree with its cigar-green pods hanging straight down and suffered Langleys to approach him until they stopped making the effort and he stood alone. Hugh would always come. He brought his son Billy, who rather than take part in the ballgames and other festivities would hide behind the barn with some other cousins and scheme to get the upper hand. Everybody brought hampers of food. We never ran out of fried chicken and squash casserole and potato salad and deviled eggs and pound cake.

On one occasion, I remember an enormous catfish, and the story had it that Uncle Chester himself, after spending years of futilely baiting his hook, had caught that catfish out of his own pond. No one, least of all Aunt Beatrice, had even believed that catfish existed. She'd thought her husband was deranged, sitting there with a pole between his knees week after week, year after year. Had divorce been an option she would have exercised it. Then Uncle Chester caught the darned thing, took it to the icehouse in town and had them freeze it for him until the summer reunion rolled around when, telling no one, he deposited it on the table with the chicken and deviled eggs and pound cake, which it dwarfed. When Aunt Beatrice saw it her mouth hung open in disbelief; then she closed her mouth and a furious pressure began to build, just time enough before she exploded for Aunt Louise to go up to her and talk her out of it. Aunt Beatrice might have gone after Uncle Chester with a carving knife, and the family reunions on his farm might have ended right there. All the time he'd wasted fishing for that ugly, whiskered thing! It's like when a storm was about to hit, Louise claimed, and you're standing out in the middle of a field. Nowhere to hide. But thinking fast, Louise stepped up to the table and cut the first piece of catfish for herself. I swan, Beatrice, she said, I didn't think Ches had it in him! This thing's as big as his leg! But tender as a sweet little drumstick. Let me cut you a piece, too.

We all ate. Hugh brought Billy out from behind the barn. My mother ate a piece with a resolute look on her face. Louise took my father a piece, planted under his tree. If I could have read her lips they would have said: Do it for me. My father ate. I knew the muddy pond the catfish had come out of and I swear I could taste the mud, but I ate too. I don't remember my sister at that reunion and I can't imagine her eating such a fish. But it became a day in the Langley family to date things from: the third Langley reunion since Uncle Chester's catfish, the seventh, the tenth. When Louise became frail and couldn't muster the energy to push things along, the catfish did the work. The thirteenth, the fifteenth.

My father was devoted to Aunt Louise, but the day came when he quit going to the reunions, too. No one stood up under the catalpa tree. No one sat up there, ate up there; children ran around it in their games. Out of bottle-bottom glasses Aunt Louise would cast occasional glances up to the tree until she admitted the truth, too. My mother attended a few last Langley reunions with a puzzled scowl on her face, a mixture of amazement that she was there at all and ill-disguised disapproval of all she saw around her, and then she stopped going, too.

But Aunt Louise never ceased to champion the Langley cause. When we were little she used to send her nieces and nephews letters with family news so that the children could keep abreast, and in the margins of these letters she pasted little cutout farmland animals, bunnies and chicks and chipmunks and ducks, in case our interest flagged and our eyes didn't want to keep moving down the page. For the adults she kept scrapbooks, and for herself she kept a scrapbook of my father's accomplishments, which she'd take out of her desk drawer—an outsized desk, with a multitude of musty cubbyholes, which had belonged to her father—and show any family member on request. But we'd have to sit there and look at it without squirming and with something like reverence on our faces, and if she believed we'd begun to humor her or if she detected something hollow in the admiration we professed, she'd quietly close the scrapbook and return it to its drawer. It was in those brittle and time-yellowed clippings I got my first indication that my father was not the man I knew. With his baseball cap pushed back off his forehead and with a savvy-smart grin breaking across his face, he seemed to be choosing sides for a game that would never end and wanted you to come play on his side, too. In his football helmet he struck a combative stance, with a stiff-armed pose, but you could see all he really wanted was to dance off down the field. On the basketball court, he bent at the knees for a two-handed set shot, a smiling farsightedness in his eyes, as if he'd already seen the ball swish through the hoop. His specialty on the track team was the pole vault, and Aunt Louise had one photo of him cradling his bamboo pole, and another action shot where he'd left the pole behind him and had cleared the bar with open sky ahead. We didn't need to read about his records because she would recite them for us. I didn't tell her that he had leaped beyond me, that I couldn't make the connection, because she kept insisting that this—and this and this and this—was the man.

I had seen photos of Aunt Louise herself when she was a teen-ager. She'd been beautiful. With a face of clear, clean lines, "elegant" might have been a better word. Perhaps Langleys were not meant to be "elegant." In her late teens Louise had been stricken with scarlet fever and had begun to suffer a life of poor hearing, poor eyesight, wizened cheeks and a bony chin. She developed curvature of the spine and scuttled when she walked. But she was brisk. She cared for her parents and kept alive my father's legend as long as she could.

There were no post war clippings. My father's success as a businessman was all conducted behind the scenes. There were no photographs of a one-legged man who with his enormous upper body strength had learned to hurtle along on his crutch. No tacklers he'd trampled and left in his wake. No diplomas, no citations, no testimonial plaques he'd won. No record of praise.

My father never took me with him when he went to see his sister Louise, but once our visits coincided. He had a car, a dark Oldsmobile sedan, that was frequently streaked with red mud since he made a point of going out in person to inspect property, almost always rural, he was about to buy. He had no chauffeur; he drove himself.

He probably had the first clutch-free, automatic transmission in the area. He wore a dark leather shoe on his right foot, which he moved from the gas pedal to the brake quickly, deftly, but with a punishing weight held in reserve in case the car failed to perform. The day we coincided in our visit was before Aunt Louise gave up the Langley house and moved to her brick bungalow, and I did not see my father's car parked out by the road. But my father also walked the town. His office was down on Main Street, looking out on one of the town's two movie theaters, but there were times when he put himself on public display and aggressively set out poling up and down the town's sidewalks. I did not think of that. I was on my bike and thinking instead of a time when as a little boy I'd been climbing one of the pecans and blue jays had chased me down the tree and up onto the Langley screen porch, where Aunt Louise had been sitting on her glider. She'd pulled me inside and, as bent and frail-seeming as she was, shooed the blue jays away. Riding by on my bike, I remembered that time, and suddenly felt the urge to visit my aunt. But as soon as I'd stepped up onto the porch, I sensed my father's presence. I had yet to knock on the door, which I wouldn't have done anyway. I would have opened it, called out, Aunt Louise, and she would have answered, Ah, pshaw! I declare! Look who's come to see me! The house was large. With both her parents now gone she'd taken to living in one corner of it, her sitting room crowded with furniture from the rest of the house, including a very tall grandfather clock that tolled the hours as solemnly as if from the courthouse or a church tower, calling on all the Langleys to reunite while there was still time. But at the door I hesitated. I hadn't heard my father. I'd simply realized something—someone—of a splintering authority sat on the other side of that door.

It was my father who opened the door to the Langley house and told me to come in. I entered the sitting room, and although Aunt Louise offered me lemonade and her molasses cookies, normally she would have jumped up, scurried into the kitchen, rattled plates and glasses before insisting I eat and drink. She said she was tickled to see me, and she remarked to my father how much I'd grown. She was about to go on in those cackling bursts of hers about how it wouldn't be long before I was taller than my father, and, if the girls would let me breathe, how I'd hit and throw and kick and pass and shoot that ball as well as he, when she suddenly stopped, blinked, and her eyes behind those bottle-bottom glasses she wore took a turn inward. I looked at my father. I expected him to give her an encouraging nudge, but instead he was sending a message to me: since I'd been the one who'd intruded, it was up to me to step in. So I did. I told Aunt Louise the truth, about how I'd been riding by on my bike, how I'd remembered the blue jays she'd saved me from when I was a little boy, and how I'd just wanted to stop in and see how she was. The blue jays? She smiled but still with that puzzling frown in her eyes, and if it was a blank she was drawing and a family story had escaped her, I realized I'd somehow made matters worse. Nonetheless, I went on. I was just a little boy, it was a long time ago, blue jays wouldn't bother me now—after all, I was a jaybird myself—but she wasn't getting any closer to remembering that day, and, in fact, there was a moment when she wore a stricken look, as if she were peering out on a blank expanse and her memory had failed her entirely and nothing was left.

Of course, I was just a kid. How was I supposed to know what was really going through her mind? And the room was shadowy, and her frustration and the look on her face might have had more to do with something she'd eaten, something that hadn't set well in her stomach, and forced her to turn all her attention there. Or maybe she hadn't been able to sleep the night before. Anything. But, of course, the real reason for her disconcertedness was my father, my father's presence, the three of us together in the same room, without the clippings and the tales that went with them that would have brought that opened-mouthed smile of astonished good fortune to her face. There had been such a time, such a man, and here were the crinkled and yellowed scraps of paper to prove it. The grin, even when he was trying to look fierce; that look of an endless summer day he stood at the center of, whether on the baseball diamond, the football field, or releasing a pole, clearing a bar, and vaulting into the sky. With a sadness that was strange to me, obviously influenced by my aunt, I turned to my father whose sandy hair had turned to iron shavings now, and whose cheeks and chin were weather-hardened knobs. The eyes didn't blink, small and flat and two-dimensional as tarnished coins. My eyes fell, as they would have to, and settled on the empty space where a leg had been and a pant's leg was folded and pinned. The pin was out of sight, but I had seen it, as children will always catch forbidden glimpses of the things their parents want to hide. It was a diaper-sized pin with a rubber-protected head.

My father said, "Don't mention the blue jays again. It's not a story to be proud of. Louise has forgotten about them and so should you."

I didn't reply. I didn't bow or nod my head. I don't remember what I did, or what my aunt said, surely something to soften the blow, if she spoke at all. I remember a heavy-laden air, a difficulty in breathing, and a period of silence, which might have lasted as long as a sermon in church.

BUT THERE WERE MOMENTS. I do remember moments. Judy says you add them up and get nothing. She says every child is entitled to make up her own burdies. And I say if the memories are real and you add yours up, you'll get a sum. One and one make two.

I remember as a little boy being with my father in Uncle Raymond's furniture store. It was just possible my father had been working there for a while, perhaps selling used furniture out of the dusty, dimly lit back of the store while Uncle Raymond worked out of the shiny and wax-scented showroom up front. It's possible my father had taken me to work with him that day. Anything is possible. In my memory I am crawling around on the floor, exploring among the old dining room tables and chairs and somber dark chests while my father waits for his customers in an easy chair, like a bear sitting back in his lair. I must come on him unwittingly for when he says, "Where do you think you're going?" he takes me by surprise and I don't have an answer. The light is so dim back there that he seems to be part of the chair. The armrests are massive and end in what look like an animal's claws, with deep grooves between the fingers. The chair's fabric has a staleness about it I'll later associate with the staleness of caves. My father sits there, almost daring someone to come in and give him reason to rise. One foot is planted squarely on the floor, and there isn't another, of course. His hand briefly grazes the top of my head. "Where do you think you're going?" may be the first words of his I remember, a rhetorical question, for surely he knew the answer. I was going to him.

The memory continues. My father insists he didn't hear me and asks the question again, but before I can even attempt an answer he has picked me up and sat me down in that gap his missing leg provides, and there is nothing spooky about it, nothing to be kept out of sight—as though in the darkness at the back of a store—and I remember in that instant it being the most natural fit in the world. My father lost a leg fighting for his country, and I sit there in the space provided making up the difference.

The second memory is more complex. I am older. More is at stake. And it all takes place out of doors. Even with that loss of a leg my father remained an outdoorsman. For a while he had a few friends left he hunted with, but he never took me out with him then. I saw him come home with game, quail and rabbits, mostly, and I saw the breached shotgun and could smell the spent shells, and I especially remembered the muddied end of his crutch, red mud, the stain sometimes a foot high. Because I'd seen the implacable way he hurtled around town, I could easily imagine him out in a cornfield, moving down rows as he flushed out quail. He'd hammer the crutch home and in the second half of the motion raise his shotgun and fire as the quail whirred up before him. His hunting companions might be stumbling over clods of dirt and stumps of corn stalks and get off slightly delayed shots, but it would be unfair to compare them to my father. It was not just his powers of concentration that were fierce; his powers of compensation were, too. He'd lost a leg and made of his crutch a fulcrum for any activity he wanted to undertake. In comparison, his two-legged hunting companions would seem under-equipped. It wasn't their fault, and they wouldn't hunt with him long. Others would, men my father came to do business with. And then they wouldn't either. And I, of course, never hunted with or without him a day in my life.

But he did take me out of doors for I remember walking through the shadows of a pine forest and then emerging into the open of an overgrown field of some sort, corn or cotton, abandoned now. I remember coming out into the light, an unsunny gray day but a great expanse, and the light under those clouds seemed equable and clear. We were not alone. Another man was standing on the other side of my father, whom I didn't know. I remember he was not dressed for the forest or the fields. Perhaps he had a suit on and a pampered sort of plumpness to his cheek that would have led you to believe he'd spent most of his life indoors. Now, I have reason to believe he was a bank official of some sort, but in my memory he simply stood on the other side of my father, and when my father raised his free arm and with a visionary authority divided up the field, I assumed he was doing it for me, that there was a lesson to be learned, man subduing nature, that sort of thing. My father and the man exchanged some words, and then my father raised his hand again and, altering its line, divided the field differently. His tone of voice was more patient than normal, but still instructional, and even though he wasn't expressly addressing me, I believed the lesson to be learned was mine. I nodded and tried to stand up taller. My father and the man continued to talk, and the word I heard again and again was "future." The field, I began to realize, would not always lie so low to the horizon and that lid of clouds would not always be there to take the harshness out of the light. Something would have to be done to accommodate oncoming events, and that was what my father was explaining to the man and marking off with that hand. The future. Then the hand fell on my head for perhaps the second time in my life. A large hand, perhaps as large as a preacher's, but with a burly, root-like strength in each of the fingers. In the dimness of the used furniture section of the family store, he might have placed his hand there once before, but this was out in the open, there was a witness, and in the name of the future my father and I stood together, hand to head, bound by a common cause. I believe the man made some sound or motion to indicate that he understood. I don't remember ever meeting his eye. The truth is I disregarded him. He was a mere accessory to whatever my father had brought me out there to do. And I have to believe the man disregarded me, or regarded me as a mere prop for the show my father was mounting to get what he wanted from the bank, which was a loan, of course, to buy the field, which would be divided up according to the dictates of his hand once he'd raised it off my head.

But I was not a prop. The town banking man was wrong. I was an accomplice, and with his fingers spreading out over my head my father is telling me to play along, to look out over that field and see what he sees, an expressway passing by, with its off-ramps, over-passes, clover-leafs, shopping centers, neighborhoods of curving streets and handsome houses with glistening front lawns and cars glistening in the drives. Schools and ballfields and boys with their balls. The fingers breathe, vibrate, send out their code. We make up a team, son, you and I. This fellow standing at my side is a lifetime minor leaguer, but we'll use him to take a step up. Don't worry. We won't be seeing him again. And I don't have my hand on your head because I need you to be my crutch. I need you to stand there and smile and nod and look like a boy who wants to ride a bike down one of those streets, and who wants to jump off in front of one those houses, and who wants to be there when his father drives up one of those drives. You could be that boy, couldn't you, son? And if your father were coming back from a war, you could be standing there like a little soldier yourself waiting for him, couldn't you? At attention like a little soldier? Without blinking your eyes? For however long it takes? Sure you could, son.

⌇⌇⌇

THE STORY OF HOW MY FATHER MADE HIS FORTUNE I did not have to go to Hugh or Aunt Louise or any other family member to get for I observed it myself. For all practical purposes, my father's career as developer began in that field. And one field ripe for development led to another. How my father learned where various expressways and roundabouts would be built, instantaneously converting barren land into very valuable property, is another story, and a darker one, or perhaps its darkness is nothing more than the last light left from the Bob Langley legend, what not just the town but that whole area of the state felt it owed the man before the curtain came down and the debt was paid in full.

It helps to understand the location of the town, called Russellville. The town itself was nothing special. Six or eight blocks of businesses, with a clustering of multi-story buildings at the center. To the east, a textile plant, a tannery, a grain elevator, the feed stores, and out beyond them, the black neighborhood and less reputable churches. To the south, the tracks and the train station, with its long brick depot. Across the tracks, the highway and its filling stations, a couple of car dealers, a barbecue restaurant, and a coming and going of repair garages. To the north and west, the stately homes, with their ample verandas and flower-bearing urns and venerable shade trees. The old established churches. Farther out, the humbler houses, cottage-style, block after tidy block, until you reached the weather-grayed shacks, still intact, still inhabited, with sand and no grass for a front yard. At the town's limit, an improbable mansion, down to its last flecks of paint, with verandas both upstairs and down. At the town's center, an outsized county courthouse. Behind the courthouse, a jail. And that was all. A smell of age, deeply settled, mixing with the heat of melting asphalt and exhaust from the cars.

And still, although less frequented and strangely muted, as though from an era long past, fields of play.

It was the town's location, not the town itself. And it was the lay of the land. That flatness of fields lay mostly in a child's memory, for the land around Russellville was choppy, with some arable plots on the hillsides, where corn and even cotton and later soybeans might be grown as cash crops, but land mostly used for truck farming and cattle-grazing, with run-off ponds down in the folds. The soil was eroded, sandy, and what I remember best were rows and rows of poultry huts on that scratched-over land, huts I'd pretend were soldier's barracks, only with the car windows down and with the sole highway into the city a crowded two lanes, you couldn't escape the smell, a thin stench that had nothing to do with dung and that I associated with an extreme degree of privacy, like an ancestral smell of closed rooms. Then the pine forests began and the sour stench came from the lumber mills, and that was a smell without many likenesses other than the smell and taste of what your mother called "upchuck." Except the smell was vigorous and fresh and didn't bother me as much as the smell of all those chickens did, which was embarrassingly thin, stifling and closed. It was to the south of the city, where the last wrinkling traces of the mountains disappeared, that the land lay arable as far as you could see. That was a part of the state that owed my father nothing, where he was known but not beholden to, and where no one had fed off his glory. But that forty-five mile stretch between our town and the city, where the highway ran along the train tracks and where the poultry farms and lumber mills held sway, was another story.

And the same was true for the twenty-five miles on the other side of our town. The land didn't change—if anything it got even choppier—and there was that same string of whistle-stop towns with storefronts and bedspread stands along the tracks, but going in that direction you arrived not at a city but a town not much larger than ours, where the state university was located. That was also Langley country, but of a different sort. You excel on the sports fields of the state university and you immediately have a wider reach and multitude of admirers outnumbering any you have known. Your picture goes off in newspapers around the state, and with your baseball cap pushed back on your head and your football helmet unobstructed by the bars of a face mask, you are known wherever you go, upstate or down, on the coast or up some mountain hollow. But the small town intimacy is missing and your fame is mostly hearsay. You are like some fair-haired abstraction whose existence off the sports fields is your own. You provide weekly thrills but no one lives off your blood. My father's life was bound up with his town. He knew it. He went off to war and came back, and, to reclaim his life, there are those who say he sucked the town dry. And there are others who'll say that without Bob Langley the town wasn't worth saving, and it was his to dispose of as he saw fit.

What he did was lay a sort of siege. Even before Eisenhower was elected president, everyone knew an interstate highway system was destined to be built. Eisenhower wasn't the only one to note how Hitler had been able to use his autobahns to move men and materiel around the country, from front to front to front, for before it was over the Germans were fighting on three, and even though Bob Langley had not made it across the Rhine, he'd studied the movement of German armies so closely that he'd learned the lesson, too. By my father's calculation, two American autobahns would pass close to our town, one to the west connecting the city with other major cities up and down the east coast and the other practically on the outskirts of town connecting the city, with its state capital, to the university, whose football games were massively attended. Between those two expressways any number of bridging links would need to be built. With all these motorways in place and with factories pushing out cars and trucks instead of half-tracks and tanks, our town would lie in a section of the state soon to be known by the numbers of its off-ramps, where subdivisions would quickly be built and malls would take up the shopping slack. Subdivisions pre-dated the war while malls didn't, but any child could see that a man with his life now set at the speed limit was not going to crawl into the center of a town like Russellville to do his day's shopping. Or his day's socializing in a barber shop or at a drug store counter, or his day's horse-trading at a buggy shop converted into a car dealership, or pay his day's respects to a time now past in the shadowy reaches of a prominent family's furniture store. Plenty of other men understood what my father did—that towns like Russellville were relics in the making and that those stately family homes would soon be boarding houses for transient workers—but other men didn't have the chits to cash in that he had or hadn't had their natural bonhomie converted into something calculatingly cold. Other men might have the inside track, but other men weren't on a mission. Some might call it a score to settle, but I call it a mission.

How else was he going to get the inside information he had to have to make his deals? You can bribe or cajole or sweet talk just so many highway superintendents or statehouse higher-ups before the word goes out that you've had your fill, but only a man on a mission with a vision at the back of his head can keep winning converts to his cause. I don't know how my father got all the information he did, but it was as if he'd sat down and plotted out the whole superhighway grid himself, down to the last entrance and exit and cloverleaf, and all the bypass belts, then anticipated to an uncanny degree the distances at which subdivisions and malls would be willing to leapfrog each other in their quest for even more abundant and strategically located terrain. He did his homework with a concentration and a cunning that must have been extraordinary, then he went out and beat all his two-legged competition to the punch. No quarter asked and none given. The jackpot and the pocket-change—he wanted it all.

IV

Finally, it was Karen Ambrose who called me. She knew how long it had been since Judy had given me her phone number, and the implication was that my time had expired. She was offering her condolences. She had not called when Mother had died, perhaps because she'd been occupied trying to save her marriage and had had no time or inclination to revisit my life, our eight years together. And she and Mother had never really gotten along. My mother thought her judgmental. It was Karen's judgment that my mother was passing her bitterness on to her children, and anyone who came within her reach. Her judgment was identical to Judy's, and Judy had gotten away. But my father took Karen by surprise. I had managed to avoid mentioning that he'd lost a leg.

"The War," I told her. "The Battle of the Bulge. The army left him for dead out in a snowy field, and the next morning, to make it up to him, they took off his leg." Then I uttered, perhaps, the first of the lies between us. "I guess sometimes I just forget he only has one."

A lie which she ignored. "Left him for dead?"

"No one could explain," I said, "how he survived that night, and when the army can't explain something," I added, as if I were the cynical military brat, not she, "you're dead until you demonstrate otherwise."

"And he never bothered to enlighten them, did he? I'm guessing he never told anybody. Am I right?"

"You are. How did you know?"

"Just look at him," she said.

A man that powerfully self-contained would have no reason to tell anybody anything was what she meant.

She kept her distance. And my father never went out of his way to go after her. He acknowledged her. He made what for him passed as civil conversation. The only thing he said to me was, I assume she'll want to get pregnant. Most women do. And I assume you'll finally know what you want to do then. As it turned out he was right, but it didn't happen. When we broke up she didn't single that issue of a child out. She said it—our relationship, our consensual cohabitation—had run its course. If she had gotten pregnant and given birth during her subsequent marriage, I assume I would have heard about it. I calculated her childbearing years were now behind her and the issue was moot. Once we had parted ways, my father never mentioned her again. Strangely, it was my mother who said, There goes your best chance to start a family, Jay. And the accent she gave to "family" was like a coffin lid coming down, a coffin ready to go underground or up in smoke. The point at a funeral after which it was all words.

Yet Karen had called me to offer condolences on the death of my father.

She said, "I hope he left you something."

He'd left it all to me, I had no idea how much. Or how much of it was toxic. It sat in banks, in various accounts. For reasons yet to be examined, I had not re-entered the house. But that wasn't what she had meant.

I said, "How are you, Karen?"

And she said, "I'm mad. Mad at the waste. Aren't you"?

And she sounded mad, a woman who for the years I'd known her had made an effort to let nothing get under her skin.

"How are you otherwise?"

"You mean how have the years treated me?"

"How have they?"

"I'm twenty pounds lighter, for one thing."

I wanted to congratulate her since she'd fought her weight for as long as I'd known her. Her father had been a naval officer, rising to the rank of vice admiral, and had been decorated in the Korean War at the Battle of Inchon. Karen and her mother had waited for him at various bases around the world. They had both put on weight while her father remained fit. The next time he came home on leave, they claimed, they were giving the pounds back to him.

She was a big woman—almost my height—with ash blonde hair and blue eyes. She'd had a goal-oriented personality. She'd wanted a child. With a child no longer an option, she'd gotten into fighting trim to achieve some other objective, I assumed. A loss of twenty pounds would make a difference.

"I'm glad for you," I said.

"Really? Would you like me to send you a picture?"

"A picture?"

"On your cell phone. On your computer. You are on line, aren't you, Jay?"

"Yes, I'm on line."

"But not ready for a picture of an old flame twenty pounds lighter. 'Old flame.' Strange expression, isn't it? As if 'flames' could age."

"Send it, Karen."

"Old flames might not even burn. Judy tells me you can't leave it alone."

I didn't play dumb. She'd split and walked away after those eight years, and one of the ways I'd dealt with it was to assign no blame, to suspend judgment. In that way, the intervening years were like a perfectly clear solution you could see through back to the start.

"Not yet," I admitted.

"They're both gone now, Jay."

"And your parents, Karen? The vice admiral and..."

"Maureen? My father is long retired, on permanent shore leave. He and my mother have taken up golf. They travel around the world and play exotic courses. They ride in the same cart. Mother says Papa drives recklessly, that one day he'll turn the cart over and kill her. But until that day, they're both under par. 'Under par' doesn't mean they're sick, by the way. It means they're playing out of their minds."

In that moment I remembered the story of how Karen's parents had met. It was after the War. Her father had been a cadet at the Naval Academy in Annapolis, Maryland. In his naval whites he'd joined some other cadets for a weekend in New York City, but it had been Karen's father's whites that had blinded her mother. They'd both missed the wild celebrations after the War, and it was as if they'd thought, for a romantic weekend, at least, they could reenact them. Karen had been her blinded parents' result.

"Globetrotting golfers," I said. "Why not?"

"Don't be a fool, Jay," Karen said, picking up on Judy's word for me. "You can do it if you really want to," and, again, the antecedent for "it" was not in doubt.

"To answer your question, Karen. Yes, he left it all to me and so far none of it has gone to waste, none of it. It's where he left it, down to the last dime, and it's all mine."

"That wasn't the question."

"I know it wasn't."

"That money's not going to help you a bit, Jay."

"Probably not."

"There on his death bed…there was nothing? He gave you nothing else?"

"There was no death bed. He died driving his car. He had the good sense—you could even call it 'the courtesy'—to pull off onto the shoulder before he died. In a manner of speaking, he ran out of gas. Certain people had tried to get him to give up driving alone, but I wasn't one of them. And they didn't dare revoke his license, of course. Can you imagine that, Karen? The town of Russellville revoking Bob Langley's license?"

I laughed, hard and long, within which it wouldn't have been unlike her to hear a sob. But I hadn't sobbed. My laughter had caught in my throat at the sheer absurdity of that thought. Bob Langley presenting himself at the Office of Motor Vehicles; someone there, some poor scapegoat of a clerk, being asked to convey the sad news, the hard facts: 'Bob, I'm going to have to ask you to surrender that license of yours…'

Surrender? Bob Langley? His license?

I laughed again.

Karen said, "I've got some time. Why don't I drive up? We could talk over lunch. I think it's time."

And I said, "Is this something Judy asked you to do? To check on me? As if I might not be responsible for myself?"

And now Karen laughed, a rumbling laugh only a portion of which ever escaped. Preliminary to something.

But being honest, I couldn't picture Judy taking that final step and instigating anything like that, and I couldn't picture Karen taking Judy's hint.

She came within a week. It was a week during which I might have taken certain steps myself. I might have gotten my finances in hand. I might have paid a long-delayed visit to our family lawyer. I might have paid a longer-delayed visit to the house of my boyhood, of my sister's girlhood, my father's house, my mother's, too, built up on a ridge on a street called Crestview, not to impress anybody or any of us, but so that my father could look out. There lay the town. I lived beyond it, partway to the city, in a raised ranch in a development I'd always considered temporary, both the house and the development, but which Karen Ambrose knew well. I lived in a house in a neighborhood my father might have devoted five minutes of dreaming attention to as he passed his money-making wand over the land, a house he had never entered since what he bought he sold so quickly he really didn't need to wash his hands. But unless her memory had failed her, Karen knew the house well. Actually, I didn't expect her to pay me a visit even though I stayed around town and in a neighborly fashion tried to keep busy. Far behind my neighbors, I cut my grass. Turned the earth over in some flower beds. Had the hose out and might have washed my car, which sat in the drive. There were other things I might have done, touch up things, minor repairs, brightenings to offset the effect of the years. A heat wave passed over our town, and I might have called my sister and told her, You're right, I see the point of a willow and a river like yours to sit beside, otherwise how does one deal not so much with heat as with time?

But within a week Karen did come, and unless we drove the forty-five miles into the city or the twenty-five to the state university town, both accessible by interstates now, there was really no place to take her out to eat. But she knew that. She knew the town. She could stay on her diet, if that was how she'd shed those twenty pounds. It seemed as if she'd entered a whole new stage of her life. No longer capable of childbearing, she seemed now to have taken an indisputable place in the world. More concentrated, less distracted, less visibly on alert for any passing advantage. She had a "considered" look. She looked immune to "old times." The question that immediately occurred to me was: What would a woman like this want?

She said, "If it's any consolation I'd recognize you at once."

I laughed and we hugged. We held each other a moment past

that. And I remembered at once that it had never, ever had anything to do with Karen Ambrose. And it still didn't. Bob and Fran Langley had died, and it was as if the conditions of my life had not changed. But Karen had. She looked more resourceful. She was both bolder and more relaxed in the eyes. Her mouth was full. The tension had gone out of her lips. Those twenty pounds she'd exchanged not for more mobility but for a greater and more collected ease where she stood. She wore a dove-gray muslin blouse, earrings of an opalish cast, and smelled like a cornucopia of fruit, not immediately sweet.

I said, "I'm not sure I could say the same thing about you. I mean that as a compliment."

"Meaning I looked pretty horrible back then?"

"Meaning you look good."

"How gallant of you, Jay."

"You know I haven't got an ounce of gallantry in me. You look like you've come to terms and you look better for it. That's all."

"Sweeten it a bit."

"You look like you're prepared to enjoy life more now. Like you've cleared the decks."

"'Cleared the decks'? That's not sweetening it. That's naval talk."

"Then I take it all back. But it is good to see you again, Karen. I'm glad you made the effort."

"No effort," she said but with a directness I hadn't heard in her voice until then, as if she wanted to set the record straight.

I took her to a restaurant scattered through the five or six first floor rooms of what had once been an old family home. The food was strictly old family fare, tasty if what you really wanted was to nibble on the past, but two of the rooms were small and quiet where we could sit and talk. There were photographs of the town from decades back hanging on the walls. I saw horse-drawn wagons. A way of milling the people had as if about to be addressed by a politician or traveling evangelist. Eventually, fields of play. I still took my ice tea sweetened, Karen no longer did.

Before I could ask what a woman like Karen Ambrose now wanted, she announced she had no plans, shaking her head at the quiet and perhaps childish delight of living simply one day ahead.

"So you're saying you're taken care of."

"You mean are my needs met?"

"As if it were any of my business."

For those eight years we'd pieced together jobs—I'd worked for a clothing manufacturer in the city, an events coordinator in a fancy hotel, I'd tried to make a living selling shares in vacation retreats—all in an effort to stay independent. Karen had gotten up and on a daily basis driven off to work, too.

"They are. I got a generous settlement."

"Should I congratulate you?"

"You probably shouldn't inquire. It's over. I came out intact."

"Judy did too, by the way. I was up there—but I'm assuming you already know that. She spends her time—"

Karen cut me off. "That river would put me to sleep."

I heard a summary judgment in her voice, edged with sympathy. But no laughter.

She continued, "It's like a drug. You've got to stay on alert, Jay."

"If you have something to stay on alert for. But if you're taking it one day at a time, as you say..."

"That doesn't mean all days have to be the same, does it?"

I acknowledged the point. Although rivers changed moods. It was never the same river twice. I had not known that Karen Ambrose had visited my sister. Not in the flesh. "How long were you up there, Karen? Judy didn't say."

She shook her head. She slowly lowered her eyelids. She looked down at the table where we'd yet to be served our food. It was the quiet way she had—she'd had—of putting herself out of reach.

I suggested we order. The squash casserole, the butter beans, the greens, the sweet potatoes, the chicken or ham. Tea sweetened and unsweetened.

Then she answered my question. "I really don't know. A week, maybe two. Ten days. It rained twice and we went down to the little downtown and had lunch with roof over our heads but looking out over the same river. I met some people she knew, one man in particular, who owned a furniture store. I remembered that your family had once sold furniture. I mentioned that to her and we were back to the river again, as if to wash all family associations away. Jay..."

"Go ahead and say it," I said.

"I already have. You've got to stay on alert."

I looked at her directly over the table. With the lost weight the cheeks had become a little hollowed, the chin more squared. I didn't stare. The age was in her neck, a slight pouchiness under the eyes. But the large eyes were anchored. She was fixing on me, holding steady, and it became clear she'd come on a mission of some sort, but not one that Judy had instigated.

Our food came. Daily fare, no more than it was advertised to be. We ate as if to get it out of the way.

Then it was as if she'd pushed her plate aside and leaned in over the table. When the waitress came to refill our glasses, it was as if the waitress had not appeared. Karen repeated, "Stay on alert, Jay."

I admitted to a slight irritation. "There's no river out there lulling me to sleep, Karen," I said. "No one's committed a crime here. There's no investigation."

She reached across the table and touched my hand. 'Call Karen,' Judy had said as she'd slipped me her number. 'Or don't,' she'd added because she had surely slipped Karen mine.

The air conditioning was on, and Karen's touch became a warm squeeze, a light pat, and it was as if the game were underway.

"Start somewhere," she said. "Where does it start not to make sense?"

"It" again. I exhaled and sank a bit in my chair.

"I lived with you all those years, Jay. You think I don't know what a weight you were carrying around? You were in mourning the day I met you—if you'll pardon the expression."

"So what are you saying?"

"Whatever it was you couldn't do when he was alive, you can do now. Find out what it is and do it."

"Why wouldn't it be too late?"

"Because before he would've stood in your way. You know that, Jay. He was massive. He was like some massive monument unto himself. He defied anyone to take him on. You say he voluntarily pulled off the road to die? What if the car really did run out of gas?"

"He always had at least half a tank. I didn't have to check but I did."

"Still, he pulled off. But why wouldn't he just die where the car stopped and block the road? What road was it? Was it an interstate?"

I shook my head. "A country road, a county road. A road that came before all of that." Actually, it might have been a road my mother had driven him down when Claire Goltz had thought she was calling the shots.

"Where was his crutch?"

"His crutch?"

"It was his weapon, his club. Right? You always said they took away his M-1 and gave him a crutch instead. Wasn't that what you said?"

"In the seat beside him? Or the back seat? He carried a back up in the trunk."

"They didn't return it? You don't have it?"

"Karen, what's all this about?"

"Ask yourself: Where does it start not to make sense?"

I glanced around. The room we sat in was small but large enough to contain a coal-burning fireplace. On the mantle sat two sepia-toned photographs, the closer of the two of two young girls, dressed in generic white, side by side on a swing. One of the girls had her legs extended, as if anticipating a push. As soon as the photographer clicked his picture. Or exploded his powder flash. I raised my hand to the waitress passing down the hall, a woman relatively new to town, whose family had bought the house cheaply to convert it into this restaurant, which would soon, surely, fail. She saw me, started our way with the check, before I waved her back. I caught her in mid-stride, an awkward moment.

It was not as if I had suddenly remembered why I had not opposed our break-up all those years ago. It was that I had before me a Karen Ambrose new to me and had no idea what was in it for her. She'd have her goals. I suppose I was now a wealthy man, but it wasn't a fortune-hunting woman who sat before me, either.

"I don't know what you mean, Karen. Where does what start not to make sense?"

"'It,' Jay," she replied with feigned frustration.

I recited the obvious. I might have been re-indoctrinating her on the terms of our years together. "He was a cold man when before he'd been a warm and happy and multi-talented one. What they called 'a natural' in everything he undertook. The war did it to him. Mother defended herself until it was her war, too. No mystery. Just a bitter twist of fate."

"Maybe," Karen responded at once, as if she'd had it all thought out, "but you tell yourself that story long enough you might as well be sitting beside your sister's river."

"Just not as peaceful, as pretty, as non-navigable, no war-ships, if we're still talking naval terms."

"I told you. They're playing golf now."

"Karen, why did you come?"

This time when I signaled the waitress I didn't wave her back. But it seemed we were going Dutch for Karen left a twenty-dollar bill beside her plate. I left another beside mine. Outside, we stepped into a heavy humid stew, and it took an act of will on both our parts not to turn around and step back inside.

"Because I wanted to see you," she said. "And I wanted to see if I could help."

"So how do I look? You didn't say."

"You need some *joie de vivre*, Jay, some *élan vital*."

"Something foreign? Something French?"

"A jolt."

"Hugh says it's time for me to go to the mountains."

The glare off of the magnolia leaves just behind us in the small front yard added to our discomfort. Featureless white light, suffocating heat, what everybody back in the pre-cooled days had to endure until evening came and you caught a breeze on somebody's screen porch.

"Why did I think that Hugh Langley was dead?" Karen asked, momentarily taken aback.

"Because he should have never gotten off of Okinawa," I said, "and when he came home I was new-born and Bob and Fran Langley, his Bob and Fran Langley, his inspiration, were gone."

"I knew that." She was impatient and a little disappointed with herself. "But I thought he'd died up there. That that's what he'd gone up to the mountains to do. Who told me that?"

If anybody had told her that it could only have been Judy, sitting beside her river watching each Langley float downstream.

I shook my head. In that instant, the heat held us speechless, at a standstill. Finally, I asked her if she planned to come back, and she replied that I should go see Hugh, almost making it seem that she should go, too. But, perhaps, with cool mountain evenings in mind, we'd been rendered defenseless in this heat, and not entirely account-able for what we said or implied, heat I, for one, had known all my life.

V

THERE WAS A PERIOD OF MY ADOLESCENCE during which I'd been stopped on the streets of our town and exclaimed over. Hoping to appeal to my father by currying favor with me, certain older men had taken every opportunity to greet me and remark how much I was growing up to look like my dad. It was as if the Bob Langley they'd all known back in the glory days had come walking down the street. This was nonsense, of course. I might have borne some resemblance to my father in the features of my face, and by the time I was finished I was almost his height, but the way we carried ourselves and the way we took on the world, or the way that I, for one, slipped to the side to let the world shoulder past, had nothing in common. But what else could these men say? On what other grounds could I be exclaimed over? And these were not your typical town sycophants. Bank presidents greeted me that way. Pillars of the community did. Ministers of the town's reputable churches. Businessmen you'd think would be so secure in their skin that they'd never need to give a thought to what Bob Langley's unaccomplished son thought of them all took pains to get on my good side. Be sure to tell your Dad I send him my very best. You'll remember, won't you, son? These men frequently mentioned my mother, too. I heard a genuine fondness then, and something like a wistful savoring of what might have been, but my father brought out a deeper and darker mix of emotions in their voices, all overlaid by the humbling realization there was nothing else they could do. Except butter up his son.

When I understood that, I had no trouble at all in imagining the deals my father had struck with these men, how as an object of their past worship he commanded their allegiance still, if he was strong and unswerving enough to demand it. Bankers might imagine themselves saying, Now, Bob, you know I'd do anything to set you back on your feet (except they wouldn't have said that, not with that crutch of his planted at his side like a standard), but banks have to look at track records and banks have to consider collateral or they'd go out of business. Banks and hunches don't go together, Bob. Oil and water. Yankees and Rebs. You've got a good hunch there, and some interesting inside dope, but come back when you've got something solid the bank can foreclose on.

I can imagine a wink on the word "foreclose," as if the best they could offer my father would be this insider's glimpse of the delight banks took in suckering their customers along, but with Bob Langley himself seated before them, what could they do? This was a man they had thrilled to on all local fields of play, and this was a man who had gone off to a foreign field and martyred himself to their cause. Only he hadn't died. He had come back from the dead—no one could explain how—to walk one-leggedly among them and turn the terms of his martyrdom around. Now, bankers knew they were the ones in arrears. What could they do except give him what he wanted and then exclaim over his son the next time they saw me on the street?

I did have one Bob Langley-like accomplishment to my name, although no one who stopped me on the street ever mentioned it. I did do one thing my father had done, nowhere near as well, but a difference of degree not of kind. It was not premeditated. Not all the men who stopped me did so on the street. In school I was stopped, too, by teachers and by coaches who, if they hadn't known my father, had certainly seen the trophies in the trophy case he was responsible for winning for the school. One of those coaches, a man named New-some, *had* coached my father in both basketball and track and was about to retire. He claimed he had seen me playing basketball in a junior high pick up game—a memory I did not have of myself—and whether I knew it or not, I had the talent to make the varsity squad. He did not grovel, did not beg, did not even imply that as Bob Lang-ley's son I could round off his career and send him off into retirement a happy man if I would just come out for the team. But that was what I read in his face, with its baggy cheeks and eyes, a longing that if made good on might restore twenty years to his life. But I let the last basketball season go by. And what I did do had nothing to do with Coach Newsome, who was a benign and sadly beloved old man.

A day before the spring district track meet I walked out onto the track in my gym shoes and jumped over the high jump bar. I hadn't meant to, but I really don't know what I was doing out on that track, either. It was a day in May, and maybe I wanted the sunshine and maybe I jumped because something spring-like surged in my blood. Coach Newsome, who was peptalking the relay teams, saw me and moving over to the high jump pit, as idly as if he were out for a stroll, asked me if I could do that again. So I did. I backed up, jumped straight at the bar as if it were a fence in a field, and cleared it again, apparently by a wide margin. Coach Newsome took his measurements and then, still as if engaged in idle conversation, asked me if I would come out to the district meet the next day and do what I'd just done. So I did that too. I ran and jumped over the bar, and they set it up higher and I jumped over it again. I had no technique. I jumped until they set the bar so high I couldn't get over it. Then I sat down in the track infield and watched the remaining jumpers take their turns.

And that was when I saw him, saw his crutch first as I so often did, his flagpole, his mast, and then saw my father seated up in the stands. Obviously, Coach Newsome had contacted him. Whether he had come to the meet to honor his old coach in his last days on the job or to see his son do something he'd once done himself with such god-given ease, I do not know.

Most of what I know about my father I had to imagine, and that I could do very well.

Coach Newsome called him and said, Bob, the darnedest thing. Then the Coach described what he'd seen me do and allowed himself to indulge in a reminiscence. Like the men who stopped me on the street, he surrendered to a moment of make-believe. I thought I was looking at you, Bob. I said to myself, I'm getting senile, I just saw Bob

Langley sail over that bar. And Bob Langley said, What time d'you say that meet was, Coach?

I can't say he smiled. He did nod his head to me, as a greeting or praise or just to indicate the curious circumstance that we were on the same field of play, even if he was up in the bleachers and I was sitting slumped over on the grass. Coach Newsome came by to tell me my mark was the best yet and there was only one jumper left. Coach Newsome beamed at me—as if at a distance of twenty or thirty years. The sporting gods had come home to roost. I looked back up into the stands, and it seemed my father had a moment—he tilted his head, some of the iron appeared to go out of his spine and a quiet preliminary wave to wash through him. He straightened and took the next wave without wavering, as Bob Langley must.

That remaining high jumper had the bar set an inch above mine and missed on his first two attempts. He was actually shorter than I was and more heavily built, but he had technique. I ran up to the bar and jumped, but he rolled over it, and on this third attempt he succeeded. I had won second place, which qualified me to participate in the state meet, something I had had no idea about, but which offered Coach Newsome some consolation—he would be at that meet (and I would too, jumping three times at the same low bar and failing on each attempt), where the two of us would team up again. He shook my hand as I sat on the infield grass, not at all dejected, and then helped pull me up. Up in the stands, my father hadn't moved. He had a puzzled look on his face, as if somewhere out in all that distance there was something that did not conform to his wishes, but his eyes never met mine.

It took him two days, but true to his nature when he did it he came into my room and stood over my desk, where I was doing my homework. He said, "That boy was lucky. His first two tries he didn't even come close." He paused until I looked up at him, up his right side, not his left, where the leg was missing. Then he paid me perhaps his highest compliment—but by the back door. He said, "He had no natural talent."

And it might have been the only time when I openly disputed his word. I forced myself to meet his eye. His eyes were green, a brownish green, but screwed up tight, as if he had just so much eyesight left and was not going to let an instant of it escape. I said, "Yeah, but he had technique. He could do the roll."

I believe I saw the eyes soften. He was too much the man to let them drift off, but I believe I saw that tightened green take on a film. And as steady as he held his voice, I believe I detected something there, too. He said, "You deserved to win, son."

Other men—those men on the street—often called me "son," but not him. I deserved to win because I was his son? That must have been what he'd meant to say.

I said, "Hey, I got second! That's not so bad!"

Here was a man who'd been open to everything a town had wanted to pour through him. My father had been something like their distillery, not their moonshine but their sunshine distillery, and for all those years of his prolonged boyhood in exchange for their praise he'd given the town an elixir to drink. I should have gotten up from my desk and embraced him. He should have placed a hand on my shoulder and saved me the trouble.

It didn't happen.

ON A GRAY NOVEMBER DAY a man came to our door and left his car running out in front of our house. It must have been a Saturday for Mother, Judy, and our cook Pearl were all there, probably Saturday morning, for by the afternoon Pearl would have been gone. Sunday, Mother would have had us in church; a weekday, of course, and Judy and I would have been in school. It could have been a holiday, but there wasn't a trace of festivity in the house. Pearl left the kitchen to answer the front door, and even before the door was fully open I heard my father from down in his study, with the same view I had of the street outside, say something practically unprecedented in our house. He said, "Yes, he may come in."

I had seen the car running, not the man. I wouldn't see the man until he left the house and returned to his car. He wore a long gray overcoat and his head was bare. He was bald. Even though he was heavy-set he gave the impression of being sickly, or in pain somewhere, and he also gave the impression of having come from a long ways away. It was the way his overcoat hung open, as though he didn't know whether to button it or not, and it was the shambling way he walked, tilted forward, testing his footing, as if on unfamiliar ground. It was probably also the running car, the way a man might step out of his car to ask directions or use the restroom before he drives the next hundred miles. The man got back into his car and sat there.

Well before the man had driven away, Judy came into my room, and Judy was at that age when she'd come into my room only if I'd taken something or hers, something she really meant to get back. Or if somebody had held a gun to her head.

She said, "That makes me so, so sad. How can we stay in the same house with him?"

I didn't say anything, although what I'd heard had made me sad, too. Or maybe I was too shocked to answer, uncertain why our father had let the man go on.

Judy read the uncertainty on my face. "He felt guilty, don't you see?" she emphasized each word, as though underlining a bitter truth. "He didn't shut that man up because he knew he was right. Daddy shuts everybody up, for nothing. But this time he knew that man was really, really right."

And she was right, I knew that. But telling her so meant I was giving up on my father entirely and joining her camp. And she didn't want me in her camp—I knew that too. She'd kick me out and I'd be in no man's land.

I said, stalling, "He didn't come from around here."

"You figured that out all by yourself? You should be on The Sixty-four Thousand Dollar Question! He came a long way to say what he had to say, and Daddy let him say it because Daddy knew he was right."

"Well, that means," I replied, struggling to say something intelligent, "that Daddy can be right too, if he let him come in and say it. Don't you see?"

Our mother appeared at my door. She stepped inside and closed it, took a breath and settled her expression. Her eyes, so used to restoring calm, seemed emptier than usual, as though there were little to back them up. She said, "We shouldn't be quick to judge. We won't know the full story until Bob decides to tell us himself."

"And here's something else," Judy continued, "Pearl's heard all that too. She goes back and tells everybody in…" and in her building rebellion she was about to blurt out 'niggertown,' as Mother had warned her not to. Judy yielded just that much. "…in that neighborhood she lives in and it'll be all over town in a minute. Not that it will shock anybody. Will it, Momma? Who could be shocked by anything Daddy does now!"

"I'll wait to hear Bob's side of the story," our mother repeated, with a trace of petulance in her voice.

Which Judy picked up on. It was as if a young girl had been backed into a corner and said what she'd been schooled to, refusing to admit she'd been tricked or trapped. Our mother might but Judy would never allow herself to become such a girl. She said, "We won't hear it. No chance! Daddy doesn't explain himself. Why should he if everything he does is always right?"

"No one does everything right," Mother replied.

"Daddy does!" Judy shot back. "Whaddaya want to bet?"

I said, "Maybe that man was making things up and Daddy let him go on so he could 'hang himself.'" I liked the phrase. I'd heard Perry Mason say it, and it was a tactic he used in court, letting a witness go on and on until he'd convicted himself and the jurors began to shake their heads.

Judy looked at me and made a tight-lipped screech of disgust. Then she let herself go limp and dropped her head. "I could cry," she confessed. "I really could."

I looked at Mother, who, as her daughter mimed defeat, stood her ground. Then she left Judy to her theatrics and looked at me. Whenever it was just the two of us and the world was either behaving or misbehaving—it didn't much matter which—I'd get that fine crease of a smile at the corner of her mouth. That smile always meant there was an alternative to the prescribed way of things. But that smile did not appear. Instead, Mother looked like a captive staring out through the bars of a cell, the bitterness of the years to come beginning to take hold.

The three of us were standing there when we heard my father walk down the hall outside the door to the kitchen. The sound he made as he passed by was of one enormous stride punctuated by a powerful jabbing thrust. He talked to Pearl—we heard the bass rumble of his voice, no words. Nothing from Pearl. Then my father levered himself back down the hall, and we didn't see or hear him again until lunch, where he helped himself to an extra-large helping of candied yams, a favorite dish of his, presumably what he'd gone down the hall to tell Pearl to make. Of his visitor earlier that morning he said nothing. There was not a hint on his face, nothing in his manner or his tone of voice that would lead you to believe anything remained to be said. Nothing. Judy had been right, of course—our father was not about to explain himself. She might have crowed in triumph, but she sat in a scowling silence throughout the meal. Futilely, Mother tried to right the balance by making sure all the dishes reached us in the proper order and with due speed. I snuck a string of glances at my father, so many I might as well have stared. Nothing.

The candied yams, I concluded, had been the treat he was awarding himself.

That man had come to my father's home and not his office, not on a working day but on a weekend, to plead his case on the grounds of common decency. Legally, he had grounds, too, he believed, but common decency was where he stood, and because the grounds were common they necessarily included my father. In that he was mistaken, mistaken with the first words that escaped his lips. But my father had left his study door open, even though his visitor might have preferred to have it closed, and let him go on. The man, whom my father addressed as Mr. Howell, had a barrel-toned voice with a sickly, scratchy echo, a voice that at one time had been overused, as though it had belonged to a preacher. The grounds of common decency Mr. Howell spoke of were both moral and concrete. Moral, in that they pertained to rules of behavior that had governed civilized conduct for centuries, and concrete, in that they referred to a particular piece of ground. A family cemetery. Mr. Howell made a significant pause, and my father asked his visitor to continue. Clearly, Mr. Howell had not been expecting such open-door compliance, for he hesitated a moment, cleared his throat and tried to adjust his tone. In the interval my father asked him if, by any chance, he was related to Miss Imogene Howell, if he might have been one of Miss Howell's brothers who lived out of state and had come to visit a sister he hadn't seen in years. These even-toned questions destabilized my father's visitor; his voice thickened and his breath came short as he pleaded the case that Judy claimed had almost brought her to tears.

Our father had taken advantage of Mr. Howell's sister, her brother maintained. She was an old woman who had lived in that house her entire life, and when siblings had moved away she had stayed behind to care for her parents. She was an old woman with a saintly nature who preferred to see the good in her fellow man, rather than dwell on the bad, and she deserved special consideration. Perhaps my father had a sister like that (he did, and her name was Louise). Common decency demanded—and my father interrupted his visitor to utter a phrase he would repeat two more times. In *compos mentis*. What my father meant was that Miss Imogene Howell was legally of sound mind, and if she wanted to sell the property she and she alone held the deed to that was her affair. Mr. Howell protested that she held the deed only because their parents knew she would always keep the property in the family, she was safeguarding it so that brothers and sisters would not have to spend time and money in lawyers' offices... In *compos mentis*, my father uttered again. Mr. Howell protested, But you offered an unconscionable amount of money to an old lady...Which only means that your parents miscalculated, my father responded. And we were not notified until the sale had gone through! That was not fair, sir! And my father pointed out it had been Imogene Howell's decision to make, and he was not about to tell a lady like that how to conduct her affairs. Was there anything else?

There was, of course. There was the family cemetery, where Howells had rested for generations. A sort of foggy reverence entered Mr. Howell's voice now, and the house went exceptionally quiet. Mr. Howell began to name names, starting with great grandparents, and to each he added a phrase or two to personalize it all. Mr. Erastus Howell, the grandsire of them all, who had cleared the land for farming, his nature as steadfast as a plough. His wife, Henrietta... and my father did not stop him. By the time he had finished Mr. Howell's indignation had succumbed to the weight of his memories and his voice sounded spent. That cemetery was holy ground. Mr. Howell's sister had no right to sell it to my father, not for all the money in the world. In *compos mentis*, my father replied, for the last time, and Mr. Howell seemed to release a low long breath, so deep-chested it sounded like a distant howl. But he must have been asking about the bones, on that last long breath he must have been making a piteous plea for his ancestors' bones, for I heard my father say, with a sort of biblical finality, Dust to dust, ashes to ashes, sir, and it was shortly after that that Mr. Howell got up and shambled out to his car.

Why did our father leave the door open on that pitiful scene, and why did he let his visitor go on and on? I think he was teaching us a lesson. My father was a businessman, and being a businessman required a clear head twenty-four hours a day. People who weren't businessmen only cleared their heads occasionally, and when they did a lot of cloudy sentimentality could come gushing in. With a more consistently clear head somebody like the downtrodden Mr. Howell would have realized that his sister had no business holding the title to that property exclusively, that a day of reckoning was close at hand. And when that day came, Mr. Howell and his other aggrieved siblings might discover they didn't know their sister Imogene at all. A woman who had seemingly denied herself all her life might try to get it all back in the end. A clearer head might have alerted Mr. Howell to that possibility. This was not a story of abstract acreage with survey statistics that would cause only real estate lawyers and courthouse functionaries to shake their heads. This was a story we could all understand. Our father was testing us. Would we belong to the clear heads of the world or to the Mr. Howells, left shambling out to his car, which was still running because he really didn't know whether he was coming or going?

But the family cemetery? You can't buy somebody else's ancestral bones—even I knew that. Say Miss Imogene Howell needed money for an expensive operation and took out a mortgage on her property, and say the bank eventually foreclosed. The bank couldn't plow those bones under. They'd have to relocate them, bury them anew. Unless...unless...after a barren life of service to the family's cause, Miss Imogene Howell had said to my father, and had had it written in to that effect, too, Get rid of those bones, sir. I intend to live my last days as far from a cemetery as I can get, particularly if that cemetery is full of ungrateful Howells. Clearer heads might have alerted Mr. Howell and his siblings to that possibility, too.

A lesson on life we were getting. Perhaps our father had left his door open because he couldn't bring himself to give us the benefit of his wisdom face to face. Perhaps he looked at us and saw something like a family cemetery in the making. I don't know.

I do know I looked in the county phone book just to see, and found a Miss Imogene Howell listed and noted the address, and then talked my cousin Paul into riding our bikes out there—just to see. It wasn't far, but straight out in the country, down a narrow crumbling road that looked as if it hadn't been used more than once or twice a year. The house was like a hundred others I had seen, a small dog-trot of a house that had been built onto so often it had reached an ungainly shape only those who lived there would be able to find their way around in. The trees in front were covered with scaly lichen, and a bank of withered kudzu crowded in from one side. On the front porch were the unwatered remains of geraniums and a couple of spindly, cane-bottom chairs. The front door was closed, but I could see past a gauzy gray curtain down the dogtrot become the main hall, and no one was home. Paul wondered how I could be sure. He knew as well as I did that old women frequently materialized out of such unlikely surroundings. Until a bulldozer knocked such a house down, the chances were good you'd find an old woman in it. Doing what? Haunting it, contributing to its grayness. I stepped off the porch and took a look around. With the clear head my father might have wished on me, I should have seen an expressway running above me and, down where we stood, a filling station with a gift shop attached, specializing in divinity fudge. Or a broad yard like the setting for a sparkling jewel, which would be the swimming pool, of course. I should have heard the muted roar of expensive cars passing or children splashing in the pool.

Paul, already a purposeful boy, who would go on to have a purposeful career, asked what we'd ridden out here for if I was just going to stand there like some cigar store Indian. I told him there was a cemetery out back, which would be neat to find, which made no sense to him at all. His parents, like the parents of most of our friends, were always dragging him off to a cemetery somewhere to stand before the gravestone of a distant relative, whose name meant nothing and whose life story, which he'd be forced to listen to, sounded like all the other life stories he'd heard. All you had to do was change the name of a town or two, upstate or downstate, and the names of children who came and went, while the adults lingered on for hours, untangling and re-tangling the web of kinship. Still, I persuaded Paul to help me look out back past the listing shacks and a barn as weather-grayed as a hundred Novembers in one, and we didn't find it, of course. The fields were overgrown, and if there'd been any gravestones out there the earth had taken them under. A little wrought-iron fence, giving the cemetery the distinction it deserved, had never existed. It was a picturesque detail, a cemetery like that in a homestead going four or five generations back, but if it had never existed, then there was a chance that the improbably admitted Mr. Howell had, with his preacher's empty barrel of a voice, been trying to put one over on my father and my father had called his bluff. Which should have made us, his wife and his children, proud, although by the time Mr. Howell had been admitted to our house it was far too late for that. Mother was succumbing to the bitterness that would claim the rest of her life, and Judy was more than halfway out the door. I was proud, but not entirely, and very privately. Even at that young age, I knew I occupied a camp of one.

VI

After he'd survived Okinawa, Hugh had sent a letter back home which the military censor had let come through word for word, with a note written at the end: "Somebody should get this published in the biggest newspaper in the country." The letter was addressed to my mother. By that time my father would have been back home, but Hugh probably didn't know that. The letter was "a war to end all wars" letter; it was about the horror of war and the basic goodness of man—if somebody wasn't shooting at him and he weren't being forced to shoot back. It contained this sentence: "If it weren't for unbridled greed and a childish refusal to admit when one's wrong, this planet of ours would come to seem like a big beautiful ball of plenty." The censor must have thought Hugh had the greedy Japanese in mind, swallowing islands like some unbridled whale with an insatiable maw. Mother took the letter to perhaps the only newspaper she knew, the *Russellville Herald*, which published it proudly, and then when Hugh returned offered him a job.

Hugh took the job, then went back to school and took a liberal arts degree, returned to newspaper work, branched out into other jobs, other professions, went back to school again and studied architecture and city planning for a while, became a builder, a contractor, saw the wisdom in shopping centers when they were regarded as communal hubs and designed at least two that sat on land my father had purchased, designed a golf course, dabbled in speed reading, horticulture, helped get two local television stations up and running, became a motivational speaker and returned to his university to offer a lecture in how to succeed while doing justice to this big beautiful ball of plenty that was our world. Without exerting himself he sold himself and lived in various towns, all within driving distance of ours. He attended Langley reunions. He fathered numerous children and was the first Langley to divorce, after which he remarried and fathered another family. He suffered no shortage of *élan vital*. He was too resourceful a person to make common cause with his own father (as he aged, Uncle Raymond took on the looks and ways of a heavy-lidded snapping turtle), and even when his son Billy had disgraced himself in Bob Langley's eyes, Hugh never renounced the great lasting shower of good fortune that Bob and Fran Langley had rained down on his life. To me he kept alive what he refused to let die, and when he went to the mountains he gathered his whole life behind him and took it up there, too. The fact was, Hugh Langley never gave up on anything he'd once invested belief in. As the years passed he got rounder and rosier and hardly had to open his mouth any more to make you a believer. You believed, even though you might not stop shaking your head.

I left the heat of our town behind and drove up to see him. It was hot in the mountains, too, but up there the heat was clean, direct, you stepped out of the sun into the shade and a coolness greeted you, smelling of the mountain streams, the damp earth, and pines. I climbed up his mountain road into that coolness and parked my car beside his cistern, the clearest, cleanest, and coldest water on God's green earth, or so Hugh claimed. I should dip my hands into it and drink. And if I wanted to know what I really was, and what I still had time left to become, I should spend a moment studying the reflection of my face I saw there.

I did cup my hands and drink, scattering my reflection.

Hugh did not know I was coming. But his indestructible Range Rover was parked just down from the cistern, and his second wife Evelyn opened the door with a finger to her lips. Hugh was sitting out on his deck in the shade, eyes closed, listening to water run down his hillside, the nearby cooing of doves and the distant downhill screech of some bird warning that there was an intruder in their midst. But Hugh was playing possum. I sat down as noiselessly as I could, and Hugh, eyes still closed and in a voice as quiet as if I were sharing a foxhole with him and all the big guns had fallen silent, said, "What took you so long, Jaybird?"

So I closed my eyes, too. "I think I'm going to need some help," I said.

"And it took you all this time?"

"When you left so soon after the funeral..."

"Wrong time, wrong place," Hugh declared, sadly, but in no uncertain terms.

We listened to the hillside, the birds, the subdued stitching of insects, the absence of children, the breeze scraping in the pinecones, the sound of a shallow stream flowing around rocks, the boards of the deck taking on the day's heat. Evelyn brought us iced tea. Hugh had had four children by his first wife, three with Evelyn. She was a woman who mixed a bemused tolerance for her husband with a devotee's devotion and was at least twenty years his junior. When she smiled her cheeks balled up and her eyes puffed shut, making her expressions difficult to read. I did not know whether she had been a willing convert to mountain life or not. When she saw me it was as if I'd been expected and as if the wait had led to minor disappointments. She seemed to be saying Hugh had told her things about me I might not know about myself.

But she left us our tea. Neither of us drank until Hugh took a long swallow of his followed by its successful passage down his throat. The tinkle of ice I barely heard.

Hugh said, "I think I should show you something. Maybe the time has come."

"Just tell me one thing first," I hurried to get in. "Is something missing or is the story complete?"

Hugh laughed. It was only then when the rosiness seemed to rise back into his face. "It never ends, Jaybird. The whole secret is to find some place where it doesn't matter, where you can sleep at night, where dreams…how do they say it, 'are entirely fictitious, the characters resembling no one you know, intended for your amusement only?'"

I let him lead me down off the hill. I am not entirely sure why.

When he got into his Range Rover and began to move things off the passenger seat I told him not to bother, that I would follow him in my car. Did I think at his advanced age his driving skills were impaired? Was I thinking of my own safety? Did I think he would run us off the road? Or was I positioning myself to make a break if it came to that? I followed him around switchbacks, downed tree trunks, perhaps intentionally downed to make access to his mountain retreat forbidding, and over a shallow stream that twice crossed the road. The forest was dense until we reached the highway where a barbecue restaurant had boarded up its windows and padlocked its doors and whose sign stood lusterless and tall in a parking area where the weeds had already broken through. Hugh turned left and led me into the town.

It consisted of a string of businesses along both sides of the highway as if thrown up for gold rush days. But these businesses were all open and the traffic flow here was steady. We passed a real estate agency on the right, Mountain Vistas, which I knew to have been his. Past that was a small park with a pavilion, situated on the shore of a lake. Across the street was a restaurant, whose second floor, in a cantilevered effect, practically protruded over the highway. Hugh turned in there. Would I like to eat? Would I like to sit at a table in that protruding part which Hugh Langley as good as had reserved for himself?

His favorite waitress's name was Carole, with an "e." Hugh identified me as his cousin and then not as "Jaybird," as I'd expected, but, with a wink, as "Bob Langley's boy." Carole, the waitress, was roughly my age but she kept up a youthful banter and more than once brushed Hugh's shoulder as she passed. Bob Langley? Bob Langley? Hugh didn't mean that legendary four-letter man from back in the Golden Age, did he? About whom she had heard so much? Back across the Great Divide? Carole, the waitress, brushed my shoulder, too, as she leaned in to take my order. Bob Langley's boy.

Hugh Langley was grinning for the staging. I would forgive him this piece of theatrics.

I said, "Can you think of any more stories, Hugh? Any more? I mean stories from back then."

"Back when? From before the war? There's no end to the stories, Jaybird."

"I don't mean home runs or touchdowns, anything like that. No fly balls caught climbing the fence. No pole-vaulting into the great beyond. Nothing like that. No father or father-substitutes playing catch with deprived little boys."

"You mean a story to end them all."

"Do I? Do you know such a story, Hugh?"

"Did I ever tell you about the time Bob and Fran Langley, née Knowlton, ran off and got married on the sly?"

Hugh Langley had never sailed over water as blue as the blue I saw shining out of the slit of his eyes. With the years and the searing mountain sun his face had become as cured and pebbly as an old fruit rind, but his eyes were a deep-sea, relishing blue, and I told him, no, such a story he had never told me.

Our lunch first. Carole brought it to us on a stream of her banter. A couple of Hugh's acquaintances stopped by. Someone waved up from the sidewalk below running along beside the highway through town. I got the impression my uncle-aged cousin, now retired, did not make everyday appearances in the town and when he did was regarded as being on display, fair game. After lunch he walked me across the highway into the park with a pavilion out beside the lake.

He said, "There's something I want to show you."

I said, "You were going to tell me a story first, the one to end them all."

"I was?"

"About my parents marrying on the sly."

"Oh, that story. Everyone knows that."

"I don't."

"I bet you can get Judy to tell you that story."

"Judy's gone. She's not coming back."

"She's not? Well, that's a shame. She was the prettiest little thing. She couldn't have been more than two years old when I came through town and she jumped up on my lap—"

I interrupted him. "Before you went off to the Pacific, before Okinawa, you mean."

The name of the island itself seemed to trigger an involuntary reaction in my cousin, something like a hypnotic response. For a moment everything stopped. No traffic noise, no boats on the lake. Little waves, if there were any, lapped soundlessly against the shore. Hugh might have just awakened from a nightmare, a strange mixture of apprehension and relief clouding his eyes, in his voice a distancing effect, as though he were speaking under the calm of a temporary truce. "...that was where it all ended, every day the end of the world. Easter Sunday, April fool's, the biggest amphibian landing in the Pacific, and the Japs let us walk up onto the beaches. Not a shot was fired. They let us climb up onto the cliffs. We looked out on a bay and had the biggest light show in the war to entertain us. Search lights. Tracer bullets. Exploding bombs. Kamikazes going down in flames. Battleships going down. We dug our foxholes and took in the show. Then it turned around. It really was April's fool day, Jay. 1945. Their planes began to bomb us. The bombs when they fell made a swishing sound, this quiet 'swish, swish, swish,' and you waited. Then their artillery came in. The Japs had an artillery school on the island and had the entire terrain mapped out in tight artillery squares. Their accuracy was incredible. We slept in mud and rainwater. If you survived the bombing and the shelling and crawled out of your foxhole to try to find a dry place to sleep, they'd shoot you, if your own men didn't. You stayed put, dug deeper into the mud, and in the dead of night a Jap might slip in beside you and slit your throat. But you didn't get out. Small mortar fire would come right down a row of foxholes, shells the size of your fist, they could fit one in each of your pockets, their marksmanship was that good. But you lay there freezing wet, afraid to crawl out, really nowhere to go, waiting for it to get light. You were never sure it would. You know what it was like, don't you?"

"There was a story you were going to tell me, Hugh."

"Sure you do. A watery hole? You lie there in the dark waiting to see the light of day? This went on for months. It was as if we'd dug our own graves. The sad fact is, most of us had. I don't think it was until I came up here that I finally got the stench of death out of my nose."

"Hugh, that story."

"Look up there first, Jaybird."

My cousin was pointing up the lake along the unbuilt-on, left hand shore. The houses and boathouses were all built along the right. It's just possible he saw the lake as a vast watery hole and the mountains as an elevation far beyond the reach of bombs or guns. In the middle of the night no one slipping in beside him to slit his throat. At last, the smells of the seasons, each a distinct delight.

"As far as you can see. That point way out there. The last one. Now keep that piece of land in your mind's eye."

We went back to our cars and this time he wouldn't let me get into mine. We'd need the Range Rover to get up that left-hand shore. A dirt road had been graded through and then abandoned, it seemed, and storms had washed deep ruts in the road and brought limbs down out of the trees. Hugh drove his Range Rover as if it were a tank, blasting through obstructions that would have caused others to turn back, and I soon suspected that the tracks I saw in the hardened clay and mud must have been his from earlier trips. We took our jolts. The expression on Hugh's face was committed, concentrated, but on the edge of some deep and satisfying pleasure, as if he calculated with each turn of the wheel just how far we had left. We saw no one else. Through the trees and brush on our right no trace of a house or car or dock. Occasionally, when a stream came down from the hills on our left and entered the lake, some lake-light broke through, a glittering, effulgent expanse, quickly gone. We smelled the lake, though. Its rawness, its freshness, its natural taint. Just a flavoring of fish. All that Hugh said during this ride was, "It's worth it, Jay. Just hold on."

The road swung to the right, the underbrush thinned, the tall trees, mostly oak and ash and hickory, just a scattering of pines, gave way, and we drove out into the open on the point of land we'd seen at the limit of sight from the pavilion down in the town. Hugh directed my attention away from the town and toward the mountainside rising out of the lake across the way. I knew where I was looking even before he said, "In the winter I can sit on my deck and see this point with my binoculars. It will be at least ten years before anyone builds out this far, Jay. Maybe longer. Here's where you want to be."

We got out of the Range Rover and walked across a mica-glittering clay out to the shore. With the Range Rover behind us and no boat anywhere near us on the lake, the smell was pure, a musky and manless blend of fresh growth and decay, fish and crayfish from a nearby entering stream, animal life and animal death from farther back in the brush. The smell of sunlight on the water, hot and then cool with the uplift of a breeze, the suggestion of an untapped and inexhaustible natural fund.

I said, "Let me guess. This is that piece of land you've been telling me I should buy, isn't it, Hugh? When it was time to come to the mountains."

"This is it, Jaybird."

I looked up the lake toward the distant, newly founded lakeside town. I looked across the way to Hugh's mountainside.

"Except you can't buy it."

"No?"

"It was the last piece of land I sold before I retired."

"I see," I said. "Who'd you sell it to?"

"I sold it to myself."

"And?"

"I walked over to the town hall and put it in your name. The land belongs to you, Jay. The time has come. If it's those sweet dreams you're after, you need it now."

"You're sure."

"You haven't got a day to lose. "

"What was that story you were going to tell me, Hugh?"

He put his hand on my shoulder. For an instant he regarded me with a look impossible to read, it was as if the contours of his highly animated face had suddenly been struck still and caught in an expression corresponding to no emotion he'd known, certainly nothing I'd seen there before. It was a face of excrescences, a moment's alien natural growth, which gave the glint of his eyes a pleading and imprisoned look. I had to look away. I took refuge in the touch of his hand on my shoulder, where he wouldn't squeeze, but where in both the vastness and seclusion of where we found ourselves there was a sense of intimacy unlike any I'd felt before.

"I think you know," he said.

In that, I replied, he was mistaken.

"It's those towns down there, Jay. Every one of them has to have its hero. Someone who can excel in what the townspeople can only dream about. Russellville chose your father. In exchange they gave him everything. They gave him his four letters and his perfect spirals and his thirty foot set shots and his great gliding range in center field. They gave him his good looks and they gave him your mother, even though Fran was doing the driving and thinks she caught him fair and square. And they gave him his decency, his generosity. They gave him his capacity to be everything to everybody in town. Remember, he was my hero, too, when my own father was as tight-lipped to me as that wound he carried in his shoulder. Anything wrong with that?"

No, nothing. But Hugh was right. I did know about all that. What marriage on the sly?

"Just a little something your mother and father took for themselves when the town wasn't looking. Although the town found out—eventually those towns down there will discover it all. One courthouse to another, downstate to upstate. Then someone in Russellville's courthouse passing on the word to someone in the family for safe keeping."

And that someone would be Aunt Louise.

"The downstate town was called Chandlersville. South, southwest, on the state line. They drove down in the morning, married in the courthouse at noon, and were back in Russellville by supper. Bob ran the risk of being recognized. To reduce that risk all they'd have to have done was step across the state line. I don't think they cared, or the town did much either. If Bob Langley and Fran Knowlton took a little something for themselves, no complaints, as long as they were back by supper time and the town got the church wedding it wanted."

Minus the honeymoon.

"There were hundreds of photographs of that wedding, and every one showed your mother married in a dress as white as the driven snow."

In effect, just a day's outing.

"They remained within bounds. A little act of rebellion that had already been written in. Something they took for themselves before the town took its due. Except…"

I waited. Hugh looked away, he looked around, as if to assure himself we were alone. We were so alone that only in winter with the most powerful binoculars money could buy would we be detectable, little twig figures barely identifiable as human, on a tiny spur of land raised up to the sky.

"…except the town didn't count on a World War. What do you do with a hero then? These towns don't always know what they want. Come a war, do they want your Dad with them to keep him safe? They've got a big bomber plant nearby and they've got a draft board that knows the score. Or, on second thought, do they want him over there? And once he's over there, what do they want him to do? Win a few medals he can show around town, until they begin to tarnish like everything else? Or die gloriously on the field of battle, to keep the illusion alive? Remember what the poet says about a timely death: 'And now you will not swell the rout/ Of lads that wore their honors out,/ Runners whom renown outran/ And the name died before the man.' I'm willing to bet that it never crossed Mr. A. E. Housman's mind that his athlete might decide to come back from a war as a one-legged man, to rub the town's noses in the mess it had made. You see what I mean? See what I'm driving at?"

I neither nodded nor shook my head. I stared at him.

"Bob Langley had a little taste of rebellion when it hardly mattered. But when it did, it changed everything. He rebelled and instead of getting married on the sly he went to war on the sly, and there was nothing the town could do."

At that point I woke up to what I was being asked to believe. It had been Hugh who, long ago, had told me the story of how my mother and grandmother had sat my father down and informed him he would not become a professional baseball player. Henceforth, he would become a respectable man. Why couldn't his wife and his mother have sat him down again? You will not go off and get yourself killed or maimed just to satisfy some boyish streak of rebellion a man like you has to quell. You will cleave to your wife and daughter, town and country, and do as you're told. You will obey that citizen's committee known as a draft board, keep the bombers rolling out, and rebel against your rebellion. Of course, there was something the town could have done, and had not done. Why was that?

With my insistence, Hugh's eyes had opened wide. They were filling up. I had to remember his age, the emotions of the moment, the point of land on which we stood, his gift to me, what all these years he'd been planning to pass down. His hand was no longer on my shoulder and I hesitated to place my hand on his.

"What was it?" I said. "There was something, Hugh. Is it something you've chosen not to tell me or is it something you don't know?"

"Jaybird," he murmured. It was as if he'd reached out to make sure I was there and discovered I was. Then his hand was back on my shoulder, his emotion-filled eyes on mine. "You like it up here, don't you? You truly do."

I assured him I did. I nodded. I might have paused a moment to look around, to take on the distances, but I didn't.

"You can live in those towns down there just so long, then if you want to stay sane you've got to come up here. You understand that now."

There was no arguing with him, nor did I want to. For an instant I closed my eyes, and within that vast and secluded stirring of nature all around us what I heard was a hissing and a puckering sound, as if we were both under fire. I felt that muddy water that Hugh, night after night, had bedded down in rising around us. All so that Bob and Fran Langley might be kept safe from harm.

My existence had hung in the balance. I opened my eyes.

Hugh's were filled with rheumy tears.

I said, "I can't accept this land as a gift, you know that, don't you?" I was thinking of Hugh's seven children. And no telling how many grandchildren. It had been many years since the Langleys had held a family reunion.

"No gift. No freebees," Hugh said. "It will cost you a dollar."

I smiled and shook my head. This was to have been my purchase on our big beautiful ball of plenty.

"I like you, Jay. Don't know why but I always have. Tell you what I'm gonna do," Hugh spaced it out, affected a salesman's cadence and chumminess, "I'll make it ten bucks, but I won't settle for a penny less."

I continued to look at him, continued to smile. I thought of all the ways I was indebted to this man, who, in the face of what had become the town's disapproval and, even more unforgivingly, my sister's, had kept the Langley legend alive. He had amassed such a fund of approval for himself he could afford to spend a portion on what, sadly, had become a lost cause. His cause had been to redeem

Bob Langley from an overreaching sort of disgrace and Fran Langley from an associate's guilt. His cause had been to unpoison me, to bring alive for me a time I'd never known. Then, perhaps, with that same Langley lore, to poison me again. Judy certainly thought so.

"Jay," he said. "Jaybird. Don't turn me down."

There was a nakedness and a need I'd never observed in him before. He was an old man, beloved by everybody in his mountain town, but no longer counting the years, now more likely the weeks and days. As a very young man he'd come back through town on his way to the Pacific and the last assault on the Japanese to tell Bob and Fran Langley to sit tight, not to worry, he would protect them from harm. In turn they were to keep the legend alive for him to come back to. Fran Langley had met him at the door in angry, confused, and accusing tears. Bob Langley had deserted her and gone off to war, leaving a two-year old daughter behind. To console her, hoping somehow to console himself, Hugh had stepped through the door. I was not there. I was not yet.

Hugh Langley, nipping at my father's heels, basking in the glow of my mother's out-of-reach beauty.

A war-bound boy. Blinded. Boyishly in love with them both, my sister had said.

And now it was all being handed down to me. His love was. His devotion. He would bring me to the mountains. He would set me down on a choice piece of land, lakefront and neighbor-free, as far away from those soul-constricting towns as I could get, all because I was Bob Langley's boy. It was hero-worship a generation removed. It was a way of proclaiming that, try as it might, the world could not kill or corrupt or maim or disfigure a real hero, regardless of what the poet said. A town couldn't either. If it tried to turn its back on a hero, it would hear the plonk-plonk-plonk of Bob Langley's crutch bearing down; it would turn back around and there I'd be. Bob Langley's boy. A non-heroic hero in the guise of an implacably old but somehow ageless man. But Hugh would save me from that. If I would let him, he would give me more than the town had ever given my father. I was beginning to understand. Hugh wasn't hero-worshipping me—when he closed his eyes and imagined a figure gliding back against a field of green, tracking a white ball across a sky's summer-blue, it wouldn't be me he'd see, but it would be me that allowed my father to take the field, I would be the seed out of which my father would spring as long as the town in which I continued to live didn't steal my soul before Hugh could spirit me up here. From his vantage point halfway up a mountainside he could then train the world's most powerful binoculars on a point of land, which would be as good as a stage, three sides surrounded by a body of shining water, and watch me perform. My performance would consist of standing there, saved, and allowing my father to emerge out of me. Just that. No more. It wasn't asking too much. It wasn't asking anything at all.

Then there was the other explanation for why I was being bequeathed this choice piece of land. It went as follows. In Bob Langley's absence, Hugh Langley allows my tearful mother to lead him into their wartime quarters. He allows her to make him dinner. A ration-restricted wartime dinner—and while the Spam is frying Judy forsakes her daa-dee's birds and climbs up onto her uncle-aged cousin's lap. Her cousin has sailed the seven seas, he's seen some very exotic stuff, but Judy is only two and no one is in the mood for tales of faraway lands anyway. Still, even when dashed in his hopes and caught in a self-questioning turmoil, Hugh can be an engaging and enlivening presence, and it takes a while before Judy, whose father is not there to tell her a story and kiss her good night, can be persuaded to go to sleep. And even then she might wake up to the twenty-four-seven clamor that plant must be making as it keeps the B-29's rolling out. Judy might call out in her sleep. Already, she might be dreaming of something as quietly flowing and restful as a river right outside her window, and wake to find she's been betrayed. So many things. It would depend on how intemperate my father's departure had been, how displaced, strange to herself and exposed my mother had felt herself to be, and how shattering the times. I could imagine a time when deaths and births were thrown back on each other with kaleidoscopic speed. A time with no mooring, when you simply clung to what was nearest at hand.

Or nearest of kin.

It would have to have been my mother who cried, who pleaded, who asked only to be comforted and, insatiable for comfort, asked again and again. And it would have to have been my cousin Hugh who couldn't stand to see her like this and who couldn't stand not to do her bidding—still, in spite of his Merchant Marine service, in so many ways a boy, but a boy who kept a man in reserve for some once-in-a-lifetime feat. Hold me, Hugh! No, don't let go! Hold me tighter! It's all right…it's all right… Anything can happen now, the world is turning upside down, no one is where they belong, Hugh, we may be the only two people left alive…and am I then to assume

that Hugh Langley made love to Fran Langley as if both were clinging to a raft in war-torn seas and hoping only to survive until the
seas calmed and Bob Langley walked back through the door? And,
incidentally, engendering me? Consider the math. And Bob Langley
did not walk back through the door—at least, on two legs. Consider
how betrayed and how disconsolate my mother must have felt and
how anxious Hugh Langley must have been to console her and how
tempted to lie in the arms of his hero's bride and be Bob Langley, if
only for an hour. Inconsolable himself, perhaps, when it was all over,
but for that hour, at least...

And I couldn't consider it. The ecstasy done, the betrayal full-
blown, Hugh Langley lying there with his arm thrown over his eyes
and Fran Langley mothering him back to life so that he could be
shipped out to Okinawa and a foxhole, where he had one chance in
ten of being born back into this world. I couldn't hold it all in my
mind. This piece of lakeside land was not my birthright, was not a
father's bequest to his son. It was a cousin's gift to a cousin, an uncle-aged cousin to a much younger one who, in spite of the math, was
unmistakably his father's son.

"Forgive me, Hugh," I said. "Of course, I'll accept your gift. You
can imagine me right here, on this point of land, and when the winter
comes I'll wave."

It was as if I had given the gift to him. He did what seemed to be a
little dance of relief and delight there on the clayey sand. He beamed
at me, his mouth hanging partially open, and for an instant I feared
for him, as if such good news was all he was living out his last days
to hear. I went up and put my arm around his shoulder. I was a good

half-head taller. Broader shouldered. And, as everybody said, I had my father's cheekbones and chin.

Hugh recovered enough to say, "There're a couple of papers you need to sign in the town hall. We still have time."

I led him back to the car. He didn't protest when I climbed into the driver's seat of the Range Rover. He docilely took his place in the passenger seat, buckled himself in, and it was in his tracks I found myself driving as we worked our way down the heavily rutted and obstructed road. Once I realized there was really no harm I could inflict on his car, that it was powerfully enough built to withstand anything I could ask it to do, I gave myself over to it, plowing through any and all resistance, yes, following Hugh's tracks but also creating my own. I would come back out to this point. I would buy a Range Rover myself and revisit my isolated point of land, looking out on a lake the smooth low-luster of jade. The building of a house never entered my mind. As Hugh had, I pictured the point unbuilt on, the smell not of lumber, paint and concrete, but of what lived and died in those weeds and crawled or washed up onto the shore. I pictured Judy sitting beside her river. What a curious coincidence, I thought, and what a world of difference. I looked over at my cousin and benefactor, who hung in his seat harness as though deeply asleep, so deeply that I reached over to give him a gentle jostling shake. But before my hand reached his shoulder, he addressed me. He said, "I want you to go talk to Billy, Jay. Now that Bob's gone, it's time we all made peace. Will you do that for me?" For my information he then added, "Billy's better now."

Later, with the deed to the land we'd visited in the glove compartment of my car, I pulled off the road and instead of calling my sister

Judy, as I'd intended, tried to call Karen Ambrose instead. Between towns and still in the mountains, I was told I lacked coverage. The next town was named Carlson, and it had a little square and a bandstand and a statue of a Confederate soldier erected beside a cannon, as if a cannon and a soldier with his musket were all it was going to take. This time I got through to Karen, who said she was doing nothing, which I found hard to imagine, and who said she'd been waiting for my call, which I found harder still. We had such a span of years between us. As unattached as she now felt herself to be, that she would be swinging in her concerns back to me seemed almost self-contradictory, unless, of course, there'd been something in our relationship binding us still.

Had I gone to the mountains?

Had I seen my cousin?

Had I stayed on alert?

Had I discovered where it started not to make sense? Did it make more sense now?

I stood directly before the statue of a man—a battle-hardened boy—in a kepi cap leaning on a musket propped at his side. Where a crutch might have been. As if every soldier needed one. I smiled, but I now had an answer to her question.

"I don't know why my father went off to war. I really don't. If there's a place where it starts not to make sense, it's right there."

Not a surge of patriotism? Not a seizure of able-bodied, home-front shame?

"That's what I'd always thought. The truth is I hadn't thought, but now I believe there's something more."

And I needed to know? She reminded me that her father, the vice admiral, had arrived late for the big show and had had to be content with the Korean War instead. Like a consolation game. Third place. War does strange things to men's minds, and a World War…

"Karen," I said, "I've got to hang up. I'm about to lose coverage. I'd like to see you again. I don't know how you feel about that."

Did I mean see her now that we were both free?

But she said it in such a way that I was led to understand we both weren't—free. I didn't argue with her. What would have been the point?

I said instead, "Hugh Langley is still alive. He could die any day, but right now he's in his element—if anybody is."

She was glad. She was glad that she stood corrected. She told me not to forget her and asked to be kept informed. Then she hung up.

It was a mystery to me, and before I reached the next town the mystery had built to the point that I didn't want to wait. I stopped for gas which I really didn't need, then moved the car over to a shaded area, beside a dumpster, which gave off an odor of lubricant waste and fast food trash, and this time I did call my sister. She answered, and before I identified myself I listened to see if I could hear the background flow of water, in a single living unturbulent stream. I believed that I could, and, as I pictured it, that was where she sat.

I said, "Why didn't you tell me that Karen Ambrose had visited you up there?"

And she replied, "I thought I did."

"You said she'd called. Or that you had."

"No, if I remember correctly, I said we'd stayed in contact."

"Contact? You sat her down beside that river where you're sitting right now."

"Actually, I'm inside. It's raining up here. Coming down in sheets. Can't you hear it?"

"Do you talk now? She's back in my life. Did you know that?"

"Well, good for her… No, I take that back. Good for you. For her we'll have to wait and see."

"She said that river of yours put her to sleep."

"Jay, I've got a little secret for you. Nothing puts Karen Ambrose to sleep. Not any more. What she might have meant to say was that the river dulled her edge."

"She's different, you know."

"I know."

"Do you know what she wants?"

"In so many words, I suspect now that she's free she's out to see if she can keep those eight years she spent with you from being converted into an absolute waste."

"Retroactively? And what's to keep her from wasting her time again?"

"Only you, Jay, if you cooperate."

"What's that suppose to mean?"

"Don't fight her. If she talks sense to you, listen to her. She's down there and I'm up here."

"You're asking me to treat her as your proxy?"

"Did I say that? We're about as different as different can be. She's sane, and we both know I'm not."

She suspended her tone, held a space, waiting for me to laugh.

The woman in the carriage house. I heard the rain come down, except it sounded like the river to me, in close passage, as if she'd moved her chair to the very edge of the bank and was cooling her feet, perhaps more than that, venturing Ophelia-like out under the willow, downstream, bending this way and that, until, her hair streaming, she floated out to sea. But Judy's hair was cut short, an alert salt and pepper gray.

"I want to ask you something," I said. "Did you ever hear a story about our mother and father running off to get married before they gave the town the wedding it wanted? Running off to get married on the sly, just for themselves? Did you ever hear that story?"

More rain poured down or more river flowed by. Finally, in a voice strangely clear because something in it was spent, she said, "Jay, leave it alone, please. There's no end to those stories, you know that."

"But did you?"

"I've heard them all."

"So if there was a marriage was there a honeymoon, or was that something only the town could give them?"

She exhaled heavily, seemed on the point of hanging up, but then revived. "There's no way of knowing, is there? Which means we could always make one up. Or you could. That's your department, not mine."

"Meaning?"

"Meaning when it comes to Bob and Fran Langley, you seem to never know where to draw the line."

I held a pause. The water came down, in sheets, or the water flowed out in one glassy stream.

"All right," I said, "here's something entirely yours, only you can answer. At two years old, were you the prettiest little thing?"

"What?"

"You have at least one memory from those times, you told me so. So do you remember looking in the mirror at that age and thinking, what a pretty little thing I am?"

"Jay, what are you insinuating? What are you cooking up?"

"After our father went off to war, maybe taking the cardinals with him, I don't know about that, do you remember being bounced, say, on a kinsman's knee and being exclaimed over. 'You're the prettiest little thing' or maybe 'the cutest little thing'. Something sweet, something you wouldn't want to forget."

I listened to the water again, the flow, either down from the sky or on out to sea, it really didn't matter. Out at sea the river water would evaporate, mist up to the sky, then rain down and create the same river again. Which you could step into as often as you wanted. Or simply sit beside.

In a voice hard as stone but hollow, as though despairing at the core, Judy said, "You've been talking to our cousin Hugh again. You've been up there, haven't you, Jay."

"So you do remember Hugh. You were two, maybe two and half, and he stopped by on his way to war."

"I'm hanging up. Don't call back."

"A simple question. A second memory to go with the burdies."

She paused, drew breath, then as deliberately as she could she pronounced the words, "I'm up here because I don't want to have to deal with all of that. Don't you understand anything?"

When I didn't answer immediately, she added, "Yes, you do understand, which makes it worse. Goodbye, Jay."

I waited, breathed down the mixed aroma of thickening motor oil and rancid French fries, and held it. Listened to the water and, just to see, waited for its cleansing effect. Even had time to imagine myself out on Hugh's point of land with a mountain lake all around. Then I heard a click, but discreet, as if one person hanging up on another—slamming a receiver down in anger, in disgust, in sorrow, in an act of utter impotence—were a thing of the past. As if, henceforth, there never could or would be a clean and irreversible severing of the ties.

VII

MY FATHER DID NOT SMOKE. The woodsy odor of the sun shining through fall leaves Judy had detected as a two year old child I had not. I do not remember any particular cologne. He was always clean-shaven but never seemed to smell of shaving cream. I remember a background smell of dust and dirt and then the sheer exertion of human heat, a state of combustion more than anything else, which was particularly strong every time he picked up that crutch.

The crutch remained propped on the windowsill of his office, a window which looked down onto the street and the town's second best movie theater, always about to close, or on the verge of being converted into something else, and I smelled that combustive smell then.

My father had never invited me to come work for him. He had never hinted I should stop by to help out after school, or in some way that I should apprentice myself to him. The only time I'd made common cause with my father was when I'd stood as a child on one side of him and the banking man had stood on the other, we'd looked out on that first field, and my father's hand had fallen on my head. It was the hand that had said, Do this and don't do that. Stand there, wait for me. Stand there for as long as it takes. My father had not uttered a word, but the fingers had taken root. Can you do that son? And I'd stood there, as I would have stood by one of those suburban driveways waiting for my father to return home, until the banking man, who considered me a prop, part of the pitch, something my father had brought along to put a wholesome face on it all, gave in and the field was ours.

The future.

But my father had never offered me a job. For some reason he'd asked me to come by his office, a request I didn't recall him making before, but he'd never said, Come join me, learn the ropes, work your way up, father and son. Come be me when I can no longer be myself. And I thought I understood why. I didn't know what resources he could call on when I turned him down, my father never having been turned down before. He'd been shot, not said no to, and once I'd said it we both knew I could never take it back.

My job, perhaps even my profession, was to understand my father, and standing at the center of the maelstrom that was his life, how was I supposed to do that?

But he needed help. His office was a mess, his desk a chaos of property abstracts, title deeds, survey maps, maps of all sorts, some of which he'd drawn, aerial photographs, not a single family photograph, of course, but photographs of the lay of the land, manila envelopes stuffed with them, and business envelopes containing letters, some of which would be important, some bearing the statehouse seal, thrown in with the rest. My father's office looked like a Quonset hut out on a field of battle, which could be carted off to another field as the battle waxed and waned. The outer office where his secretary had her desk was conventional and clean, if without the first decorative touch, but his secretary was gone for the day, and it was as if I'd been blown into my father's presence and had to hold on while he told me what he had in mind.

Maybe I was simply there to restore order. Clean up. Finally make myself useful. Maybe he'd sat me down before him so that I could establish a beachhead on his desk.

Then he surprised me—but he shouldn't have. The fact is, my father was never without resources. Not really. There was always a way. Small eyes steady, mouth firm, shoulders squared, neck erect, his amputated leg out of sight but his crutch within easy reach at that window, he announced that he wanted to consult me on a matter. I'd been called in as a consultant. If it was my future he had in mind, I'd have to insist on it, but it was another sort of family matter that concerned him now. It took the form of a question. My father was not given to dramatic pauses. He paused just long enough to draw a breath and then announced he was thinking of bringing Billy Langley into the business, and his question was was I surprised.

If I'd said, Frankly, yes, I'd be a better choice, my father would have said, Convince me. If I'd said, You're using Billy as a stalking-horse, why don't you make the offer to me, he would have said, Convince me.

If I'd said, Remember, Billy Langley was once a southern version of a sixties' radical, which, granted, wasn't saying much. But Bob Langley was a one-man Establishment in himself, and if Billy had any revolutionary ideology left his great uncle Bob was the enemy. If I'd said all that my father might have laughed, but beneath the laughter he would have made no effort to conceal his disappointment. He would have finished by demanding, Defend yourself, son. Don't let Billy Langley take it away from you. Claim what's yours.

Instead, I said hiring Billy to be a sort of backup would make an interesting experiment. He should keep me posted. I assured him I wouldn't be an indifferent observer.

At that point, my father made a vacating sound, a rocky avalanche of a sigh, intended to bury me, I suppose. He shook his head once, and that quickly, his patience was exhausted. He'd provided no time for me to think it over, to reconsider an offer he hadn't made. The consultation was done. He reached for his crutch and that combustive smell filled the room.

But before Billy Langley was a campus radical he'd been a little boy at family reunions wandering off by himself, whose father had had to herd him back onto the field of play as if he were a stray sheep. My father stood straight, his crutch seemingly as deeply rooted as the catalpa tree that shaded him, while my cousin Hugh joined us in play out on a field, where dried cow pies sometimes served as bases. At that age—seven, eight, or nine— Billy was quick to go off by himself, not easy to round up, and had a thin, bony face and lank black hair he'd gotten from God knows where. Get in the game, son, get in the game, Hugh cheered him along, but I always felt Hugh was looking at me and saying, Get him in the game, son, get him in the game. See what you can do.

Then Billy Langley was a thin and bony twelve year old who,

when he wanted, could tear around the bases, but who could just as easily stroll between first and second until some earnest, little rule-enforcing cousin would run up and tag him out, at which point Billy would grin, say something like, What's the big deal, and stroll away. All this before the eyes of grandparents, aunts and uncles, and almost always some long lost kinsman making a once only appearance, and my father, of course, taking up his stoic position under that tree. Hugh hadn't given up on Billy yet, and had to take him off behind the barn and have a heart to heart talk. At which point Billy would return as if he were perfectly rehabilitated, and his father would give me a look that said, You can't trust this kid. You're Bob Langley's son, see what you can do. Billy ended up back on my team, and when he hit a grounder to the second baseman, a notoriously bad fielder with a very poor arm, and stood at home plate daring to be thrown out, and eventually was, I did what Hugh wanted me to and took Billy aside. But I didn't chew him out on the field; I, too, took him out behind the barn. I said, "No one wants you on their team. Why can't you understand?" And Billy responded, "My Dad's gone ape-shit for your Mom and thinks your Dad's a one-legged superman or something. What sort of cousins does that make us?" Then he laughed, a yippeeing hoot you might hear at a roundup and that years later would become his battle cry, and ran off before I could disown him once and for all.

Then Billy Langley was a degenerate fifteen year old, whose goal at that summer's reunion was to turn our Aunt Louise on. He brought with him a plain girl with a doughy face and a wrinkled man's shirt, who nonetheless had a supercilious air and who stood off to the

side and observed the Langleys as if she were completing an assignment in an anthropology course. Now, Billy was doing the talking,
and out behind the barn was for getting stoned. Every other word
was an exclamatory variation of "trip." He must have rolled half a
dozen joints before he'd come, and his preliminary mission seemed
to have been to wean his cousins off of lemonade and marshmallows
and onto pot, culminating in his main mission, his great aunt. Aunt
Louise neither smoked nor drank—very few of the Langleys did—
and that was because, Billy claimed, she had already blown her mind.
For Billy she was one step away from becoming a kindred spirit, and
to take that step all she needed was a little nudge. His girlfriend had
baked a batch of brownies laced with marijuana for the occasion.
Get a woman like Aunt Louise stoned and suddenly those little bunnies and chicks sporting at the margins of her letters would go crazy.
I shook my head at his antics and made a weary, disgusted face. He
gave me his crooked grin and went off to make his offering to his
great aunt—family chronicler, when the facts were to her liking, and
family fabulist, when the Langleys failed to live up.

I didn't intervene. Hugh saw Billy make the offering, and, whether
he trusted his son or not, gave him a wink of approval. My father
from his sentinel's position under the catalpa tree observed it all, too,
and most certainly made a mental note in the family ledger he kept,
but let it pass. Aunt Louise looked at the thin-faced Billy—he had
the face of a small burrowing animal, his eyes narrowed as though to
see in the dark—and at his pie-faced girlfriend, and then she looked
over at me, accepted the brownie Billy had offered and took a bite.
At that point, Aunt Louise got rid of Billy's girlfriend and Billy's

father and her own favorite brother and narrowed it down to Billy and me. Her eyes, behind those bottle-bottom glasses she wore, grew larger, bolder, and full of a crackling light. She was clearly amused and seemed to be saying, If this is the best you two boys can dream up you better go back to your cow pies. If you're lucky little Langleys you might make it home.

That was the last time I saw Billy at a family reunion. The next time I saw him may have been at the University when I walked into a dark basement room in a fraternity house where I was not a member, sank down into an old leather sofa to take a break from the party I was crashing, and heard a voice at my ear say, "Hey, cuz, this the Langley room, or what?" Billy Langley was sitting down there in the dark, a bigger party-crasher than I was since he hadn't even graduated from high school yet. Somebody had brought him to this party, and he had gone off reconnoitering on his own. The chances we would both sit down on the same basement sofa in the dark were not good. I didn't ask him if he were stalking me, but my tone of voice almost certainly said, There better be a good explanation for this. Billy responded with a question, to the effect of, Any way for a Langley to be a big man on campus without being a jock? He implied he'd find a way, and he gave me fair warning: he'd be enrolled and ready to go next fall. I was not drunk, not stoned, just out of my element. It was Billy who moved in and out of the dark. I wished him good luck, but certainly did not say, If there's anything I can do. Then I did have a few beers and the next morning could almost convince myself that that basement meeting had never happened. Or, since I was not a fraternity member and not much of a partygoer and drank less than my share, that I had somehow willed that meeting on myself from the dark part of my psyche and, therefore, could un-will it. If I'd brought Billy Langley on stage, I could usher him off.

But he came to the University, stayed his four years, and did indeed make a name for himself. The university sports teams got more press, but Billy Langley was quoted in the school paper as often as the school quarterback, from which I deduced that student protest had become a serious spectator sport. I did not doubt the genuineness of Billy's political convictions. The Vietnam War was a self-perpetuating nightmare from which no one could awake. While world leaders argued about the shape of the peace table in Paris, back in the jungles and rice paddies of Southeast Asia thousands were being killed. Only these were not deaths; they were "collateral damage." This was not war; it was "pacification." The war tainted everything at the time—there was no such thing as an innocent, unaffiliated act—and I did not doubt that Billy believed everything he attacked deserved it. The Establishment waged war, and the Establishment was a world complete unto itself. The ROTC belonged to it, of course, but so did that chain of fast food eateries, and so did that nine to five guy who shuffled back and forth to work and kept his brain turned off.

No, it was not Billy's convictions I questioned, it was the vehement and the high-pitched delight he took. In the two years we overlapped I tried not to be anywhere near where he might be participating in a protest. It was that roundup, rallying cry of his, clearly meant to provoke a stampede. To my knowledge, he never named my father in speech or in print, but everything he said about men out to amass fortunes at the expense of the little guy and the downtrodden races and the future of the planet, and every time he used his favorite phrase, the "tentacle-reach of the Establishment," I had no doubt whose face he saw. And when he excoriated men of conscience for falling under the sway of such power-hungry men, he might very well have meant his own father. And when he attacked anyone so bound to the paths of the past they were afraid to break new ground, he might have been reading someone like Thoreau or Emerson, but he was thinking of my weakness for family lore and family reunions and he meant me. I was an American history major, and for Billy history was what I'd become.

I remember one other meeting before I'd completed my four years and left campus. This was not an innocent encounter, and I don't quite know how he managed to catch me when I was alone, but there came a moment after my graduation ceremony when my father and mother and my aunt Louise, who had come along, too, had gone to get the car and, diploma in hand, I was going back to my apartment to change clothes when Billy came out of nowhere and fell into step beside me. It was a warm, late spring morning, almost noon, and he brought with him his chill. I was still in my gown with my mortarboard tilted on my head. When I glanced to the side I saw Billy through the tassel.

He said, "How's it feel?" And I told him if felt fine. Belatedly, he said, "Congratulations," and then we walked along in silence for a while. Billy wore jeans, a plain, discolored white t-shirt and sandals, but beside my gowned presence he might have been naked. He looked as if he hadn't slept in days; he always looked a little diseased. Then he said the most uncharacteristic and least declamatory thing I'd ever heard come out of his mouth. He said, "I hope I make it." I couldn't believe he wasn't mocking me although that was certainly not his tone. "Why," I said, "should you care anything about graduating from this institution? Aren't institutions all the same? What do you care about this?" And I held my diploma under his nose. He ignored the diploma and looked me in the eye. His eyes looked sleepy and unrequited, as if he'd maintained some sort of fruitless vigil all night. "I saw your Mom and Dad," he said. "Aunt Louise was with them. That's..." He paused, and then gave me the word. The word was "nice." And I told him he should have come up to us, he should have made his presence known, although I quickly realized everything that was passing between us at that moment was off the record. I almost got angry with him then. His public persona would not allow him to show up at anybody's graduation, much less a family member's. We were his secret attachment and his shame. I remembered the way he'd materialized at my side on that sofa in that dark fraternity basement. This was a bright, late spring day, but he'd materialized again. I said, "I'm sorry it has to be this way, Billy." From my lofty graduate's perch I was about to go on, Maybe when the war is over and we see things from a different perspective...but I didn't. Nor did I shake his hand; nor did he offer it. People had begun to pass us on the sidewalk, other graduates with family members of theirs. Billy and I didn't belong. Father and Mother, Aunt Louise and I were going out to lunch. I could have invited him, and the stranded way he stood there, neither in one world nor the other, told me I should have. But I didn't. I wished him good luck and kept my diploma and my celebration for myself.

Two years later Billy got his own diploma. I didn't attend his graduation and later learned that he didn't either. Walking humbly forward to essentially bow down before the school president and assembled faculty and have a scrolled piece of paper placed in your hand was not something he was prepared to do, but he did fulfill all requirements and his name was among the other graduates in the state's main newspaper, because I saw it there. I had taken the trouble to look. Later, I heard that he had gone off to continue his schooling in another state, but that might have had something to do with his draft status. To my knowledge, he had never made a public point of burning his draft card. When the lottery system started, his number must have placed him out of harm's way. There'd been a couple of years there when I'd waited to see what our local draft board was going to do with me. Then the lottery gave me a high number, too. Finally, with bodies hanging off the last helicopter out of Saigon—of all the horrible images that war had given us that might have been the most shameful and surreal—the war ended. Dissidents reemerged in hopes of resuming their lives. I had met Karen Ambrose and begun a succession of jobs. Billy went to work for my father, taking my place beside the "one-legged superman or something" and his lovely wife.

—⁓—

I WAS LED TO BELIEVE that Hugh had interceded with my mother, and my mother with my father, to get Billy hired. I wasn't there. It was done behind my back, but I can't imagine it happening any other way. Hugh, yet to move to the mountains, would have driven from whatever town he'd been living in at the time over to ours. He would not have taken the expressways, one of which would surely have been completed by that time. He'd have driven the country roads, and meanwhile he'd have thought it out. The favor he was going to ask of Bob and Fran Langley was immense. In going to Fran first and not directly to Bob he was aware he could be accused of subterfuge, of shameful opportunism, of preying on the weaker sex, really of cowardice in not confronting the man himself directly, but he simply didn't believe in acting alone he had much of a chance. Bob Langley was barely approachable. He approached you and dictated his terms; you didn't approach him. Family still mattered to him, and if Aunt Louise had not been bedridden at the time and within three months of her death, Hugh might have approached her. Bob Langley had not become a renegade to the family, an apostate. He had become a force, and forces were faceless, they bore no immediate resemblance to people you had known, you had to deal with them on a whole different plane, and the truth was that that saddened Hugh Langley deeply.

He and his uncle Bob had already crossed professional paths. Or, rather, they'd come close because at the last moment Hugh had stepped aside, but the shopping center he had helped design with its terraced gardens at its center, where shoppers could stroll and find a secluded place to sit and take relief from the give and take of commerce down below (before re-entering that world, of course, and buying more), almost didn't happen because Hugh had had a sure presentiment that Bob Langley would not allow family and business matters to mix and would prefer to sit on his land instead. But Hugh had done a disappearing act and the deal had gone through. It was as if he'd been blacklisted. The first shopping center was followed by a second. No, it was as if he'd had to blacklist himself. Not that his uncle hadn't known that his nephew had been employed in the firm responsible for the centers' designs, it was simply that Bob Langley had waited for Hugh Langley to excuse himself, after which things could move ahead.

How to put a face on a force?

Bob Langley had a secretary in his office. He had surveyors and lawyers and landscapers and part-time jobbers he called on. He had a network of contacts without whom nothing would have gotten off the ground. But he didn't have a lieutenant, a second in command, and Hugh must have reasoned that if he could smuggle in his outcast of a son, Bob Langley might come to resemble the man he'd known, a family link might be restored, and the force might take on a face. And Billy Langley, after all his years as a sideline heckler, might assume his place in the world.

But Hugh Langley went to my mother first because he'd never ceased to recognize her. She remained Fran Langley. The wrinkles furrowing across the forehead, the crow's feet, the lusterless hair, the dimming eyes, the darkening veins on the back of the hands, the wasting away and the futile shoring up of the little that was left—he recorded all that but quickly looked back to the woman he'd known and saw Fran Langley again, too. She served him lunch. Pearl's special egg salad sandwiches, except Pearl would surely have been gone by then. He expected Fran to sigh, to shake her head and murmur, Hugh, so good to see you, where in the world have you been, but she didn't. She waited until he'd eaten—she only nibbled to get past the time—then went to sit in her favorite chair, a wing chair with floral upholstery, where she centered herself as though on a throne and asked him what she could do, what in the world she could do that he couldn't do for himself. She was no help to him, but she was Fran Langley, the same woman who'd once snapped a picture of him after he'd snapped one of her, as though they were forever bound by that single reciprocal act. My son, Billy, he said, your husband, Bob, I can see, Hugh said, how they might be good for each other, how Billy might learn what it means to make his way in the world, and how, once the dust has settled from all these years we've lived through, Bob might give him a clearer view of the way things are now, of how even a one-legged man can survive, and thrive, and Billy, almost in spite of himself, can bring Bob back to…I won't say back to the fold, but closer to where we all began before the world blew apart… maybe how the Langleys once were, Fran, a family where we all gave a little but got a lot, how does that sound, I have to admit I'm struggling for words…

My mother might not have remembered the phrasing but she wouldn't have forgotten the thought, that once you got rid of unbridled greed and learned to admit when you're wrong, we sat on a big beautiful ball of plenty, enough for us all. She just didn't believe Hugh Langley was struggling for words, believing instead that like everybody else who'd come up against her husband, his only recourse was to play dumb. That could not have been Bob Langley. That's not the man I knew. I am at a loss for words.

She thought instead Hugh was willing to sacrifice his son to redeem his vision of a once illustrious man, and told him so. With no pity in her voice and no gratitude either for the sacrifice the man sitting before her had once made, she said, Hugh, Bob would eat your Billy alive.

And thinking of mortal combat, hand to hand, in a night that would not end, Hugh was about to say, No Langley would eat another Langley alive, but he didn't. He looked at Fran Langley, sighed, held steady and waited for her to retract those words. To bring back a glimmer of those bygone years. And she didn't. My mother sat there in her wing chair, her flanks secure, and waited in turn for this no longer young man to come to his senses.

Hugh said, You won't help me, Fran?

I'll advise you to come to your senses, she said.

That means you've given up on Bob, then. That's what that means.

She looked down, measured out a long pause. Then she said, Hugh, even when he was golden, Bob always wanted to win. He may have looked like he was having a fine time, all for the love of the game, rah-rah and the cheering fans, but never doubt he wanted to win. Now that he only has one leg to do it on, he wants it even more. That's all.

If Hugh said to her what he should have, he said then, Yet, you fell in love with him, Fran. You and the rest of us, too.

I'm just not sure that Hugh did.

But if he did, if that was what he said, my mother took a jolt in her favorite chair. Her head snapped back, just a bit, just enough. Enough for Hugh to add, Help me, Fran. Help Bob, too.

She shook her head. Silently and motionlessly she began to cry, but then she fought it, and it was the fight she waged against herself—in her tightened jaw and trembling neck, in her vein-darkened hands on the armrests—that brought Hugh to his feet. He started to her, and she waved him back. You poor fool, she said.

He stood there, stopped in his tracks, as with a fine, fierce containment, Bob Langley's wife rode out the storm. Hugh sat back down. She raised her eyes to him. At the end of winter she'd once looked ahead to spring, and he'd snapped the picture. He hadn't thrown that snapshot away. He'd try to find it. He'd dig it out and pass it on. Meanwhile, winter was on her again, and this time there was nothing he could do. It was all gone now; she bore witness to the way all beauty darkens and hardens and dies. He was about to say, heedlessly, Save my son, save your husband, too. But he didn't. Never before at a loss for words, not really, he was now.

Otherwise, how have you been, Hugh?

Her joke. He had always laughed—with an excess of good spirits, he'd needed a vent, and his laughter, it could be said, was who he'd become. He summoned his conviction and laughed again.

But it wasn't a joke. She meant it. There had to have been an "otherwise." Otherwise, why utter another word?

He said, I'm thinking of moving to the mountains, Fran. I'm thinking of taking the whole family up there.

And start again?

She made no attempt to disguise the scornful disbelief he heard in her voice, tempered by weariness of her own and an anger so distant, so diffuse, she couldn't bring enough of it to bear against any one person, at any given time. It made Hugh want to rise and comfort her again and run the risk of having her anger directed solely against himself.

He remained seated. He said, Something will come along. It always has.

No time limit? No expiration date?

There doesn't have to be, Fran.

And when would you go?

And something in her tone of voice, some forced show of bravery, some mockery holding off a willingness to believe, some echo of a time in her life when desertion had been the rule, some bleakness, some old domesticated despair, tempted Hugh to say, When you're ready, Fran. When you're ready to come with us. But he caught himself and declared instead, I'd like to see my son settled first. Not until then.

Time passed. From somewhere close by a clock marked the minutes, although to my knowledge a clock like that, grandfather or otherwise, did not exist in that house. But the house was that quiet, so quiet that time somehow marked itself, and only ceased to sound when Fran said, I'll talk to my husband—but not for Bob's sake, and not for Billy's either. I'll do it for you. So that you can go to your mountains.

Later, Bob Langley took his nephew out for a drive. He didn't tell Hugh to look to his right or his left, at that farm or sawmill or what remained of those poultry huts, he simply rode around over land that both knew so well it would seem impossible to see it with fresh eyes. For that reason it was barren land even though corn and soybeans and produce of some sort and what remained of cotton might be growing there. It offered no yield. In the present tense, it had ceased to exist. Then he drove back into town and parked beside the courthouse square. There was a bench there, and when the two men seated on it saw Bob Langley bearing down on them with his crutch, followed by his nephew Hugh Langley, they got up and left. Catty-corner across the intersection from the bench was the Langley furniture store, no longer owned by Hugh's father, who had died, but by Raymond Langley's long time assistant, a sweet-tempered and unambitious man, entirely identified with the town, named Donnie Abbot. It took no act of the imagination, nor the influence of any melancholy mood, to see that the store was diminishing before their eyes. Around it other businesses were abandoning all pretense. They were seasonal, like H & R. Block, or they were little ethnic holes in the wall, or they bought and sold gold. Above their heads the court-house clock was ticking too, and at the quarter hour sounded its vacant and rusted chime.

With an interest not at all avuncular, rather more speculative and investigative, as if he were keeping tabs on an experiment of some sort, or covering the terms of a bet, Bob Langley asked his nephew, Why would a young man like Billy Langley want to spend five minutes of his life here? I still see Billy as a little boy, out behind the barn, creating mischief, scheming to get the upper hand, getting sillier by the year. And now that he's a man he wants to come back here? Bob Langley raised his crutch and pointed it, point blank, at the old Langley furniture store. I worked over there when I came back from the war. Maybe a year. If your father'd had me up front I could have sold out the store. Instead he put me in back with the antiques, which is what the store has become. The whole town has. An antique no one wants to buy. The saddest thing in the world, and it's almost all you see any more. Who has the strength to keep things going now? Those shopping malls you had a hand in? They'll be howling ghost towns in ten, fifteen years. Can Billy stand that sort of sadness?

Hugh knew that no one could, not indefinitely, not over a life. He himself had moved from one enterprise to another, recreating himself and not looking back since there'd been nothing to look back to. Except the Langleys, Bob and Fran. His stomach clenched and held when he looked at his father's old furniture store. But it was as if his stomach wept, pleaded and wept, when he looked at his uncle Bob.

Not unless you teach him, Hugh said.

I'm not running a school.

He'll learn from you. He's smart. If he's been spinning his wheels all these years it's because he's never been in the presence of someone who engaged him, who commanded his attention and his intelligence, and who maybe frightened him, too. Do that, and he won't give up.

Frighten him? Again, Bob Langley pointed his crutch across the intersection. Isn't that frightening enough?

Again, Hugh looked along the crutch to his father's old store. Its façade was a dyspeptic and discolored aqua green. The "g" in Langley had lost its lower curl. The bed through the showroom window was bare. The overhead light fell on it like a fluorescent sheet. The store was neither opened nor closed and no one appeared inside.

Hugh turned on the courthouse bench, squaring up to his uncle. He'd been in a war, he knew the chances of survival were always slim, but Hugh took his heart in his hand and said, My father was a cold man, who had terrible troubles in his life, but who never shared a moment's warmth with me. He lived in that store, and like all these businesses that can't last, that never quite succeed, it became a sort of tomb. But the Langleys took me in. You did and Fran did. It meant everything. It was all I had. And what I'm wondering now is if some of that Langley magic might be left for my son.

Langley magic? my father, Bob Langley, said, staring directly at his nephew.

And Hugh didn't flinch. He studied his uncle's face, determined to recall it—to restore it—in his mind. Past all that had weathered into a façade of blunt protuberances and fissureless stone, he saw the reddened cheeks, the parted chin, the green gleam of the eyes, the mouth open on the tip of the tongue, always about to exult, to release a joyous song of praise. What he would call outlets for the Langley magic.

Why'd you go to Fran first, Hugh?

Because she's not as scary as you.

And there, to top it off, was the famous Langley grin. For the risk he'd taken, Hugh had caught a glimpse, and on the strength of that single flickering glimpse of a grin he sent Bob Langley his son.

—◆—

I don't know exactly what Billy did to bring on his disgrace. But I have no trouble imagining the series of miscalculations that brought it all to that point. Hugh miscalculated when he thought enough remained of the Bob Langley he'd known to work redemptive wonders on his son. Billy miscalculated when he concluded that Bob Langley, far from being the Establishment's main man, was in fact a one-man wrecking crew, a rogue, a mole within the system. And my father miscalculated badly when he assumed he could take Billy the maverick and imbue him with enough family loyalty to make him do his bidding. My father wanted someone combative to replace his contemplative son. Billy wanted a Nietzschean naysayer. Hugh wanted back what he'd lost, a vision of humanity he'd hunkered down in a foxhole for, a son in the image of an extraordinary man; in effect, his purchase on that big beautiful ball of plenty.

I do know that it wasn't one thing and that it took place on both ends of the stick. The stick extended from the land my father bought up at cheap prices to the land he resold to men who wanted it for their eye-blights: their subdivisions and shopping centers and exit-ramp conglomerations. A man who gave back to the land's original owners a portion of what he took from unscrupulous buyers could walk away with his conscience clean and, perhaps, no small sense of satisfaction. How do I know this? Because the stick was long enough to accommodate both ends of human nature, as long as someone remained faithful to his word. Someone might say to a little old lady whose family had moved out of state—to someone like Imogene Howell, for instance—you sell me this land cheap so that I can show the numbers I'm required to, and I'll go out and sell it for an exorbitant sum and come back and quietly cut you in on the profits so that you get what you should have had from the start. We play the system against itself and come out ahead. All we need is someone at the top who can't believe someone with a heart will work one end and then go out and put the screws to the sons of bitches at the other. Not the same someone. A land speculator with a heart is not supposed to be able to look a buyer heartlessly in the eye and say, You want what

I got, pay for it, you contemptible bastards, or you can watch your shopping center turn to synthetic dust before it's even built and this field covered in kudzu. If it were up to me, it would be rolling in kudzu right now, but I'm going to give you a break. Just how badly do you want to fuck this country up? Now you know the price.

Not the same someone.

It would have gone something like that. Billy kept his goodness alive by giving vent to his vehemence. If he hadn't had a buyer to berate he wouldn't have been able to befriend and reward the seller. It was a middleman's consummate balancing act, and my father must have known about it and allowed it to go on because…because it worked. Billy got the deals he had to have because he kept a version of himself beyond reproach. What businessman doesn't aspire to find a self he can live with so that he can go out and that much more vehemently wheel and deal? The vehemence was what my father wanted, and if Billy got it by being a sort of Robin Hood in your face, my father must have said to himself, Let's see how long he can keep it up. I do know that Billy Langley himself became a force in our part of the state. As I went from job to harmless job, Bob and Billy Langley simply became the Langleys, one no less formidable and feared than the other. Lazy reporters in the press might refer to them as father and son. When the reporters' mistake was pointed out to them, they didn't always bother to correct it.

Billy Langley's mistake lay in thinking Bob Langley gave a damn about what Billy may still have thought of as his "values," and that Bob Langley had succeeded because from the outset he'd been intent on undermining the system from within. When a stoned Billy Langley had claimed his Aunt Louise with her storytelling loops as a near-kindred spirit, he'd probably been closer to the mark.

What happened was what had to happen—someone died. I seem to recall the name of Morton, which I know as a name has death built in, but Mortons die, too, and that is the name that has stuck. This was a Mr. Morton, and of course he was old, but unlike Imogene Howell he had family he did not plan to disinherit, and when he died before his transaction with Billy Langley could be completed, Billy had a decision to make. Old Man Morton had scribbled out an addition to his last will and testament in which he'd mentioned money due him from the Langleys he wanted to go to certain family members, but that agreement with Billy Langley had not been put into writing and there'd been no witnesses. It was Old Man Morton's handwriting and his word, and Billy had been called to a meeting at which Morton beneficiaries were present, and the question had been put to him. I am assuming thousands of dollars were at stake. Billy took one look at the Mortons and saw faces like fists closed around a clutch of dirty dollar bills, and said the old man was delusional, there had been no secret agreement, nothing beyond what the purchase contract had called for, which had permitted Mr. Morton to get out of that shack his family had allowed him to rot in and—here Billy heard himself repeating words my father would have drilled into him back in his indoctrination days—into a new triple-wide mobile home with the conveniences he'd gone without for so long. A kitchen with a microwave oven. A living room with remote controlled color tv. A bedroom with a comfort-controlled bed. A bathroom with space-age shower head. Heat in the winter and air-conditioning in the summer. Progress, all at his fingertips, for every finger something to give comfort to his old age. And Billy kept that portion of the money he'd agreed to return to old man Morton for himself.

Was it what Mr. Morton and his dollar-fisted brood got for not making sure every codicil and every side agreement was spelled out in the contract? No, it was what Billy got for being so persuasive out of both sides of his mouth. It was the reward Billy earned for balancing on that tightrope of his nature and not falling off.

He didn't so much convince himself he'd earned all that Morton money as he did that the surviving Mortons didn't deserve the once agreed to share. And if they didn't he did, until a more deserving person came along. I don't intend to make light of this, but as Billy's vision of the average American man and woman darkened, his bank account grew. He'd married and had children of his own, but all that was beside the point. When my father, as upstate's number one sports hero and number one war casualty, got tipped off where the next superhighway was due to be built, he'd send Billy out with the names and all the data they could gather about property holders along the route, and it became a sort of judgment day assignment for Billy. He would appear at some doors willing to talk large sums of money, willing to distribute largesse, but at others he'd experience a sort of tightening of his being that gave him a powerfully concentrated and intimidating presence. Look at me, old man. Twenty-four hours, forty-eight. When the state wants to claim something by eminent domain, they might not even wait that long. Look at me, ma'am. No time to be sentimental about it. This land has been your curse. Tell me the last time it gave you a minute's worth of pleasure. Pleasure! Have you forgotten what the word means?

But if the person before him stuck his sympathy's chord, he'd get around to proposing that between the two of them they get the bad guys before the bad guys got what they were after.

It was an exciting moment for Billy, it kept something in him vitally alive. It gave him a purchase on who he'd been. If he got that special tingle, he'd lay himself open to this old man or woman, and if a certain chemistry ensued, he'd keep that tingle going until it became a wrathful current and he was spewing venom, as he'd done back in the old days, at those assholes that would cover this land with one huge carcinogenic growth, even as he prepared to sell it to them at his exorbitant price, and even as he calculated how much he'd take as his own cut, the price for exposing himself again and again.

When my father finally called him on it, Billy was about to say, So what? No big deal, as if he'd been tagged out between bases in a game he'd long since outgrown. But Bob Langley had so many contacts in the state and so many people still anxious to get on his good side that he would have a complete record of Billy's misdeeds. He would have taken the time to write them out, one column for the price Billy supposedly paid for the land, another for what he was supposedly paid, and then the columns that mattered: the chivalrous kickbacks to the original sellers and the unaccounted for remainder in the fourth column, beginning with the Morton money, what Billy paid himself for being a middle-aged radical and a vigilante of times past. This paper lay on my father's desk, surrounded by the usual mess. Had Billy thought my father such a turbulent force he was incapable of keeping good books?

It was mid-afternoon. Autumn. Whoever the secretary at the time was, she'd been sent home. Down below on the street the movie theater had become a shoe store and a number of other businesses before going back to a movie theater again, this time showing X-rated films. The only rigor to be seen anywhere thereabouts was in my father's face, which had gotten harder and knobbier and more fiercely contained over the years, just as Billy's had begun to flesh out and break down. My father's small eyes did not blink. They bore back through the world and, at times like these, seemed to repudiate everything in sight. Billy tried not to quail.

My father stood. He invited Billy to sit or stand. Billy sat because he suddenly realized he couldn't trust his knees.

My father didn't say a thing. He simply pointed at the four columns of figures and let them speak. Billy took the time to go down the columns and do the arithmetic, as though he were balancing his checkbook. Then he laid the page back on the desk.

For a moment he mustered his courage and became the one-man movement he'd been in college. He said, "It's how I do business. You do business another way. The numbers come out the same in the end."

My father did not say, My way or no way, as Billy must have expected him to. He simply bore in on Billy until he'd taken his fill, then turned to look out the window. He took his fill there, too, until his disappointment filled the room, which Billy experienced as a palpable pressure in his chest. He found himself protesting.

"I didn't steal a dollar, if that's what you're thinking. I got more from the bastards than you ever did because I took them to the limit.

I showed them who they really were. The only thing they could do then was pay up. So I gave some back, and so I kept some for my efforts. I never stopped hating them, that's the difference…"

The difference between you and me, was what Billy had meant, but he left the sentence hanging for my father to complete. My father didn't. Instead, he stood there on his crutch like a monument to difference, like an indestructible testament to his own singularity, until Billy said it for him:

"The difference between you and me."

Then my father spoke. He measured out an uncharacteristic pause, as if he were about to make a full-voiced pronouncement, yet he had never said anything as quiet, clear, and intimate to me in my life. He said, "Billy, I hate them all."

My first cousin's first son now knew that hatred included him, and he might have realized that hatred so pure and private could not find expression in the country's courts, and that as far as prosecution for the crime of embezzlement went, he was off the hook, but he did not know my father as well as I did, who had studied him all my life. I assume Billy assumed his irregularities in how he did business would one day be discovered, and that since Bob Langley had such contempt for the whole corporate system he'd pitted himself against, Billy's kick-backs to the little guy and pay-outs to himself would be taken in stride, if not applauded. Or so he believed. And he was wrong. Corporate systems for my father were just so many words. He'd pitted himself against individuals, not abstractions. It was safe to say my father had never taken the time to watch an abstraction form. No, Billy was wrong and Billy was crushed. It wasn't even a matter of money. It was the clear and unimpeachable story those columns of figures told as they lay on the mess that was my father's desk. A story of sophomoric grudges and sentimental hopes and venom turned almost sweet with age. Billy's story. A Langley give money back? A Langley take money on the sly? As fierce as he'd thought himself to be, Billy had shown himself to be a soft touch and a sticky-fingered sneak, and that my father couldn't forgive.

PART TWO

"WHEN HUNTERS LIE IN WAIT"

VIII

I TOOK A DRIVE. I could have gone back into the mountains, for the weather, for the cooler, cleaner air, but I found myself driving the old two lane road into the city. The chicken farms were gone, with their barrack-like huts. The sawmills had disappeared, or the trees they timbered had. Tracks still ran alongside the road but apparently trains didn't. Or perhaps they ran at night. There were no more stands selling bedspreads. There was no cotton in the fields. The whistle-stop towns were still there, and behind the front row of brick businesses a large house or two with verandas still stood, but the businesses were no longer in business and the houses hadn't seen fresh paint in decades. The trees in the yards, mostly water oaks, were grayer than green. Gas stations with convenience stores had cropped up along the highway where commerce still got done, but you couldn't drive too far without asking yourself what was the point, where was the hunger, where was the need, where was anything at this late date likely to roar back to life, demanding to be fed? I wasn't the only one on the road, but, with an interstate two or three miles away, perhaps I was the only one driving this road with a purpose, with a real thought in mind.

I kept the window down. Even with my speed nearing fifty, in spots the air barely stirred. I stopped beside the road and got out. Other cars and pickups passed—I could have counted them—but the stillness was absolute. It was a warm day, but it wasn't heat. It was a distillation of years and years and years, and it had persisted until this day, but there was nothing and there was nobody to give it a spark of life. The day hung suspended. I could drive and drive and get nowhere, and when I reached the next town, not a whistle-stop town but a town with a courthouse whose name I knew, I waited for a life, a presence of life, a gathering, generative force, to find me. It was like a refueling, and then I could go on. Which I never failed to do. Eventually I covered those forty-five miles to the city. And before I reversed myself, turned around and drove back, with yet another courthouse behind me, I called Karen Ambrose, as though to register a claim.

She'd remember she'd asked to be kept informed, so I told her I was getting close. With nothing really to back me up, I felt as hunters must feel when they lie in wait and game begins to come near. Of course, there was game and there was game, and little game might end up crawling all over you while the big game bided its time. But the fact that the little, unsuspecting game had come so near was a good sign, didn't she agree?

And she laughed. She'd never hunted and she thought she knew for a near-fact that neither had I. I explained. It was a way of seeing past the sham of the moment, past the garish, dull come-on of what paraded before your eyes to what lay behind, that gave an astute hunter the awareness of the proximity of big game. And she laughed again. And I insisted, it's all dull dazzlement and loud noise and one thing vying to outsell another, and then it passes away, you see the time clearly, the people, step by step the decisions they make, each of the seasons lifts its curtain and you see them, the man, the woman, the child, the big game, once the little game has had its sport with you and caused you to spend your ammunition and make a lot of needless noise. She asked me to name the town, and turning on my bench I was able to read it off the courthouse door. She was close, she said, she lived close, and I said I thought I knew that. What if she drove up? Would I mistake her for big game or little game? I told her, Karen, I wasn't hunting you, and she said she didn't know whether to feel offended or not. And I said, No, no, you reach a point when it's not hard to see through all this, but then you have to wait for something else to appear. It was the one great modern-day consolation, it was all so easy to see through. But then what do you do? Most hunters play games, or they drink a lot and plot out their grudges and without pulling a trigger eliminate their enemies one by one, but the big game comes quietly, disguised in the guise of every-day, and just as quietly disappears while you're dreaming of some trophy on your wall.

And if she did drive up? Would he give up his hunter's perch and get into her car? They could have another meal. Or better yet, she could cook them one. Just how many years had it been since I had eaten her cooking, and I didn't count them, not sure that I could, or sure that in the count I wouldn't hurry those years aside, sitting in wait on a courthouse bench while petitioners, lawyers, minor traffic violators, couples out to be married quickly, on the fly and on the sly, filed past me and went inside. I wasn't hungry, I said, and she reminded me I had to eat. Karen, I said, it'll go away, if I just sit here quietly in its midst, time would pass by and all of this would fade from view and the right people would appear. Up in the mountains you could barely see your own reflection in a cistern, or a lake, but here it was a matter of patiently wearing the years away until the world came to its senses and the right people appeared. At that point, we would all be next of kin.

She continued laughing, I don't think she'd ever stopped, but I knew that she was out the door and had started the motor of her car and had joined in the stop-and-start traffic that would bring her to my bench. Before it did, before she stood there reminding me I had to eat, I brought her on as she'd been, her long legs, her size, her weight, her ash-blonde hair whitening the sunlight, her resolute movement ahead. When she danced, though, she held her ground, with a side-to-side step that was really a gyrating grind over a fixed point. The loose dresses and smocks she liked to wear swayed and flowed, but she didn't leave that point. Karen Ambrose, daughter of globetrotting golfers, one day teeing it up in Hawaii, the next day in Hong Kong. She drove by first, but I pretended not to see her and she observed me out of the corner of her eye as she passed, a curiosity on a courthouse bench, which was where most of the curiosities in these towns sat. I allowed her to leave and prepared for her to reappear, I performed the necessary preliminaries. When she walked by in the presence of townsfolk, all with petty grievances and petty petitions of their own, she did not blend in. She was past that point in her life, past the marriage grievance, the child-bearing grievance, the profession grievance, and it occurred to me that if I was sitting in wait for the people who mattered, for the big game to appear, it could be said that she had become a grievance of mine. I didn't have a shell to waste on her. She sat down beside me. She was wearing a scent of some herbal astringency that couldn't be found within a thousand miles of this town. She had a no-nonsense rigor about her, but she was an old song. And she was good-humored, a game-player, which meant there had to be rules, which, when it suited her, she would be pleased to bend. For a while we waited together on the bench. Karen Ambrose, to her credit, always gave the benefit of the doubt. But, aggravatingly, she was frequently fast to express that doubt. She was fairer-minded than almost anyone I knew, but there was a limit, something was ticking, we'd had good times together, a mostly affectionate life, but that ticking had gone on.

She said, I'm thinking of barbecuing some ribs on the grill. Some corn on the cob, too.

They're out there, I said, all this you see before you is just for show.

Your big game? If you see them, Jay, what are you going to do? You won't fire on them, you won't do that. You can't call out to them. With all this noise you'd have to shout like a madman to make yourself heard.

I'd join them, I'd fall silently in step, I said.

And if they won't have you, if they ignore you, what would you do then? Would you shoot them then? Your big game?

Look over there. That two-legged man, that lovely woman, and that fortunate child. Do you see them?

Not clearly enough to shoot at. I know you, Jay. I know you well enough. The play's the thing—isn't it, my dear? She took me by the hand. C'mon, let's go eat.

I never left her rear-view mirror, she made sure, as I followed her to a home she had her ex-husband to thank for, and she gave thanks, she told me, every day. I looked around for a screen porch, an amenity from times past, which barely existed anymore. Instead, she sat me down outside beside the pool, and a grill with more dials and switches and time-settings than airliners have, and a vaulted, sarcophagus-long lid. She could have roasted an entire pig in there, in addition to the ribs. I wasn't sure exactly where we were. The neighborhood was new, the houses all large, the trees recently planted and slow to catch up. We were in the outskirts of the city in one of those gated communities built just ahead of the sprawl, but with a guardhouse, and a guard, to keep out the game, both large and small. And each resident with her own body of water. I'd sat beside a river and then a lake and now I sat beside a pool, and it was as if Karen had left me there so that I could come to my senses and from the three available bodies of water make the correct, up-to-date choice. At that moment I remembered an incident from my childhood, my youth, and when Karen appeared to fire up the grill and then to serve the ribs and corn on the cob, I told her that something had occurred to me that, amazingly, hadn't before and that I should tell her, not because it offered the key to anything but because it provided an exclamation mark past which it was hard to proceed. Was I still talking about game, and, if so, big or small? And I explained to her that that had been a manner of speaking, that when you're looking for something with, so to speak, existence on the line, it was always a matter of game, whether hunting came naturally to you or not. And she laughed, but more sadly and wisely now, and for the first time in that span of years, if you excluded a pat or a semi-distanced hand on the shoulder, we touched.

She laid the warmth of her right hand against my left cheek, and I covered her hand with mine. Her hand smelled of barbecue sauce, which was also at large in the air. We smiled. It was an old familiar touch, and I could just as easily have said she was holding me off, but there was that welcoming warmth, and that cooking smell competing with the smell of a hand lotion brought to mind a life we'd shared for eight years.

She asked me to correct her if she was wrong, but hunters had to eat, didn't they, and then they had to rest before they went out on the hunt again. The time had come to eat. We had a salad, too, and with a slight hesitation, perhaps a certain misgiving, she opened a bottle of wine. I ate from the pork, the corn, the salad, and took a sip of her wine, not really hungry, at least for the food she'd served, but to allay her concerns. Hunters did have to eat, and to do her justice I ate it all.

Evening fell. No insects hovered over the water, or dimpled its surface. No fish rose. No swallows swept low, dipping their wings. The chlorination unit hummed into life, released its sterilizing fragrance, and then fell quiet. At the predetermined twilit moment, lights around the pool came on. Underwater lights came on, too. An oval-shaped pool, not large, seven-eight-nine strokes from end to end, a pool to cool off in, most likely heated in the winter, too, whose primary purpose would be to serve as the property's jewel.

Women divorced men and got for their efforts a body of water. I laughed at the coincidence. Judy divorced her husband, Karen divorced hers, and each body of water came with a house, which was the least of it. I continued to laugh, and Karen said she was pleased, to see me laughing again, as she refilled my wine glass. Eventually she asked why.

I don't know how I'd forgotten, I told her. All these years. Some hunter, I said.

I was referring to that exclamation mark past which it might not make sense to continue?

I was referring, I told her, to a trip our father forced us to take.

A story, she said in anticipation and settled back in her chair. She seemed to clear a space before her, space enough to house a theatrical event, then nodded.

It was summer, I said. I was about to enter junior high school, and Judy senior high, so maybe it was a rites of passage trip. No one knew where we were going. Mother didn't know. We were herded into the car and I was stunned to see my father appear without his crutch. He had a suit on and inside his left pants leg he had strapped on an artificial leg. I'd seen the leg before. He'd attended certain funerals with it on, and at least once when the Chamber of Commerce or the Rotary Club or some local organization had tried to win his favor with an award. And I'd seen the leg by itself, with its hinged harness and straps and long wooden shaft and its flat toeless foot, which had to fit inside a shoe, but I'd turned away because wearing it my father seemed like a cripple any boy might knock over. With his crutch, of course, he had always seemed fully armed, and before I got into the back seat of the car I snuck a glance into the far reaches of the trunk. My stomach unclenched when I saw the crutch packed there.

The four of us left town driving west. For maybe half an hour we treated it all as a game and let the suspense play out. Then Judy reached her limit and I heard her defiant screech. "All right! That's enough! Tell me where we're going or I'm getting out!"

Judy knuckled down in her seat. Some time later she shot up. "I mean it! You think I don't?" Then she pleaded, "Why won't you listen to me!"

With a certain knowing sympathy, Karen at that point laughed. I didn't say a word, neither to Karen nor, at the time, to my sister.

We crossed over a mountain and drove down through tobacco country. We went around a big city and entered an area known for its caves, one so big it was called Mammoth. There were parks, there was a national park, and the idea crossed my mind that our father was going to take us on a summer tour of the nation's parks—the Rocky Mountains, Yellowstone, Yosemite, all the way out west. We were going to get an education. But we didn't stop in any of the parks.

At a roadside diner we pulled off and had lunch. You ordered your sandwiches from the menu, and our father left our choices to our mother. Before we'd finished he'd risen and with his missing left leg walked to the cash register to pay. His suit was a light brown, he even wore a tie, and when he stood there with his cash in hand he settled his weight on both his feet, his real one and his artificial one, and the woman taking the money didn't know, and there was an instant when I might not have known either since there was no wind, no motion, and the pants leg fell straight and bodied-out around its stick. The woman looked up into my father's face, smiling. Her mouth was half open. She seemed honored. Then my father turned, and before the pants leg could fall straight and full-bodied again, I saw—I thought I did—the shape of the stick.

Late that afternoon we came to a town built behind a river wall. An iron staircase led up to a walk along the top of the wall. After supper I climbed that staircase by myself and stood looking out over the river at dusk, a large river, wide and full. I watched a barge carrying mounds of coal traveling down river and another, empty, its tugboat chugging against the current, going up. In both tugboats I saw men taking the evening air out beside their cabins, and I saw wash hung out to dry. I understood they had made for themselves a kind of home.

I shared a room with my sister, who was outraged and as close-mouthed as a stone. With the lights out and from her side of the room, Judy did say one thing. "I'll bet you he's going to take us to the smallest hick town he can find and dump us there. The way you go off and leave dogs and cats when the litter's too big. Whaddaya want to bet?"

Again, Karen, who knew my sister and could get inside her skin, chuckled and shook her head.

The next morning our father began to talk to the three of us. He became instructional. He found an opening through the floodwall and drove the family down there. "This is the Ohio river," he said, and named the major cities upstream, east of us, until he came to the city where three rivers converged to form the one we were all sitting before. Then he drove us out of town, across a bridge, and in another state now turned the car west so that we were following the course of river he'd just named. We came to another town, a town built into a fork of rivers, which we passed through and out into a park of some sort with a prospect. There we got out of the car and stood looking out at the green Ohio, the green of a pup tent, only brighter, and at the other river that joined it there, the brown of chocolate milk. For an improbable stretch the two rivers ran side by side, the line between them clear, then the brown swallowed the green, and the smell that rose was so heady it stung in your nostrils.

"That big brown river is the Mississippi," our father said. "It's brown because half the country is pouring into it. It's the biggest drainage ditch in the world."

Still in good humor, Karen laughed, perhaps surprised to hear the man she'd known as my father make anything resembling a joke.

A bridge led over the river, with cars crossing back and forth. But instead of joining the cars and crossing over, he pointed us north. We passed the entrance to the bridge, and drove along a narrow road shrouded in summer foliage, where in the breaks you could see the river out to the west, big and close and brown enough so that at any moment it might rise out of its banks and shoulder you off the road.

We passed other bridges, of course, even passed a ferry, and, more than my parents and Judy, much more, the river was my closest companion for the rest of that day. It was full of things, big things, trees and sheds and the shattered remains of boats, and innumerable little things like bottles and cans, dead fish and birds, but in its massive broad flow and its playful eddies it could seem so friendly you could imagine it, with its cool river breath, whispering in your ear, *Why stay in a stuffy car with people who'll never understand you when you could ride with me to the end of the earth?* I had its smell in my nose even when the road took us far back into bottomland, which might be planted in corn, which gave off a powerful odor of its own. The bridges rose over the river, and those big stone piers were sunken into it to break up its flow, but it became a sort of lesson on life at how little fazed the Mississippi was by any of it, not even by the barges and tugboats that rode it or churned against its current. At bridge after bridge our father might have joined the string of cars and crossed safely to the other side. A big city was coming up, which is where I assumed it would happen. But then St. Louis appeared and disappeared and we remained on the other side.

A shame, Karen sighed, a real river city if there ever was one, and I informed her the town we stopped in was called Alton, in the state of Illinois. This was in a motor court, situated on a low bluff, looking out over the river to the farmlands of Missouri, and maybe, at the limit of sight the glimmer of another river, which would be the Missouri. And that, I remembered, was the river those two larger than life explorers, Lewis and Clark, had ridden up in their quest to cross the continent. The bridge below us bore their names. It was alive with late afternoon cars.

I ate supper and shared another room with my sister. I fell asleep and dreamed not of rivers but of the school I'd be entering at summer's end, where students streamed up and down its halls, their heads bobbing like fishing corks, until they all went still before a trophy case where little football and baseball and basketball players struck their characteristic poses atop their gleaming pedestals. There were nameplates fixed to those pedestals, but as hard as I looked I couldn't discover a name. When I woke it wasn't because I'd given up but because the stream of students had moved me on.

It was early. The gray at the window was neither light nor darkness but some undeclared state in between. I dressed quietly so as not to wake my sister, whose face was buried in her pillow. As I stepped out the door into the open, I saw that beyond the line of cars pulled up before the rooms another dawn-breaking pioneer had preceded me. There was a crescent of lawn out there, some flowers and a couple of small ornamental trees. Around the crescent's curve was a wrought-iron fence, past which you had your view of the river and the great beyond. My father stood with one hand resting on a knob of that fence. Only the hand wasn't resting. The first thing I noticed was that the hand was gripped there, as though my father feared the wind might blow him over the bluff and into the river. He was wearing his light brown suit again, but the grayness of the night not yet become day cast him in an indeterminate color, whose lines were all blurred. He was more shadow-man than father in that moment, the farthest thing from a pioneer. Then I saw—because I had avoided looking until that moment —what the wind did to the empty pants leg. It whipped it around that stick. It made of my father a scarecrow, some lonely stick figure standing in the center of a field. If I believed my sister, he had brought it all down on himself—his loneliness, his scariness, the cold bare bones way he had of driving everyone back behind the farthest fence. Twelve years old, I had begun to realize that my mother, my father's very wife, was just one of many people he had driven back, and that, as I counted them up, he had no one left. Of course, he had kinfolk, he had his sister Louise and he had his nephew Hugh, but of those in that closest circle who should have defended him until death, my father had no one.

I walked out to him and stood beside him, my hand on the nearest knob in that fence. With him I looked across the river, which I discovered was the quick, glistening source of that grayness itself, to the broad reach of the land. I couldn't see far. There were the occasional car lights on the country roads out there, but that western half of the continent was still asleep. At the farthest reach of my vision the darkness rose up in a towering sort of wall, which might have been the Rockies themselves, for all I knew. No, I knew better, on the maps and on the grade school globes the Rockies were hundreds of miles away, but the darkness was mountainous and the darkness was close and I believed I understood the question our father was asking himself: Do I take my family into that? What are the chances we'll all come out into the light of day?

The wind blew in a sudden gust, and like my father I tightened my grip on that wrought iron knob. At my side, my father made a sound, a low whistle or a sigh, a marveling or a self-cautioning release of breath, a sound I had not heard him make before. The other sound I heard was instantly familiar, although I might not have heard it before either. I heard the empty pants leg flap.

I had a decision to make, and I decided to leave him there. I found our car in that line drawn up before the row of rooms, and then I had to plant my rear foot and push hard with the heel of my hand against the silver button before the trunk's switch would release. It was pitch dark in there, but with the suitcases removed it was possible to half-crawl back as though into a cave and run your hand over loose items—the out of place shaft of a beach umbrella was the first thing I touched—before I found what I was looking for. In the closed air of the car trunk I smelled it, of course, the sweat-stiffened cushion that fit under my father's arm, and once I had it out and the trunk closed, I did something I'd never done: my father had been a pole vaulter, and to be sure the crutch was worthy and hadn't suffered any cracks during its period of disuse, I took a couple of practice vaults. It was as stout as ever and I took it to him.

I wasn't sure of his expression. Was he angry or startled or deeply disappointed, at me or at himself? His head snapped up, as if he'd either just been rebuked or was about to exact an exemplary punishment. There was a chill in his eyes and a dark line at his mouth, but he took the crutch. He fitted it under his arm, as if he were trying it out, and I heard its rubber tip crunch in the gravel of the path. Then he turned back to me. I was about to say, The wind and the night and the river down there, that artificial leg you've got s'no better than tinkertoys, it's crappy, it could snap like that! and I would have snapped my fingers, too, but he looked down at me, and the light in his eyes and the line in his mouth gave way, just a bit, and he said, "Wake your sister and mother up. It's time to get back."

That was brave of you, Karen said. Making that decision for your father like that.

We did not cross the Mississippi river. We did not stop at any of the nation's parks. There came a moment late in the afternoon when driving through Cincinnati we came upon the city's major league ball park, all lit up, and from the elevation of the highway you could even see the players down on the infield grass. They were practicing, which meant the game hadn't started yet, and, whether my father looked for me or I looked for him in the rearview mirror, our eyes met. All I had to do was make a needy smile and plead with my narrowed eyes and he might have stopped and taken me and my outraged sister and long-suffering mother to the game, but that was what I couldn't do. I returned his look in the mirror, man to man, and the players and their white lines and green grass and brightly dressed fans passed from view. We crossed the Ohio again, that army green tributary to the mighty brown river we had not crossed, spent one more night on the road, and then went home. I can't be sure, but my sister, my mother, and I most likely went to Daytona Beach and spent two or three weeks splashing in the foaming white waves.

While I was there, in those tedious hours of digestion when I was forced to lie on the sand, I asked myself what my father had had in mind. At vacation's end, he would come and get us and deliver my sister and me to our respective new schools, but there was time to wonder about that four-day interlude. And I concluded he'd been showing me the way. History books are full of heroic figures pointing off into the distance, as if to say to their more cautious countrymen, There, there is where you want to go. These two-legged countrymen would eventually stumble forward, but by then the trailblazer, who had brought them to the very edge of the promised land, would have disappeared. There were people like that, frightened and as dug in as mules, who had to be carted off and shown where their best interests lay, people who had to be brought to the river's bank. There would be a warm-up river to cross, the way you warmed up for a game, but the river that mattered was for you alone to master. And when you saw people blithely driving across in cars, that was an illusion and belonged to another age. Real rivers mixed darkness and light, raised winds and cut continents with their onrushing flow, and the world could be divided into two camps of people, those who had crossed them and those who hadn't. Our father wanted us to know.

Karen looked skeptical, not entirely convinced, so I concluded my story by invoking those different bodies of water—including her father's open sea—and I hypothesized that everybody had to choose one body to measure himself against, beginning with this pretty little pool of hers. I got up and ran my fingers through its luminous clear water. Its coolness was carefully regulated, as was its scent. A leaf or an insect might have fallen onto its surface, but none had.

Seated over the remains of our meal, Karen said, What if your father was afraid of his river? Not just for his family but for himself? What if he realized he didn't have the courage to cross over into that darkness and all that was behind it? Hunters track their game right up to the water's edge. What if that's what you'd done? But instead of shooting your father you rescued him and brought him back. You said it all came to an exclamation mark. So why isn't that the end of the story?

Because it's still going on, I said.

Did you really bring him his crutch? Not just in fiction but in fact? I said, Yes.

And you stood beside him, the two of you together, both of you holding onto that fence and facing that river—that big brown ditch of a river, wasn't that what he said?

Yes, again.

End of story, Jay. It doesn't need to go any further.

I sat across the table from her. I must have sighed.

You were never a hunter, you know that. I doubt if you've ever fired a gun.

I nodded. Quietly, but not quite under my breath, I said, Something's still out there, Karen. Hugh—my cousin Hugh—went all the way to the mountains to get away from it.

Hugh's a romantic, a homegrown mystic, Karen said. Nothing wrong with that, but that's why he went up there.

I think it's fair to say he's still crawling up out of his Okinawa foxhole.

All right. And my father's out to play every golf course he can find so that he can get off the deck of that burning aircraft carrier. He won't have time to play them all. Good, Jay.

Karen's property was enclosed by a wall. Adjoining houses were close and tall enough to look down into her back yard, where neighbors would see the two of us lit by citronella candles, lingering over the remains of our meal, but no game, game as we knew game, could get over that wall. Still, the game was there.

Jay, I'm not going to say we wasted eight years, but it didn't have to be the way it was. I think we can both say that.

Her elbow rested on the table. Her hand was up as if she were about to wave. I reached across the table and held it.

Was it a good marriage at least for a while? I asked. Were you happy at the start? Don't answer if it means opening fresh wounds.

She squeezed my hand to the point where I thought she might wring it. She might have been preparing to arm-wrestle me down to the table. Her strength had always impressed me, it had made her seem more vital, not at all mannish, and there'd been times in bed when so much physical force had been brought to bear I couldn't imagine how we'd failed to conceive that child she wanted.

You fool, she said.

Just what Judy called me.

Everything leaves a wound. Every day a fresh one. It's what life's all about. You want to revisit old times, you open a wound. Jesus, Jay, are you so much your father's son you haven't figured that out by now?

There are wounds and there are wounds, Karen.

Oh, please! I didn't rescue you off a courthouse bench to listen to you moan and groan about wounds. We've got scars everywhere you look. I was happy with Oliver for a while—that was his name. Ollie. Then it wore out. Whereas you and I we really didn't get a chance, did we?

My voice trembled and not, I would have insisted to her, because I was about to tell a lie. I was happy with you, Karen.

She tightened her grip, as if to hold me accountable; for each falsehood or half-truth I uttered, I could expect to hear a small bone snap. Well, then, damn you, she said, right into my eyes, for giving up on eight years like that.

You left, I reminded her.

But you were a missing person long before then.

I wanted to defend myself, but like one of those little whistle-stop towns, with its rows of empty stores and its weather-grayed houses without a breath of fresh air left, there was nowhere to start the rebuilding, the refurbishing, the bringing back to life. Still I felt it, in the onrush of the moment I did, and stepped around the table and took Karen Ambrose into my arms and said nothing into her ear. Then I kissed her, and that was when I did say, deep in my throat but, perhaps, not so deep that she couldn't make it out, the word "Please." The breath seemed to go out of her, or perhaps it was a sigh a long time in coming, and for an instant I felt as if I were holding her up and was relieved to discover it was something I could do. Then she had a resurgence, and for a moment, there at poolside in her back yard, we were matched strength to strength. Mine came from my father, as every ingratiating citizen who had ever addressed me on the streets of my town had reminded me. It had been a kind of chant. Whoa! I looked up and who did I see come walkin' down the street but a two-legged Bob Langley! Spittin' image! The man himself! A four-letter ghost!

Her bed was almost as big as her pool and it was oval-shaped, too. It was hard to hold a homecoming in such a bed so I held onto her and tried not to let Oliver or Ollie or anybody else get in between us. Twenty pounds lighter, she'd said, and a part of me mourned that missing weight. It was missing in the thighs, the arms, the midriff, the breasts, the hips. I was a fool to go in search of it, and I didn't, but never ceased to note its loss so that we made love in the absence of what had passed away. I can only speak for myself. She moaned to me as if I were opening a fresh wound, it was how she saw life, a wound for each pleasure reenacted, for the folly of each attempt, but she held me close and would not let me pull away until I'd bled her wounds dry. I missed the missing parts of her, but we'd been different people then, and when I let go it was as if I were calling her across some broad expanse, across past fields of play. I called her name, two, three times, then it all went quiet. A coming up, deep breathing, famished breaths, and then it all went profoundly quiet and stayed that way. It was as if a season had ended. I slept and woke. It was still dark. Karen called out to me from her sleep, a night sound, never fully accountable in the light of day. But I heard it, her voice, unmistakable, coming out on breath she'd drawn from a fund of all we'd left unfinished in our time. Then I dressed and drove away.

IX

I'D NEVER UNDERSTOOD CAROLINE LANGLEY. How does a man like Billy Langley, whose need for another would seem like only a momentary lapse from the man he professed to be, persuade a woman to marry him? The rumor was that Caroline had proposed to him. Or that she had met him during that time he'd spent out of the state, bided her time, perhaps had another marriage, and then reappeared in my cousin's life shortly after his father had persuaded my father to take Billy on. This I'd learned from Hugh, who hadn't disclosed any more. Keep an eye on Billy had been a refrain in his life. The more eyes the better. Mine had been two of them, and perhaps Caroline's had been two more.

When she stood before you and subjected herself to family talk, her eyes moved left and right as if to make sure it was just you, you weren't a locomotive pulling a train of relatives behind, or you were the end of it, she'd stood her ground, earned her reward, and you were the caboose. On those occasions, she could be relaxed, gracious, warm, and capable of a laugh. The ridgelines in her face seemed to soften and her eyes got languid. Bedroom eyes. Blue shading into gray. You might have entertained a fantasy then of another Caroline Langley before the "Langley" got attached. I looked for that other woman that morning I called at their door, but her neck stiffened and the sleepiness in her eyes turned caustic, and I didn't look again.

Her husband Billy was having breakfast out on the sun porch of their expensive home, built with money my father had allowed Billy to keep. She led me there, where she became a hostile witness to everything I said.

I said, "Billy, you know I've never asked you anything about your relationship with my father. You know that, don't you? Nothing about business, nothing about any special deals you had. You and I haven't exchanged many words over the years, and I'm sorry for that, but not one of them has been about my father."

Billy sat there in his bathrobe, still unshaven, a bleary-eyed, sallow-fleshed, deeply dispirited man. He hadn't expected anybody to show up at his door at that early hour, much less me. Of course, it wasn't hard to believe that if I kept looking I would find the man who waited only for me, who longed for and dreaded my visit, and made it a point of honor to be there every morning for what remained of his life, just in case.

I went on. "Don't tell me anything about business now—if you can keep from it. But tell me what you know. Some moment when you caught him off guard, something like that. Something he said when he thought he was saying something else."

Billy grinned, sourly. He scoffed and shook his head.

"I know," I said, "he was not a man who let himself be caught off guard. He said what he wanted, no more. I know that. So what did he want? I don't mean the money. He had power and could make men scared—I saw enough of that when I was a boy. I mean something else. Something he lacked. Something he wanted he didn't have."

Billy looked up at me then. There was a flicker of light in his eyes and some movement in the corner of his mouth. For an instant I was reminded of the boy Billy as family provocateur. A feeble surge of something behind the gray of his skin. I would have bet he was about to say, "A leg."

"And don't say 'a leg,'" I said.

Caroline said, "Jay, would you like some breakfast?"

Billy said, "There was nothing hidden. He just didn't mind taking his time."

"Ah," I said. "And finally he got what he wanted, if he waited long enough. Is that it? He lived a long life. Which means we probably buried a satisfied man."

"Jay?" Caroline said.

"What? No, no breakfast."

"Your father was not a satisfied man," she declared in a dry and very deliberate voice, trying to keep the vindictiveness out it, to make its neutrality into something like a judgment knell. "He was a bitter man. He didn't care what people thought of him. He wouldn't care if you sat here all morning tormenting my husband, trying to figure him out—"

"I know that," I cut her off. "Everybody knows that. Billy?"

Billy said, "I think you need to lie down."

"I know that too. A sleepless night," I added, and then went on.

"He was the last of that whole generation, the very last, Billy," I said. "Those reunions we had when we were kids. When you try to make sense of the Langley line—"

That brought him to life. "You try to make sense of it, I don't," he said.

I ignored him and continued, "By the time we got added on it was already fraying out. That's what we were, the frayed ends of the Langley line. But before the War, and there were two wars, but before the second one, back then..." And I paused, not so that he would pick it up, at least that hadn't been my intention. I was tired, and just the thought of a war, and then of a second, brought me momentarily to a halt.

Finally, with a trace of fellow-feeling, which seemed to belie his words, Billy said, "Family never meant anything to me, Jay. Not the way it does to you. I know it's hard for you to believe that."

"I never doubted it," I said.

"All right, then."

"But you played your part, much more than I did. That's what's funny."

But, funny or not, he wasn't laughing. He shook his head.

"You," I said, "took the bull by the horns."

"Your father, you mean?"

"You could have stayed away." I glanced at his wife, who could have kept him on her side of the state line. Beyond the Langley pull, the Langley gravitational field. What my sister had said: make that first big push then float free, come to rest somewhere else. If need be, enter another family's gravitational field. But that was Langley hostility I saw in Caroline Langley's eyes. An early morning stiffness and coldness, not natural to her. She was lovelier than that. She came from out of state. A tragic mismatch—it was enough to make you cry. "You didn't have to come back and work for him," I told her husband. "Don't tell me why. I know why."

"My father..." Billy said.

"Yes, your father. Of course, your father. All our fathers. I was up there not long ago, by the way. He had some land he wanted me to see. An isolated point out on the lake. In case I felt my sanity going and needed to get away. But before I left he asked me to do him a favor. He wanted me to persuade you to come back to the family. Now that my father was dead, he wanted us to make up. I suppose what he really wanted was for us to behave like brothers. Brothers, Billy. Any chance of that? "

'Cuz' he had always called me, and always in a mocking and disqualifying way. He wasn't listening to me. He was looking back inside. "He told me what kept him alive when the Japanese were trying to kill him was your father and mother. He said he had to see Bob and Fran Langley one more time for life to make sense."

I knew this. But coming out of Billy's mouth it sounded like the most puerile of fantasies.

"This was when he was trying to get me to take that job. He told me then."

I gave in to my exhaustion and for a moment closed my eyes. I'd been looking at the toast crumbs on Billy's plate, and the yolk-hardened half of a poached egg I hadn't allowed him to finish, and that's what I carried inside. Then I saw Hugh, curled like a fetus in the foxhole he'd dug, with the kissing-close sound of those bullets passing overhead. Through his terrified closed eyes I saw the beauty he clung to, my father and mother, sitting with their heads tilted in toward each other on a bright winter's day, so close to spring they might have been first flowers themselves, her gamesome smile, his confident, all-clear-to-the-horizon grin. I must have made a sound, and when I opened my sleep-deprived eyes, I realized they were wet.

"Jay," Caroline said calmly, as if she were measuring her sympathy out.

Billy said, "But I knew that ever since I was a kid. He loved them."

"Yes," I said.

"Then Dad came back and they weren't the people they'd been. He never got over it. He was fighting his war so that your father and mother wouldn't have to. He said that one night to me, in just those words. I thought he was crazy. Bob Langley was supposed to be the strongest man in town, if we wanted to send our best soldiers against Hitler and his storm troopers. Your father enlisted, but Dad blamed the draft board. Especially its chairman, a man named Moody, whose son worked in that bomber plant, too."

"How's that, Billy?" I said.

"A man named Moody and his son. Dad came back and went to work in the town newspaper and wrote a story about how the Moodys claimed the Enola Gay came from our plant. Turned out it probably didn't, probably came from one out in Wichita, but that didn't keep the Moodys from crowing about how we'd made history right here."

"The Moodys," I said. There were Moodys in town. The name

was not unfamiliar to me. The Moody my father's age had been known as Cholly, or Jolly Cholly. I remembered that, too. "What did they have to do with my father?"

Billy shook his head. A heaviness seemed to settle over him, a blanket of inertia. His shoulders slumped. He drew a long breath, but instead of rising, his chest fell. Anybody could look at him and tell he was sick. His face was pouchy, ashy. There was no light left in his eyes. It was all those drugs he'd taken as a kid. It was the battle he'd waged and lost against my father. He'd helped bury my father, but one look at him and, really, you knew it was the other way around.

I felt the urge to embrace him then, as I might have a brother, one returned many years later from a war. Instead, I said impatiently, "Billy, forget the atom bomb. The Moodys, my father?"

He cleared out a space, he made the effort, but it was his way of telling me this was all I was going to get. "My Dad came back and your Dad was already in town. They'd cut off his leg. Old Man Moody ran the draft board that'd kept your Dad out of the war. Maybe it was a kind of cover so he could keep his own son out, too. I don't know, but at the last minute, your Dad decided to enlist. My Dad had to blame somebody when he got back, and there sat the Moodys. I guess they made a good target."

Billy bowed his head and slumped. He made a show of shutting down. It was as if he were closing the cover of a book.

"And that's it, Billy?" And even I could hear a note of long-standing grievance in my voice, as if this man to whom I'd once relinquished my place at my father's side was only willing to give me crumbs in return. "That's the end of the story?"

"Is that what you wanted me to tell you, a story?" My cousin rallied and raised his head. That was probably the last trace I'd ever see of the flickering, scheming, little sideways Billy Langley grin. "No storytellers left in this family, cuz. They all died out. All dead. You just told me so yourself."

Eventually, I got up to go. Leaving her visibly aging husband to the remains of his breakfast, his wife walked me to the front door. I was through it and onto the porch when she called me back. Her tone was impartial, a little detached, as if she were musing in my presence, but I didn't doubt her intention. "I never believed it was 'a stray shot' that wounded your father. That seems to have been the talk around town, what amounted to the official version: a terrible snowstorm, a stray shot, and on a night any other mortal would have frozen to death, your father heroically survived. I happen to believe he fell over stumbling through the snow, shot himself, and then spent a night alone trying to overcome his shame."

"My father was a star athlete," I reminded her. "He'd be the last person to stumble and shoot himself."

"Nevertheless, he came back and made everybody he met pay the price. If he couldn't live with his shame, why should anybody else live a shame-free life either? It's time someone told the real story about your father, Jay. Don't you agree? Someone with a marksman's eye, someone who won't blink? Get free of your family, take one step out of this town, and you'd have to be blind not to see it." She moved up to me, close enough that I saw all the wear and tear being Billy's wife had inflicted on her. She lowered her voice. "Do you have any idea how much I hate the name 'Langley'?"

"Did you have a happy childhood, Caroline?"

"The best," she said. "And before you ask, yes, my father was a kind and gentle man."

Out of curiosity, I asked for his name, and she shook her head. Then, before she closed the door on me, she advised me to find a place to lie down.

On my way out, I passed by the guardhouse to Billy's development, Harlowe's Crossing, it was called, and received a nod of acknowledgement from the guard. Family got in and family got out. The second I stopped and leaned my head back against the headrest, I was sure I would have gone to sleep, so I didn't stop. I laid my cell phone on the seat beside me. I might have called Karen and allowed her to track my progress, mile by mile, back into town. I might have asked her about last night, just to make sure. I remembered a small shimmering pool, I remembered a big river, and a body twenty pounds lighter than it had been, but hers, a refuge from the day's hunting I'd done. I'd been a hunter, I remembered. Close to bagging my game. But I didn't, didn't bag my game, and I didn't call to find out that, no, none of it was true, no game, no pool, river, no slimmer version of a once beloved body. I worked my way to yet another road running parallel to the interstate with its on and off ramps and huge green and white signs, pure phosphorescence in a world of weather-grayed shacks and barns, and entered our town out by its strip malls and new evangelical churches with their enormous parking lots, on my way to the center of town and the courthouse, diagonally across from which my uncle Raymond had had his furniture store. It was gone now. A dollar store had taken its place. Your father, my uncle had told me, when he was a little boy once had a billy goat that pulled him in a cart all around town. The town was empty, its sidewalks untrafficked. The only color came from a barber's pole half a block down the street, where it had always been, and I asked myself if it was an ornament the town had left in place or if hair was still cut inside. I might have driven by to find out, but instead took the route I thought a boy in his goat-cart would follow, who in leaving Main Street would want to pass by the old houses on Midland with their columned and shaded verandas and their gliders and swings and flower urns just to receive the applause. A smart goat would know the way. The churches. The magnolias shedding light. The street side ditches still damp from the evening rains. The white of the billy goat's hair and the fair hair—none fairer—of the little boy. On a trot out to a large white frame house, with pecans growing in the front yard and screen porches upstairs and down. The house still stood, its clapboards now sided in vinyl. Across the street, its windows boarded, was an old grade school, but only a corner of the ball field remained. The house had been divided up into apartments, and a visitor would have his choice of doors. But a billy goat would know the way, and a beloved little boy, expecting a welcome, would have a sure sense for home.

I drove by the Langley house on the way to the house where I grew up, set atop its terraces, looking out over a stand of pines. There were no red lights and I rolled through the stop signs. No one was about. The houses got smaller, the front yards sandier, the trees scrubbier, and then the houses petered out. Shacks. A couple of remaining barns. Surely, a mule left standing there, if I chose to look for it. The road dropped down to a creek and then rose to Crestview Drive, and the view after all the years, the stops and starts, the expansion and contraction, remained. You looked out over pines to the tops of the church steeples and the courthouse cupola and the water tank, and if you disregarded the transmitting towers for cell phones and for radio and television stations, which you only really noticed at night, you could date the town in the era you chose and populate it as you saw fit. Our family house, the redbrick house of my upbringing, was there—we'd had neighbors, we hadn't been alone, other houses had been built on the road, some as ample as ours—and I did not stop in front. I rolled down the drive and parked in back. I lowered the window and smelled the pines, and the mud of the creek from down the hill, and I smelled the untended boxwood bushes planted around the house, which had an odor of sanctity about them, an odor easy to associate with a life lived within prescribed limits and with death. I had not been inside the house since my father had died. To prepare myself, I leaned my head against the headrest, gave in to my exhaustion, and went to sleep.

━◦∾◦━

INSIDE THE HOUSE, the stillness was palpable, it had a weight, and you moved against it as you would against a liquid that was yours to breathe and whose temperature matched your own. The dimness asked nothing of the eyes. On the first breath the mustiness spoke of smells you'd known, which spoke of people and their things; a breath later you'd taken it all inside. I didn't go through each room. I walked down the hall to the kitchen, perhaps because I always had, where a coolness came off the sink and the tiles and where the refrigerator still hummed. The electricity was on. The phone would be, too. Water waited in the pipes. None of the house's vital functions had been closed down. I walked into the dining room where the table was set for six, even though in the best of times we had only been four. Occasionally, those extra places would be occupied by family members, which had led to the suspense of who might be coming when, but their vacancy was the norm. The china was decorated with an elaborate Royal Albert rose pattern and each water glass had a gilt rim.

In the parlor, where my mother had hosted her bridge games and her figurines adorned the mantle and a triple-tiered dumbwaiter table, the stillness was heavier, or perhaps its weight had a swelling and subsiding effect. On occasion, I'd been asked to serve the bridge players their little crust-trimmed sandwiches and pastries. I rarely observed the games themselves, but I was aware of the way my mother seemed to pick for her partner the most carefree woman there—usually the youngest and frequently a recent arrival in town—and, in a bantering tone, would inform her of the cunning and treachery of the other players at the table, to the point that those other players became a bridge into the town, which allowed my mother to extend her warning until it included the town's residents as a whole, many of whom would cheat you blind and strip you bare if they got the chance. All in that same mock-bitter, bantering tone, with laughter and snacks to be shared, but when it was all over those young women frequently left the house under a pall, and I noticed that too.

On the bird's-eye maple coffee table my mother loved, her glossy magazines, her *Ladies Home Journals* and her *Better Homes and Gardens,* were arranged according to their dates. Their glossiness was free of dust. The whole house seemed dust-free. My father might have contracted for someone to come in and dust until someone else called a halt. Or until someone else came in and on one breath took the dust of the house's being into himself. I walked into my old bedroom, a faithful replica, but the sameness and the staleness there gave me nothing back. My sister's room was like looking down the wrong end of a telescope. Across the door to my parents' bedroom a velvet restraining cord might have been hung, to indicate the one room in the house barred to trespass. It had been a death room and a room of some fearful foreign intimacy, but finally a room where the stillness in the house had gathered, as if to make a last stand, or as if to tempt me into releasing the restraining cord and stepping inside. I wasn't tempted. Instead, I walked down to the end of the hall and stepped inside my father's study, where his broad-shouldered presence was immediately felt, and where I smelled his crutch and heard the heartbeat of its persistent plonk, even though I knew I had placed that crutch beside him in the casket.

He had an easy chair there before his desk, low and deeply padded, where, because of the difficulties he would have in getting out, he never sat. But his visitors did. I sank into that chair and closed my eyes and immediately returned to myself as a little boy, climbing up off the floor to sit in the space my father's missing leg provided, back before he was anything other than a hero of bygone days. Sitting like that, a little boy grown into a man might believe he could take the place of all his father had lost. It was not an unreasonable thought. For an instant, it might even have been a thought my father had shared. I remembered the naturalness of the fit there, and my father, a natural in everything he'd done, might have felt it too. Hold on to the feeling, he might have told himself, and it could be enough. I sat like that in my father's easy chair until the stillness I'd stirred up had settled, and I went to sleep again.

I awoke to a more encouraging light and a keen and clearer head. I rose out of the depths of that chair and walked around my father's desk, which, in stark contrast to his office downtown, was uncluttered, clean, occupied only by a bronze lamp and a black telephone. Built into the base of the lamp was a holder for a pen, and the desk's center drawer would contain pencils, I knew, whose points would not have gone dull. There were no locks on the six flanking drawers, and I sat in the high-backed chair behind the desk and went through them all. Besides a stack of blank paper, they contained bank statements and titles and deeds and property abstracts, no personal letters, no photographs, and nothing as out of place as a memento. That the man who had sat behind this desk had once been a town's favorite son and had once fathered a family could not have been deduced from the contents of his desk. Some of the older papers had begun to acquire that courthouse smell, which was the smell of a high and unassailable courthouse wall, and I left them there. The chair was on wheels, and within rolling reach of the desk was a filing cabinet with four more drawers, whose locks were prominent, but all four opened at the touch. The contents were alphabetized. I looked under the M's for Moody and under the B's for B-29's and under the E's for Enola Gay, and then because my father had taken the time to order things at home so obligingly, I went through the entire contents. More of the same. And I realized it didn't matter. His desk drawers and filing cabinet were utterly depersonalized for a reason, and his desktop was as blank as an empty stage. The phone was there, and that didn't matter either. But because he'd left it for me, I picked it up and called my sister.

"I remember the Moodys," she said, "but I never heard anything about them and the bomber plant. No," she said. "Why do you want to know?"

Enola Gay. Did she know what that was?

"Tell me," she said.

The B-29 that dropped the bomb on Hiroshima.

"Enola gay?" she said. "Why would anyone call a bomber gay?"

It was the pilot's mother's name, I told her.

"Jay, this makes no sense. Why would anyone name an airplane that was about to drop an atom bomb after his mother?"

I told her it didn't matter.

"Where are you?" she said. "You're there, aren't you? In the house. You need to get out of there. I'm sure you've been there long enough."

I told her I was sitting at our father's desk. I told her I'd gone through all his papers. I compared it to going through a telephone book. Just numbers and names. Not even a hint of a story for a family that had lived and died by them. Her burdies. Right out her child's window, bigger and brighter than her burdies by far, had been the B-29's. I asked her what she remembered of them.

"I was only two," she said. "Maybe three or four. I don't know. I remember a lot of noise... noise that didn't belong."

Not like the burdies singing or the sound of our father's voice.

"I don't know," she said. "You need to go ask…"

She stopped, as if at the edge of a cliff, and I said it for her. There was no one left to ask, was there? It was down to us. And I told her it didn't matter.

"What do you mean it doesn't matter? If it didn't matter you'd be back in your own house, where you belong. Or you'd get on a plane and come up here. Jay," she said, "I want you to get up and walk out the door and go—"

I asked her if she had something she wanted to contribute.

"Contribute? What do you mean? Contribute to what?"

Dad and mother, the bombers and the burdies, any last thing?

"Last thing?" she said. "Like what kind of thing?"

Anything from that time. A last family effort.

"Jay," she said, "it's time for you to get up and leave. Go the cemetery, if you have to, and stand before the graves. That's what people do. That's what cemeteries are for. They take flowers. Karen will go with you if you ask her. Have you seen Karen again?"

I told her it was all right. I could take up the slack myself. I told her it didn't matter.

"Jay," she said, "if you stay there I'm afraid you'll do something really childish like sleep in their bed. Don't make me come down there. Promise me you won't do that."

So, she had nothing, I said. There wasn't one last tidbit she was hanging on to till the bitter end.

"Jay," she said, "what do you mean 'take up the slack?'"

Supply the missing parts, I said.

"What missing parts?"

I told her it didn't matter.

X

THERE THEY SIT AT THE KITCHEN TABLE. It is somewhere between eight and nine in the morning. His father, Bob Langley, has finished his night shift at the Cargill Bomber plant, and his mother, Frances, has just fed and bathed their daughter (and only child) and left her in a spot of sun. Fran has made Bob his breakfast, but it remains untouched. It's as though he regarded it as some sort of trickery, an offering made to mask a lie.

"Can you swear to me you didn't know?"

"Yes, I can swear to you I didn't know," his mother says. This will be a long day, and Fran seems to sense it even then. Her voice is measured, far from the inflections of anger. She is in her robe—a beautiful woman. In spite of a thankless shift as expediter at the bomber plant, and the humiliating news he's just learned, Bob is a handsome man. There was never any question about that. The Great Depression rained a drabness down on the world, but on a chosen few shed a radiance. Their daughter Judy, from the day she was born, has been the darling of photographers. Then came the War, and a world reduced to coupon rationing and the names of battlefields they couldn't pronounce.

"I try not to pay attention to every rumor I hear in town," Fran goes on.

"We don't live in a town," Bob reminds her bitterly. "This is no better than base housing. The only difference is that soldiers on bases get to move on."

"I'm not complaining, Bob. We do what we have to."

Spring. If they were home, really home, they would look outside and see forsythia and redbud, cherry and dogwood in blossom. Wisteria, a great cascading surplus of wisteria in this time of scarcity. Outside, duplexes like theirs line the streets. Jonquils and tulips have been planted in thin woeful rows. They've set up a swing set for their daughter in the tiny backyard, and what she sees when they give her a push is the corrugated gray of the plant and the bombers as they roll out of the hangars. At first she associated them with her father—Daa-dee. Bomber, when she learned the word, she might have confused with her mother. Baa-ma.

To "expedite" the production of bombers means to speed production up. Mostly, Bob has stayed in an office and shuffled papers. When he's stepped into the plant itself to talk to supervisors or as-sembly foremen, he's been amazed. There's no end to it. Over forty football fields, it is said, could fit inside. There are zones for the tail assembly, the fuselage assembly, the wing, cabin and cockpit assem-blies. The sub-assembly section, itself, with its endless workbenches and press punches and sheet metal cutters, is amazing. Men and women work side by side. Double-tiered scaffolds have been set up on wheels so that workers can move up and down the length of a fuselage or wing. The drilling din the riveting and countersinking make is decibels beyond anything he has ever known.

He was more than amazed when he stood with other selected office personnel and from their elevated perch looked down the length of the production plant. Only he could not see the end. It was full of finished B-29 bombers, lined up two abreast, their wing tips almost touching. The tail fins rose toward the ceiling; at any moment he expected the propellers to fire up in a blur. Their size was so out of scale he didn't know how to approach them. He needed to be down on the ground. He needed to be on the line of scrimmage. Only when a messenger girl on roller skates happened to pass by could he begin to picture himself there, and then, more than amazed, he was overwhelmed.

"I can't stay here," he tells his wife.

"What do you mean?"

"Let Charles Moody find some other way to keep Cholly out of the war."

"What are you going to do, Bob?"

Once his anger has passed and this wound to his ego has healed, she is asking what liberties he's about to take with their lives.

Her husband is no fool. He has long been the most rumored about man in town, but until something is said to his face he's learned to let rumors run their course. Charles Moody heads her husband's draft board. He has a son just over thirty, who is the father of a little boy, as Bob is of a little girl. Cholly Moody has had his nose broken; Bob

Langley a hernia repaired. As long as Charles Moody Senior can keep Bob out of the war he doesn't have to send his son, either. He can order them both to expedite the production of bombers, and give his son the daytime shift. Bob Langley provides the Moodys with cover. It wasn't until somebody at the plant asked him how his Daa-dee was doing that the rumor became real and demanded a response.

"This afternoon," he says to his wife across the kitchen table, "I'm going to enlist."

She doesn't take it personally. It's Charles Moody he's directing his defiance to.

He adds, "If Ike keeps dragging his feet I could be there when they hit the beaches."

"Bob," she says, quietly.

"That son of a bitch!"

They hear their daughter Judy. She is gurgling in a musing sort of way. It is the song she sings in the morning, as the sun begins to warm her, and as a baroque ornamentation of her single simple theme, they hear the trill of the birds that come to her window, cardinals flashing red. Her father might get up and go to her then. In a deep manly murmur, he might sing her a song of his own. But not this morning.

Fran doesn't know what to do. She's not sure she understands her husband's attitude toward this war. The Japanese started it with their attack on Pearl Harbor, but Bob has had little to say about them, and she thinks she knows why. They belong to another race, live in a world apart, and can't be expected to abide by the same standards of decency. But the Germans are Europeans, members of a common family of sorts; as young men Bob's two older brothers fought them in the First World War, and it's as if the Germans have refused to accept the outcome. No sooner has the game ended than they've demanded it be replayed. There's some insult to fair-mindedness in that that galls him, and it is this fair-mindedness, this sportsman's code, really this code among boys, that eludes Fran's understanding. She understands why a boy might take his basketball, football, or baseball, and say, That's enough, and go home. But these are grown men. This is war and people are getting killed.

She remains quiet so that he can hear his daughter. She places her hand six inches from her husband's so that he can take it and take heart.

"I hope like hell he stays right here," he hisses, "expediting bombers until there's nothing left to blow up!"

He looks down at his plate—the bacon fat hardening, the egg-white crinkling brown. When he looks up at her there's a strange ashen pallor to his face, strange because inside she knows he's boiling.

"Middleton's standing there behind those glasses of his. Glasses so thick they're like goggles, they do something funny to his eyes. Instead of magnifying them they make them smaller and harder. It's like you're looking at nailheads. Middleton says, 'Been meaning to ask you, Bob. Why don't you and Cholly Junior go over there and give Ike a kick in the ass and the rest of us rejects will keep rolling out these bombers.' It didn't take two seconds, but I swear to you that's when I figured it out. Two seconds more and I'm thinking I'm the only one who hadn't."

"No, Bob." He won't take her hand so she lays it on top of his. "I didn't know. I still don't. Ed Middleton likes to clown around. He likes to get under your skin."

"He knows. Rejects can do it. Four-eyes like Middleton can do it."

"Rejects can't do it. Whoever keeps those bombers coming is worth a lot more than one more man on the battlefield. You know that's true."

He stares back at her, powerless and perplexed. She can see Middleton's eyes, the way they leap out at you yet crouch back at the same time. She has a cousin, Irene, whose husband Mel owns a small textile plant. The government ordered him to remain on the job, manufacturing soldiers' uniforms.

She brings it up to her husband. She asks him which he thought was more essential, uniforms or bombers—if the Germans and the Japanese were going to be brought to their knees. They've seen Movietone footage. Soldiers can be mown down like stick figures, like weeds, into the mud. A uniformed weed. But bombers flying in formation out of the clouds...

Abruptly, he pulls free of her hand. It's a short movement, he's taken the six inches back, but she's not used to being rejected that sharply, much less by her husband.

"Damn it, Fran! It's his factory! If the government wants uniforms, Mel's got to stay here and get them out. I haven't got to do anything! I haven't got to stay here and file receipts and sign requisition orders! Do I?"

It's a snarl, but it's as if he can't get it out of his throat. He's snarling at himself. He's like a battery grinding down, grinding and grinding and the car won't move. He doesn't expect her to answer the question. She understands it's better if she doesn't try.

They hear their daughter, that quiet musing gurgle accompanied by the birds. In a world at war, their daughter can make those sounds.

What does he have to do?

It is still early, still between eight and nine on an April morning, and like his wife he understands this day might go on and on unless he does something to stop it. He has been the envy of a town, its four-letter athlete, its fair-haired boy. The hair is fair—sandy—and curly. The cut of the face as clear and uncomplicated as a cut of good wood. No one doubts the quality of the grain. The mouth is surprisingly sweet, delicate. The face might harden, get tough as a nut, but never the sweet flesh of the mouth. He wears this face, this supple athlete's body, like the only suit of clothes he will need in his life. Yet, he is dimly aware: at some point he made a pact. In exchange for its acclaim, and for this handsomely clothed body of his, and for his prowess on all fields of play, and for the beauty of his wife, he owes the town a life. But why would the town put him in an expediter's office and make sneering remarks? Shouldn't he be asked to carry the town's banner out onto the world's high stage? Is the town reneging on its pact? Is he, Bob Langley, being asked to take his life back, and at the point where the town's purposes cross to make a decision of his own?

He reads the papers, listens to the radio broadcasts from overseas. Before he came to work in the bomber plant he spent a part of each day at his brother Raymond's furniture store listening to the swirl of opinions about the conduct of the war. Raymond rarely joined these debates, but nothing in Bob Langley's life has remained as fixed in his memory as that tightly pursed wound his brother carries in his shoulder. That wound speaks to him of German treachery. That was the one constant in so much else that was sheer confusion. As long as he can picture the German Wehrmacht with its jack-booted infantry and its legions of panzer tanks and its dive-bombing stukas crushing the poor Czechs and Poles and Norwegians and Belgians before flooding out over France, he can keep his mind clear. But the chess play of alliances baffles him and can awaken in him a profound distaste for anything he can't get his mind around. The Germans concluded a nonaggression pact with the Soviets and then won a be-grudging sort of approval from certain of those small town debaters for turning around and invading the Bolshevik homeland. Making the Germans our allies on the eastern front and our detested enemies on the western? Could that be? And there were "American First-ers" in that group that met at Raymond's store, who had not only objected to the Lend-Lease program but gone ahead to accuse Roo-sevelt of withholding oil shipments to Japan in order to provoke an attack on Pearl Harbor so that he could then get a declaration of war and go off and fight the Germans with Churchill. Three thousand men had been killed at Pearl Harbor. Could FDR have done that? Did the Germans really try to invade Great Britain, and did the Brits pour oil on the English Channel and set fire to thousands of troops? He'd even heard that the American army had trained dogs to invade Japanese-held islands and go straight for the Japanese jugular while sparing the natives. Could dogs be trained to do that? Were dogs going to fight our wars?

When his draft board instructed him to, he went to work in the Cargill Bomber plant twenty miles away, and when he could spare the gas coupons he drove back to his town to sit at his brother's store.

There'd been an early landing by a Canadian force on the French coast at Dieppe, but it had been wiped out. Patton, a hands-on general with two ivory-handled revolvers, had prevailed in North Africa, and finally the Americans and Brits were making their way up the Italian boot. There were men in that store whose sons were fighting in the Pacific, and as far as Bob knew his nephew Hugh still served with the Merchant Marines. Raymond never talked about his son. He stayed on the job, attending to customers when they came in, doing inventory work when they didn't. But the men of the town continued to clap Bob Langley on the back every time he took time off from expediting the production of bombers to visit the store. They seemed to be saying: Stay close, son, stay close. The truth is no one knows what's going on out there. Keep rolling those bombers out that can fly around the world and you stay here with us.

He is not used to such confusion, and it's as if a world at war is a world whose tether to homeport has been cut. It is a world mindlessly adrift. He lies in his bed at night waiting for that wound his brother received slogging though the Argonne forest to tell him what to do. He might be waiting for a small oracle to speak. Instead, a soured and bored and envious Ed Middleton has made a crack. The fat florid jowls of Charles Moody have swum into view. His son Cholly, with his slack, sidling-up look. Based on everything his admirers have led him to believe, these men are his inferiors. He does not want to be in the same town with them, bound to them in ways he doesn't understand.

Whose orders is he obliged to take?

"Fran…" he all but howls into his wife's face, even though Fran can't help him.

Their daughter's gurgling song catches, falters, she's about to cry. Fran will have to get up to comfort her.

He says, "Don't go."

But he won't touch her. He loves her to distraction sometimes. It's as if every love song fell short. He knows his great good fortune then, and his abjectness. Hers is a morning beauty—the placid clarity of her wide-spaced eyes, the restful wave to her clean brown hair. The hours he's spent gazing at her. There are people who wake to the world each morning as if they've been born anew. Her beauty has played him false.

He's been the Moodys' stooge.

He knows she knew. He realizes on questions of what is good and right and proper he has never questioned her knowledge.

So he has to place her with the Middletons and the Moodys of the world, and when he does he sees the treachery that lives at the bottom of all beauty. He has to place her with the Germans.

He jumps in his chair, as if he's just been shot, as if something alien and hot has penetrated his flesh. According to the last news he's had, the Allies have made a landing in Italy at Anzio, and the Germans have bottled them up. He sits there like that, taking enemy fire, with an unnavigable sea at his back. She's been able to conspire with the Moodys because her only interest has been to keep him enslaved at her side.

He doesn't believe that. How could he? No one has been a more conscientious contributor to the war effort. She's been a scrupulous coupon keeper. To his knowledge she hasn't hoarded a single teaspoon of sugar, a can of beans. Before receiving each ration book he's watched her sit at the kitchen table and make a detailed list of everything they've had on hand. She has never fudged. She took the pledge to accept no rationed goods without giving up a coupon, which she dutifully honored on those occasions when members of her family had passed on things of theirs. Meat fat, bacon fat, she takes to the butcher so that gunpowder can be made. "From the frying pan to the firing line," the slogan went. She's combed the house for scrap metal, scrap rubber—a garter belt she once wore. She has gone so far as to bring a soldier home and, in a splurge of ration points, feed him an abundant meal.

This was a young man from Tennessee, who had trained nearby at Fort McConnell. No, he was not a young man, he was a boy, no more than eighteen, who had just acquired a lean wiry strength from his weeks of training. Take those weeks and that strength away and he would be sitting in his school library reading a book. He had never been away from home before. Fran made him a turkey dinner with all the trimmings, even though it was nowhere near Thanksgiving, but they were giving thanks for him and she wanted him to know. Bob understood this was part of a national effort. Women all over the country were being urged to invite soldiers about to be shipped out into their homes for a last home cooked meal, and Fran was complying. But she meant it. She was thanking this boy, whose name was Steve, for the sacrifice he was making. Steve Mitchell. A common name but he was not common, and she meant it. Then they took him to the train station and Bob handed him up his duffle bag, which was heavy, but he knew that Steve Mitchell would soon be carrying a weight heavier that that. He had looked apprehensive, not really scared, but aware that out on the horizon of his life a huge storm was brewing, which he was due to step into soon. Fran told him that she'd have another meal waiting hot on the stove for him when he got back. There'd been one thank you letter, mailed from Morocco; then nothing. Either Rommel had killed him or Patton had seen him through. And there were battles to come. What had he, Bob Langley, felt with that boy become a young man sitting in their house? Pride, shame, affection, jealousy, diminishment, devotion, anger at the world, anger at himself; a father's pride and shame and all the other emotions at sending a son out to do the job he hadn't done himself. None of which was the fault of his wife. His wife is blameless.

Tears spurt to his eyes as suddenly as a nosebleed.

He knocks the chair over as he lurches up. Fran says to him, "You can't do anything now—you're too worked up. Promise me you won't do anything, Bob, until you've calmed down."

He promises nothing.

His wife says, "You owe us that. You owe Judy and me that promise."

She sits back up to the table and tries to calm herself. If nothing else, that is the example she will set.

But, as she stares at her husband's back, a chill suddenly hits her and the blood drops out of her face. She's heard the plant's motors, or felt them just below hearing, as she would the first tremors of a quake. Her daughter's begun to whine and three or four words emerge. Her daa-dee's come back and hasn't been in to see her. The bur-dees have gone. With everything turned against him and only one avenue of escape left, Bob could walk out the front door and she might never see him again. She understands this isn't just any lovers' quarrel. The world is taking sides.

"Bob, look at me," she pleads.

Before he does she's tried to picture his face and gotten only a blurring of features. Like a skin-tight mask pulled over a skull.

"Please."

THE PHONE RANG. It rang until its summons filled the house, and then it rang strictly for me. I lifted the receiver out of its cradle and the ringing stopped. I heard her voice, and then in the extraordinary quiet that prevailed in my father's study I heard over the wires my sister's breath. I understood. It was meant to be an infusion; all it would take for me to regain my health would be to time my breathing to hers. Then her voice came out of her breathing, just above a whisper, bespeaking an intimacy which as brother and sister we'd never really shared.

"I told myself if I called and you answered it meant you'd been there all this time. In that case, I promised myself I'd come back. It's what you wanted, isn't it?"

I told my sister she'd be welcome.

"Because there really is," she said, "no one else."

No, she was right, no one.

"Well, there are people scattered around," she said, "but no one who counts."

I agreed. If you looked long enough you could always find a Langley. There was Billy, for instance, and all his brood. But to find a Langley at this stage of the game who mattered…

"Jay," she said. "Do you really want me to come back down there now? Is that what you want?"

That would be nice, I said.

"Because I'm worried about you," she said. "I don't like what all this means. If you'd get up out of that chair right now…That's where you're sitting, isn't it, behind his desk?"

Yes, I said, that was where she'd caught me.

She measured her breath. "If you'd get out of that chair right now and walk out the door, I'd feel a lot better. I'd still come back, we could settle things, I just wouldn't have to drop what I'm doing, you know, and come right now because I wouldn't be so worried. I *am* worried, Jay."

I leaned back in my father's chair and looked out over his empty desk. I understood. No one leaves a desk that clean unless he's inviting someone else to occupy it. The lamp shed some necessary local light, but the phone seemed plausible only if the previous occupant assumed the one to come would need to maintain contact with the outside world.

My sister let her worry show. She added, "Jaybird."

I spoke her name, Judy. She didn't really have a nickname, that little darling of photographers.

"What's wrong, Jay? Tell me what's happening to you."

I told her nothing was the matter.

"Something is," she insisted.

Things had been left undone, I said. That was all.

"You make it sound," she replied, "like he forgot to pay some bills. You're sitting at his desk, paying his bills. Then you walk out the door and that's the end of it. Is that what you're telling me?"

In a manner of speaking, it was. Paying bills was a way to put it. So was settling affairs.

She held a pause. I heard her river flowing by—but at a great distance. She was no longer seated out doors.

She sighed, a sigh of resignation, not quite the real thing. "You just can't give them up, can you?" she said.

To her sigh, I responded with a slightly stock answer of my own. I told her there was a story left to be told.

"Told to who? You don't tell stories to yourself—sane, healthy, adult people don't! You tell a story to somebody else!" Her temper flared and her voice sounded hoarse. "He's not worth it! When are you going to understand that? Mother was a victim, everybody knows that, but she made her bed—"

I interrupted my sister to inform her that I had not slept in it. In her bed, or in his.

"So where did you sleep, Jay?"

I'd slept in his chair, I said, then corrected myself. In his visitor's chair in his office. Humbly, I had been one of them, my father's visitors.

"You're playing games!" my sister shot back. "Why should I be worried if my little brother is playing games? He comes from a game playing family. He's been looking for a game he could play all his life. He had a father who set the bar high, and a mother who had a sporting streak herself, so he's had to look for a long time, but why should I be worried if my brother only wants to keep up the tradition? That's all it is, right, Jay? You're just looking for a way to pay your Langley dues. Is that what you mean by paying a bill? No wonder you've been sitting at that desk all night."

I heard her stormy breath at the other end of the line.

Then her voice went low and confidential and never more vehement. "How many times do I have to say it? He ruined everything. He lost a leg and came home and took everything back from everybody else. That's what he did! He's not worth it, Jay! He's not worth it!"

I waited until she'd concluded her rant. I told her our father hadn't taken everything back. He hadn't taken back her burdies. I myself had heard them singing. She'd mouthed her two year old's gurgling words, and her burdies had made their trill, and our father had gone into her room and sung to her out of the manly depth of his voice. Just not on that final, fateful morning…

I heard a hush, only a hush of the river flowing by. Either she had stopped breathing or taken her mouth far away from the mouthpiece. I decided she was mastering her emotions, and only when she had would she say, in a mildly curious tone, "What did they sound like? The birds, I mean."

They'd been sharp and clear and joyous, I told her, and combined with the sound of her two year old's voice they'd made a beautiful song of spring. The plant's motors and all that heavy clashing of gears could be kept underground, so that for just a moment, at least, her burdies and her sunny little voice were all you heard.

She held another pause. "Jay?" she said.

No, I'd gone on, on this particular morning, it had not been a trio. Sadly, thanks to the Moodys, our father had not joined them.

She tried for her emotion-mastered tone, but didn't get it. She sounded weary, this time truly resigned. "What is the matter?"

Nothing was the matter, I told her.

"All right. What do you want me to do?"

Maybe a little arithmetic, I said. Or maybe she'd already done it. I told her I was doing it right now, seated at his desk, and the way it had come out—

"What arithmetic?" she said. "Jay, please remember, I'm not inside your head. What are you talking about?"

The first numbers, the most private, the oldest in the world, I continued. After that, the world got to count—

"Jay!" she pleaded.

Conception date, birth date—those numbers, I replied.

She laughed, but her laugh sounded hollow and I could hear her shaking her head. Then she drew a long steadying breath. "There are flights every two hours, as you know," she said. "I'll catch the first one I can if you'll promise me one thing."

I told her it was an inexact science, really just another game, but one all historians must play. But determine the date and a good enough investigator could always discover the place. The precise time of day, the peculiarities of the place—

"Promise me you'll hold on. Will you do that, Jaybird?"

She was my sister, and, really, there was no one else. I wasn't forgetting Karen, but Karen wasn't blood. Karen was a soft-spot, Karen was a traveling companion, given the day and given the weather, Karen was along for the ride. So I made Judy that promise, hung up the phone, and remained at his desk, whose surface continued to shine, as though in the footlights of an empty stage.

LATER, FRAN'S PERSUADED HIM TO SLEEP. She's put her daughter down for her afternoon nap. The light on their bedroom blind is a parchment-orange, but she slips in bed beside her husband and positions herself a short distance from his back. Another six inches. Immediately, she's praying that when he wakes this tumultuous interlude will have passed, but while she's praying she is keenly aware of the rhythm of his breathing and of the heat he gives off. His breathing is troubled, she thinks, and the added heat of his body can only be explained by the fight he wages inside. She intensifies her prayer. His breathing sharpens, and so does his heat, as if he's entered some decisive battle-phase. She waits for him until she can't stand the anxiety and what he's doing to himself.

She lies along his back now, his entire body length, those six inches bridged. Her breath, and the wordless fervor of her prayer, have become a whimper, which at first she's not aware of making. She is repeating his name. Already, she is calling to him across oceans. Her voice is lost in the drone of B-29 bombers, the only sound of war she knows for a fact. They are, of course, bombers he himself has expedited through production, and the irony is so neat and merciless—as the skies fill—that the last murmured vestiges of her prayer freeze in her mouth. It's as if she's been praying to the enemy. It's as if her husband's death on a beach in France has long been ordained, and her intercession on his behalf is a spiteful joke the heavens have allowed her to play on herself. It's as if a war has been staged just so Bob Langley can die and the gods can have their laugh.

She hears her own whimper and she crowds up on his back. Again, she is pleading for his help, but if asked to put words to her plea, to tell him what it is she wants him to do, she would fail. What can two people do in a world determined to destroy itself? Their daughter, whose song she'd once been able to set against that distant bloody roar, has already been taken from them. They are alone. She is naked under her slip, Bob, under his T-shirt, is aflame.

She speaks his name.

He awakes to discover a wife bearing no resemblance to the woman he has known. He's known his wife as a gamesome girl, a delighted mother, a scrupulous homemaker and coupon-keeper, an attentive daughter and sister and aunt, not always a pal but a friend, a partner, a mild and beneficent and firm-principled counselor, a wise force, but he has never seen anyone this fierce and this distraught. No wife that he knows, but he holds her. She wants to speak, but can't—he can feel it in her belly. It's as if she's entered a foreign country and the powers of speech that have served her all her life mean nothing now. It's as if she has to generate a whole new language, at a stage more pre-verbal than their daughter. Except out of the churning and the stifled heaves she keeps repeating his name. Bob...Bob...Bob...it goes on, a sort of wild and dreary chant, and he doesn't know what he can do. Other people name him and it means something—it points toward a course of action and an outcome. She holds on to him for dear life.

He tries to break free, and she pulls him back. The instant she does he understands she's pulling him back from somewhere he wants to go. He remembers—although he's never really forgotten— what he's promised himself to do. He will quit at the bomber plant and enlist in the army and present himself as the future unfolding in Charles Moody's fat stricken face.

She pulls him back onto the bed, flat on his back. He tries to rise, and she runs a hand up under his shirt. He knows her touch, bashful and then bold, bold because the bashfulness is so much of who she is. This is not that touch. She is frankly searching for something and is annoyed to the point of anger by his attempts to rise. What does she think he is hiding up under his ribs, under his arms? She is at his neck, shaping his jaw in her palm. She turns his head, runs a hand down the slope of his shoulder onto the knob. The hand's pressure is firm, demanding from him a comparable firmness—a solidity—which, in spite of his athlete's build, he fears he can't give. When her hand drops to his belly, his gut muscles tighten at once, as if she were touching him with fingers of ice. She leaves her hand there until he's begun to breathe under it and his muscles have eased their grip. That searching pressure of her touch likewise relents, and for a moment the hand rides on his belly in a state of truce, a moment of fraternization that has him relieved and intrigued, almost childishly absorbed.

She rises over him. She's looking directly at him but with a great questioning distance in her eyes. He remembers her eyes as they'd once hung silvery in the mirror of the Langley family car. Those eyes had looked through him, past him, taking in absolutely everything else at once.

"Bob," she says, low-toned, contained, but because of that distanced look the effect is close to a wail. Then another touch, quick and possessive, with a child's unwillingness to share. She takes him in her hand. He yields to her. She shakes him a little, as though his attention had wandered. Her voice takes on a secretive timbre that on any other occasion he would understand as an invitation to play. "This is important," she says. "This may be all that we have."

"I'm going to do it, Fran," he says.

She stares at him, all the way through him, to where he lies dead on the ground somewhere, or where as a victor he survives.

"I'm going to enlist."

She straddles him. He reaches for the bedside table drawer where they keep the prophylactics, and she pushes his hand away. She still has her slip on and won't let him raise it over her head. She says something whose tone escapes him and which he knows in the instant he'll never understand. "You would do that to me?" To her? His enemy are the Germans. She is not the enemy. He is inside her now, and she is his wife. She pumps him, and when he can resist no longer, she has his seed. Then they lie there in the parchment-colored light until their daughter begins to cry, and her mother gets up to see to her and her father makes good on his promise and goes off to war.

His mother. His father.

◦◦◦

I slipped out of my father's study, like a sentinel stepping off of guard duty, unsure if he was coming back. Passing down the hall I made a conscious effort not to glance into their room, then discovered it took no effort at all. I was hungry. I was curious what my father might have left for me. My mother would have left things for him he would not have touched, which allowed me to double my curiosity and ask what the two of them might be passing down.

I looked in the freezer first and discovered a whole small turkey, which, of course, would be a story in itself. My father had died between Thanksgiving and Christmas. My mother had died two years before, much earlier in the fall, but perhaps because of her rationing experience during the war she had always been a provident grocery shopper and could have bought the turkey herself when the price was low, in effect, willing to wager there'd be thanks left to give. Or perhaps it had been intended for a young soldier named Steve Mitchell, who had never returned for his celebratory dinner, which meant that it had become a *memento mori* and was older than I was. I hefted it in my hand. It was as round as a bowling ball and had a peculiar, gravity-rich weight, like a metal mined from the center of the earth. I left it in the freezer. In the basement there had once been a freezer large enough for a body to be stored, or a deer carcass, or, if carefully arranged, a lifetime's worth of meals, but I did not want to go down there. I opened a kitchen cabinet and found a can of pork and beans, which would be as close as I would come to K-rations, I knew. I heated it and ate the entire contents out of the saucepan, standing over the sink. With no effort at all I was able to place myself around a campfire, in the company of other boy scouts. In the bitterness of a winter war, that campfire might have been an oil drum, inside which the detritus of an army on the march had been left to burn. Out in a cornfield during a quail hunt men might sit on little portable stools eating pork and beans like these, which would have a gamey taste, with a smell of cordite and blood mixed in. I washed the saucepan and stood a while longer looking into a wall of pines. I raised the window and breathed down the scent. These pines had started as seedlings. My father had called in real tree farmers to plant them, but I had made a pest of myself and planted a few of my own. They were not the matchstick pines so common in this area, but bushy, long-needled white pines, and the wall they formed was dense. I left the sink and, taking the stairway down through the garage, stepped out into the back yard.

There were three terraces, then a gentle slope down to the creek. A breeze blew and spots of sunlight flickered under the pines on the first terrace. Where the sun fell I saw violets. Crocuses and buttercups grew closer to the house, a tuft of jonquils beside a downspout. Interspersed among the boxwood bushes were plots of tulips, a vibrant red. Below the insect static, I heard the chuckling coo of doves. I listened for the trill of cardinals and heard the cawing of jays, instead.

I lay back on the slope of the first terrace, in the shade of one of the pines I had planted and watered in its little moat of red clay until I'd gone on to other interests and the pine could look out for itself. The ground was damp and the grass needed to be cut. I closed my eyes. I regulated my breathing and remained there until the damp of the spring earth reached from my heels to the back of my head. Then I smelled the creek. I had never not smelled the creek, I knew, but only then did I smell its foul and fresh muddiness as an alternative to the way things were. As a boy I had caught crawdads in that creek; I had fished it and caught little suckers and shiners. All by myself I had built a dam across a branch and created a swimming hole. I had eaten lunches down there, with stones from the creek built a campfire site. Then I had pitched a camp and spent the night. The snakes and the spiders had kept their distance, and until I'd become bored or my mother had demanded I return to the house, I had created a little world of my own. The temptation was to get up and go back down there and see what of that world was left. I did get up and the breeze met the wet of my backside with a clinging chill. I was about to go AWOL.

Then I heard the phone. I heard it through the window I had opened over the kitchen sink, and I sat back down on the terrace to wait it out. At the start I counted the rings, assuming eight would be the limit. Then I doubled the count, and past that I lost it. It was my sister, of course. There was no one else. Karen had my cell phone number, but my cell phone, I remembered, I'd left in the car. Anybody else would have hung up long ago. I let the ringing go on and on, but a phone that would not stop ringing in a house of the dead was a very sad sound. I went back inside, entered my father's study, sat at his desk, placed my hand on the receiver, and took the last of the rings up into my arm. Then I picked the receiver up and told my sister that, yes, I was still here.

But it wasn't my sister. It was Karen, whom my sister, perhaps already on her way, in the skies by now if she was good to her word, had called and given my father's number, and my first reaction was to bolster my defenses, as if I were being attacked on an exposed flank. But Karen was kinder than that. She said, "Jay, where have you gone?"

Hadn't Judy told her? I had returned to my parents' house, the house of my upbringing, to air it out and close it down. I'd come back to put my affairs in order.

"No, I don't mean that, Jay. I know the house. I know where

you're talking to me from. What I don't know is where you've gone."

I held a silence. Then I said it depended on the affairs I had to order.

"We found each other again last night. Or am I wrong?"

Her voice was straightforward, very clear but very quiet. Any loud noise, as of heavy motors, might have overwhelmed it.

The Enola Gay? I said. Did she remember the Enola Gay?

She held a pause—not out of ignorance. I understood that at once. She did not want to be sidetracked, led away.

"What about it, Jay?"

She remembered it, didn't she?

"The plane that dropped the bomb on Hiroshima?"

Named for?

"The pilot's mother. I even remember the pilot's name. Tibbets, Colonel Paul Tibbets. And before you ask the plane was a B-29 Superfortress."

But she'd been a child of the military. This was like family history for her.

I expressed my admiration, my wonder, and my gratitude. And, no, she was not wrong.

"Jay, where have you gone?"

I told her not far yet. And I would be back. And when I returned, she'd be the first to know.

"You've crossed the river, haven't you? Is it something like that?" There was both a sly knowingness for the recollection and a faint shudder in her voice. A shudder for the glimmering grayness of the water at her feet, for that mountainous wall of darkness on the other side?

I tried to laugh. As if we were peering through twin binoculars, head to head, side by side.

"I'm not like a war bride, you know. I won't wait forever."

I understood. I wouldn't expect her to be.

"Judy sounded upset. She sounded upset that you'd upset her. She claims you're forcing her to fly back down here."

What Judy had to remember was that they were her affairs, too.

"Jay…"

I waited. I swept my arm across the bare surface of the desk. I pivoted in my chair to the filing cabinet, slid open the first of the drawers.

"I'm going to trust you," she said. "I don't know why… I take that back, I do know. You're not a wide-eyed romantic like your cousin Hugh…"

I interrupted her to say that Hugh's eyes were almost squinted shut. He saw what as a motherless boy he'd lived through, and he saw what a father had withheld, and rather than shut his eyes altogether he'd taken himself to a place where he saw only what he needed to see. A survivor. Maybe a squint-eyed romantic, a squint-eyed believer…

"All right, a squint-eyed romantic, a survivor, down off the world's high stage, and then back up again onto a stage of his own making. Is that fair?"

I said maybe not entirely a survivor, maybe a casualty, too. In reality, survivors and casualties were next of kin. After all, unless you'd first been a near-casualty, what could you be said to have survived?

She made an impatient but consenting sound in her throat. Then she continued. "And regardless of what you think, you're not a hunter. We've agreed you've never fired a gun. You're stranded. You need someone to lead you out of all this while there's still time, and because you're smart and something of an historian, you know how much time has passed and how much is left. You're not insane, regardless of what Judy says. You're sweet and you're almost manageable, Jay. Almost a dear. You're just in need. I'll wait, but I'll warn you again, not like a war bride. My mother was one of those. Her only recourse has been to become a golfer, and that's not for me."

I had her to thank, I began to tell her, because, if she'd remember, she'd been the one who'd instructed me to determine where it started not to make sense, and precisely there where it hadn't made sense it now did. I had begun to thumb through the files in the drawer I had slid open when I realized Karen had already said goodbye and the line had gone dead. I sank in my father's chair, then rose again. The file I had somehow missed before was not for Wallace Keaver but Walter Keaver and the folder contained a single page. It was a newspaper clipping yellowed with age, and it told the story of Walter Keaver's return to his hometown after the war. In its march into Germany, Keaver's regiment had crossed the Rhine and entered Frankfurt, where Keaver claimed the townspeople had received the Americans joyously, as if only then, after years of Nazi oppression, were they able to draw a free breath and exult. Judging from what he had seen, Keaver was willing to generalize that Germany as a whole was raising its voice in celebration. The only somber note in the article came when Keaver announced the loss of his closest friend, a man, he said, who would have raised his voice as joyously as the liberated

Germans had, a man who had given his life, and so on. Then my father's name appeared. Later, Keaver would learn of his mistake. My father would rise from the dead just long enough for his army buddy to come calling and see Bob Langley certifiably lowered into the ground.

There was a photo of Keaver, still in his uniform, receiving a handshake and some sort of scroll from a town dignitary. He was thin and stood with a bit of a stoop. Behind the graying yellow of his face I saw an array of emotions, all somehow provisional, as if his wartime caution had yet to desert him.

How my father had gotten this article was not hard to imagine. Someone who knew he'd survived the war had seen his name and sent it to him. Why he had kept it I did not know. Did he go back and reread it? Did it take its place in some ceremony he conducted with himself? Why had he never contacted Wallace or Walter Keaver? He'd once come into my room to tell me that it had not been fair that I had lost a high jump event in which I was the more natural jumper. He had not said that defiantly. He'd said it as if lamenting the way of the world. It had not been fair. The article was unmarked and showed no smudge marks around the edges. In not throwing it out my father had allowed it to stand for what it was, that was all.

The name of Keaver's home town was there on the page, and I called his house. I identified myself as Bob Langley's son. I made the mistake of asking for Wallace Keaver, and the woman who answered the phone corrected me. Her voice sounded flat and sullen and very begrudging, and I pictured the nurse who'd brought Keaver to my father's funeral although I suspected the two women were not the same. The woman at the Keaver home told me that her husband or brother or father or uncle, whatever relation he'd been, had died shortly after returning from my father's funeral. Only she didn't say that. She said five months ago and waited while I did the arithmetic. I told her how sorry I was, and then just before we hung up, to console her, although I doubt if she would have interpreted it that way, I said it didn't matter.

XI

Bob Langley crossed the Atlantic in September of 1944, approximately a year after his nephew, Hugh Langley, as a crewman in the Merchant Marines, had dodged U-boats in the same waters. He crossed on a troopship, the *U.S.S. Argentina*, so big it could hold ten thousand men. When Bob stretched out in his hammock, the closest man was not six inches from his nose. There were thirty-two other men in what the Army called their stateroom, a room the size of a garage. Wallace Keaver was one of them. Another was a man named Randy Majors, who had been a mechanic and was used to lying under cars. A fourth was Peter Brockbauer, of German ancestry, who had been a science teacher.

These four men all belonged to the same platoon of the 107th Army Infantry Division. They came from the same state and were roughly the same age. During basic training they had all crawled around holes mined with live explosives and under barbed wire with machine gun fire passing not thirty inches above their heads. A failure of nerve then and they would not be crossing the Atlantic now.

For eight days they steamed from New York City to Cherbourg, France. The weather was mild. During the day they crowded on deck, some playing cards and shooting dice, some dominoes and checkers. Some reading. The deck was teeming, but the ocean was vast. Ten thousand men was larger than any of the towns these four men came from, but it was still possible to stand off at the bow or stern of the ship and be part of the ocean, not of the 107th. Bob Langley had no thought to give to cards or dice, dominos or checkers. Any reading he did he did gazing out at the horizon as day after day they made their way across. There was still a threat of U-boats, however reduced, but it was as if the real enemy was universal sameness and featureless space. The steel-colored waves rose and fell, and the danger Bob felt was that by the time they reached France the affairs of nations and men would come to seem as fleeting as foam.

They arrived in Cherbourg just after dawn. Bob and his three army buddies had all been assigned transportation duties. Perhaps it had had something to do with their age, or with Major's ability with motors, or with Brockbauer's proficiency, or Wally Keaver's unflappable nature, or with Bob Langley's natural air of command. They were to see that the trucks and tanks and half-tracks and jeeps arriving in port got unloaded and moving down the Normandy peninsula, which meant they were longshoremen first and traffic cops second. On the docks of Cherbourg, their enemy was not the Germans but rubble. The dockside warehouses had been bombed, and in most cases all that were left standing were rafters through which the sky shone. The rubble was piled in enormous mounds. They made roads among the mounds along which the machinery of war could pass. That machinery was new, if drably colored, while the rubble was not so much old as ageless. It had no color, no shape until it was gathered into piles. That was Bob Langley's first real impression of the Old World, of how quickly it could be converted into mounds of ageless and shapeless matter, and of how a Sherman tank or an army jeep passing beside it might seem like an object from another world.

When he got off the docks and back into the town and began to notice the people, it was as if they emerged from the rubble of their houses, as if the rubble had some sort of progenitive force. They were not unfriendly. Cherbourg had been liberated by American troops from the Army's 126th division. The destruction the city had undergone had been the result of Allied bombing, but it was as if the Germans had been daring the bombs to fall out of the sky. Then Bob found himself in a street which had suffered no destruction whatsoever. These were gray stone row houses, the doors and the sash of the windows painted white; the roofs were mansard, of a sort he had not seen before, but whose slant and slate and attic windows gave the impression of a time-honored authority. As far as he could tell, every chimney pot was in place.

The 107th began to move down the peninsula, and far from being longshoremen or traffic cops Bob Langley and his buddies now served as shepherds. They marched along at the rear of their regiment, helping prematurely broken down vehicles back on the road. Frequently the road was narrow, barely wide enough for a single truck, and they saw signs left by preceding sappers: "Mines cleared to the hedgerows." The hedgerows were entanglements of vines, bushes and small trees, nothing like the privet hedges back home. Beyond them they could see dairy cattle in the fields, which were small, lushly green, and entirely enclosed. Three months earlier the fighting had been fierce along these roads, and the night before D-Day paratroopers had jumped into these fields, but the only sound of war the 107th heard now was of a single mine exploding in an adjoining field when a cow stepped on it. For an instant everything stopped, all the heavy grinding of gears and marching of men, and then a delayed and pent up cheer arose. Aircraft were passing constantly overhead, but this was an actual sound of war, a German mine, close by, in one of those hedged-in fields, and a cow had fallen over as a result.

Later, at a point where the road had come into the open, Bob Langley and his company found themselves under fire. But these were French farmers whose fields and orchards had been cratered by Allied bombing and whose frustration at the start of what should have been harvest season had boiled over. For weapons the farmers were throwing stones and the hard knotty apples that had made it through the summer. Bob Langley, who had a knack for this sort of thing and was suffering frustration of his own, reached up and caught one of the apples out of the air. Then he took a bite, made an exaggerated nod and grinned. A Frenchman threw him another and he caught it too, at which point the attack ended and a few of the Frenchmen actually cheered.

He didn't like bringing up the rear and servicing disabled vehicles. He didn't like catching apples out of the air and raising French cheers. He didn't like the ruin he saw all around him, the cratered fields and dead cows and remains of gray stone villages, without a single German in sight.

They came to Bayeux, a town that appeared not to have been touched. A stream ran through it. There were well-built bridges that could withstand the passage of tanks and half-tracks. Rising out of it, disproportionately large, were three spires of a cathedral. The cathedral was made of that same gray stone, while most of the houses in the town were faced with stucco, a shade of gray similar to the stone. On first glance it was not hard to mistake one for the other, but they were not the same. It was as if the cathedral had claimed all the stone in the town for itself, and Bob Langley found himself turning against it. His three buddies, Keaver, and the ace mechanic Randy Majors, and the clear-headed and measured Peter Brockbauer, all took a look inside and came out impressed. Not only had the town not been bombed but the stained glass in the cathedral windows hadn't even been cracked and, though dusty, shone jewel-like in the light, Brockbauer reported. Given the desolation of the day, it was something to see.

But Bob did not go inside. Troops and supplies continued to move down the Normandy peninsula, and Bob's company was temporarily detached from the 107th to direct them through town and tend to the breakdowns. The townspeople loved their American liberators who had spared their town. Women and girls brought him out pastries they'd baked while he stood in the dust directing traffic, and men offered him wine. They all called him "Joe," in an earthy, open-vowel accent that seemed less spoken than sung. The Germans had been beasts. He took the townspeople's word for it since he had yet to see one.

He saw Omaha beach where the Americans had landed more

than three months earlier. Along with his three friends, he saw it as a tourist might, in a day off. It was only seven or eight miles away, but down close to the ocean they had to work their jeep around bomb craters, which latter-day tourists wouldn't have to do. Ships were unloading supplies there on a floating causeway, and a road now ran up the crease between cliff-faces where the Americans had had to huddle that first terrible day, but what took Bob's attention were all the burned and blasted landing craft and half-tracks and jeeps and anti-tank cannons littering the beach, some riding the surf in and out. Without them the beach might have measured five miles of fine sloping sand from one headland to another. Where did this aversion to rubble come from? He had always been an excellent athlete because, even when some might have thought he was indulging in a sensational play, he wasted no motion. There were all sorts of trick plays a tailback might perform, or a base runner or a basketball guard, but none was for show. The "show" was to deceive your opponent, not to dazzle the spectators. Here, the waste knew no bounds. Of the B-29's he'd helped build to bomb the Japanese he knew a certain percentage were destined to be shot down. Yes, he understood. But when would the wreckage be disposed of? When would it all be cleaned up?

American waste, and he took it personally. He learned that if the German resistance at Omaha beach had not been so determined, the American objective had not been to attack Saint Lo, but Bayeux itself, in which case he might have been standing over the jeweled rubble of a cathedral. Driving back up from Omaha beach they passed a stone complex of chateau, barn, church, a free-standing, silo-shaped tower, and a cluster of small houses, all with white shutters and all untouched. Almost within sight down the road, they passed another complex that was devastated, where it was impossible to imagine lives having been lived. He saw an animal of some sort, a horse or mule, even perhaps a skeletal cow, standing comatose in a cratered field.

Before they'd returned to Bayeux, they saw their first Germans. They were being marched as prisoners along the verge of the road in the direction of Caen, and although it hadn't been necessary, Wally Keaver, who was driving, pulled the jeep off to let them pass. It wasn't just Bob Langley. The four of them, as though from a reviewing stand, watched those Germans pass. They were dressed in the tattered gray of the Wehrmacht and the hollows of their eyes were moribund. A number had wounds bandaged with filthy cloth. Some carried bundles of blankets and some hobbled on makeshift crutches. They gave off a fetid odor. As they passed, those who looked at the jeepful of Americans seemed to see neither enemy nor ally nor members of the same species, but alien objects of some sort whose existence was their own affair. Except for one, who, with a feral gleam of teeth, opened his mouth and delivered a string of what must have been curses, a growling, guttural sound. But that man passed with the rest and then they were gone.

Bob Langley said that two of his brothers had fought them in the First World War, the war that was supposed to have ended all wars but hadn't. Randy Majors said the prisoners looked in piss-poor shape, but they were probably glad the Americans had caught them and not the Russians. Peter Brockbauer said maybe that was what it took, getting beaten down like that before you learned to behave. Wally Keaver reminded them that Hitler himself had been beaten up pretty badly in that first war, but look at him, look at what he'd done, look at all this, look at us.

What they couldn't explain was what those prisoners were doing on this road, or where they'd been captured, and where they'd been held all these months, and where they were being marched to. They all knew the war was being fought on a massive scale that no one man would be capable of understanding. They might debate the course of the war in places like Raymond Langley's furniture store, but finally the war would come down to what was in front of their noses, and the last thing had been these unaccountable German prisoners. In that sense it would have been tempting to say that the Germans had been paraded past these Americans for the Americans' benefit alone, but that was carrying the thought too far, that was fixing the war in such a private arena it made no sense to talk of divisions or regiments or battalions or companies or platoons. Only individuals, or at most a jeepful of four.

They left Bayeux. They were in Caen for a week, which the British had fought the Germans for building by building and where the destruction was vast. It did no good to talk of rubble in a city where half the buildings had been blasted to the ground. The French continued to return to the places they'd lived, and something turned in Bob Langley's stomach and a sick taste rose to his mouth when he saw men and women and young girls crawl through a space where a door had once stood to make their lives in the remains of a home. They were like rats, whose furtive movements took them from one cramped area to the next, while the 107th moved unimpeded down the middle of the streets. Still, the French waved from their rat holes and, still, the girls ran him out things to eat.

In Caen they regrouped—as far as Bob could see that was all they did— and got re-provisioned and their machinery re-serviced for their march toward the front. Word had reached them, by way of encouragement, that Ike had bet the English Field Marshall Montgomery $25 that the war in Europe would be over by Christmas, which meant if the 107th continued at its own leisurely pace they would arrive at the front just in time to celebrate. Paris had been re-taken, it seemed, months and months ago. The front they heard was the Meuse River, separating Belgium from France. Five minutes later they heard it was the Rhine. German cities had been firebombed, and, reportedly, very few of them still stood. The Russians were swarming over Eastern Europe, and the German losses each day were said to be incalculable. You could blindfold yourself and stick a pin almost anywhere in Europe and hit a spot where history was being made. In Caen a sort of devastating preliminary history had been made, then history had gone elsewhere. Randy Major was all for putting the accelerator to the floor and catching up with it. Peter Brockbauer wanted to reach Germany, which he had never seen, while something was still left. Wallace Keaver was more philosophical. Hitler had called this horror down on himself, but in the name of Hitler not everybody, everybody and everything, had to be ground into the dirt. Bob Langley, they all knew, was governed by some sort of inner vision that weeks of training and non-stop army regimentation had not touched. They assumed that Bob Langley knew what he wanted.

And when the 107th finally marched out of war-battered Caen going east, they assumed he was pleased.

The going was slow, not because their advance was contested but because the land remained broken, hilly, and very watery, with a succession of streams and canals that had to be bridged. The roads were frequently reduced to hedged-in lanes. Back in those small, enclosed fields cattle continued to graze, and in the late afternoons formed a plodding line as they returned to their gray-stoned barns. In a lull of motor or marching noise, they continued to moo. None of them stepped on a mine—that appeared to have been a once-only event, something like an opening salvo to welcome the 107th to the war.

One morning, the roads widened, the hedges fell away, and vistas appeared. The season turned to fall and yellow-leafed poplars lit up the course of streams. The towns along this route had suffered less and less destruction. They came to the large town of Mantes La Jolie, where the last of those hedged-in lanes and small enclosed fields vanished entirely and something like a broad avenue opened, planted in wheat or some other ripened grain, and they saw fewer and fewer of those shell craters because the heaviest fighting had passed to the north. "Jolie"—Keaver knew the word. It meant "pretty," it meant something to lay your eyes on in case your eyes had been sickened by so much destruction and crabbed survival. The avenue was really a broad flat valley miles across, and at its conclusion lay Paris, a city that had famously not been bombed because they all knew that some things were too beautiful to be destroyed.

Instead of marching to the front they were marching to Paris, and a heckling voice began to sound in Bob Langley's ear. Life, in this stretch of lovely fall days, had suddenly become soft, and the word the voice repeated was "Daa-dee, Daa-dee." They still labored under their M-1's and their Smith and Wesson 45's and their hand grenades and bayonets and ammo belts and trench knives and shovels and their canteens and their rucksacks full of keepsakes and K-rations, and they still heard occasional artillery fire from some distant pocket of resistance, and overhead B-17 bombers might pass, and they could halfway convince themselves they heard the bombardments themselves, but so far out on the horizon the sound was like the muted rumble of summer thunder, which for some, as they sat out on their porches in the evenings back home, might have been the sound of someone contentedly turning in his bed. They were going to Paris to take a breather and get a good night's sleep on one of those feather mattresses they'd heard so much about, and their Daa-dee was looking out for them still.

———⁓———

WHAT DID HE WANT? Bob Langley in Paris, the Eiffel Tower, the Arc de Triomphe, the river Seine with its storied bridges, the gardens with their glorious horse chestnuts, the open cafes while the weather still held, in a city where every liberator was greeted with a jubilant song of praise and thanksgiving became an old world art—what did he want? I got up, left his study, and walked out in front of the house and stood where a car might pull up if someone got out and entered the house on a run. A one-legged run, aided by the powerful thrusting advance of a crutch. What would such a man want? Not to be forgotten? Not to be left behind? Not to be found wanting? Not to be unwanted? Not to be benched? Not to be booed? Or not to be in the wrong place at the wrong time, even if that place was judged to be a wonder of the world and even if the time was the time of its deliverance, for which abundant rewards would be bestowed?

I was standing in front of my father's house, panting lightly, when a car came to a stop behind me. The car was a long shiny Buick, and the man driving I recognized as Donnie Abbott, who had been my uncle Raymond's assistant at the furniture store for years, before buying it when Raymond had retired. Some years ago, while it was still worth something, Abbott had sold the store and retired himself. The woman sitting beside him I recognized as his wife, Thelma, small, fragile, large-eyed, smiling, and dazed, who looked to be on medication of some sort. Donnie Abbott, once as clean-cut a young man as there'd been in town, had a ruddy swollen face now, his eyes narrowed into smiling slits, and chubby fingers on the wheel.

He said, "You gave me a start, son. I'm an ole coon dog who doesn't get out of the kennel much, but for a minute there I thought I saw Bob Langley standing out before his house. I said to Thelma, 'Will you look at that!'"

I looked through to Thelma, who nodded in agreement. I looked back at her husband and shook my head. "I'm astonished," I said. "I truly am."

Donnie Abbott said, "Just for a minute, Bob Langley, the man himself."

"How far away were you?"

"Well, I drive by your house every day," he said, reminding me he was a neighbor, which I had not forgotten, the Abbott house being the fourth down the road on the right. "No more than halfway to the corner, I looked out and saw Bob Langley standing there, which tickled me pink, I don't mind telling you. I said to Thelma—"

I cut him off. I realized my mouth had been hanging open, and to the Abbotts I must have appeared something like the dim witted end of the Langley line. "That's impossible. We don't look anything alike. The hair, maybe, but my father was bigger than I am, much bigger... and there's a little matter of a leg."

This last I added in a bantering tone, loaded with a phony forgiveness and an accusing sort of incredulity, in response to which Donnie Abbott sat there and beamed.

"Must have been seeing him back when I was a boy and he was my hero. An ole coon dog lies around the kennel too long he begins to believe he's a pup."

I looked through to his wife. I was about to tell her that with eyesight like that her husband shouldn't be driving and maybe she should take the wheel. Except that she was even less fit than he was. The Buick they drove was at least fifteen years old and without a scratch. Of course, in a world of phantoms there would be nothing to crash against.

"Then we got closer," Donnie Abbott continued, "and I saw my mistake. How are you, son? How's your sweet sister?"

"Judy is fine," I said.

"Still living up in Yankee land?"

"Traveling, I think."

Thelma Abbott leaned down to look past her husband. Her medication gave a swimming effect to her eyes. "That was such a lovely funeral your father had. So many people from the town, and then folk we'd never seen before. And the flowers," she began to trail off, as if caught in a tide. "I don't know when I've ever seen so many beautiful flowers…" She swung back in. "'Rock of Ages,'" she murmured, fluttering her eyes closed.

My father's funeral had not been widely attended. It had not been 'lovely.' Whatever flowers there'd been had been beside the point. "'Rock of Ages'?" I said.

Thelma Abbott nodded in time to the music she heard in her head. "Such a fine old hymn. Why don't you hear it sung at funerals any more?"

I didn't remember "Rock of Ages" being sung at my father's funeral.

I turned back to her husband. "I've heard all the stories," I said, "but there's one thing I'd like to know. Why was he your hero?"

There was nothing devious about the man, nothing crafty about the line at his mouth as he offered me the most private of smiles, or the line at the eyes as they narrowed still farther on a pleasure all their own, nothing I hadn't seen on the faces of men and women around town, but men especially, when they wanted to express to you that they stood on one side of a divide and you on the other, and as much as they'd like to please you there was no crossing over. Those had been other times, lived by men and women of a special breed, and as hard as you might try you simply couldn't imagine.

"OK, that's all right," I finally said.

Now, the smile clearly took pity, as if to say, it's a sad trick of fate but there's nothing an ole coon dog can do. Sorry, son.

I said, as Donnie Abbott began to inch the Buick forward, "Be careful driving. No more Bob Langleys. Eyes on the road."

I watched the Abbotts roll down the street and, just before a curve in the street took them out of sight, watched them pull up into their own drive. Then I turned back to the Langley home, with the unweeded red of its tulip beds and the green of its boxwood bushes, in need of a trim. The curtains were all drawn. The front door, with its brass fixtures, slightly dulled, and its opaque lateral windows, was closed. The house was not forbidding, but it asked that you keep your voice low. What did Bob Langley want? Of his three friends, the quietest voice belonged to Wally Keaver. Bob, we're here until the army moves us out. Let's make the best of it. Churchill and de Gaulle will be coming soon to lay a wreath at the tomb of the unknown soldier. Most wars are fought by unknown soldiers, Bob. Very few men have their names on their fellow man's lips. Here, we can slip out. Here, we can take a nameless look around. This is Paris, Bob. We may never get this chance again. Quietly, without making a ruckus, even though the French may be singing that Marseillaise of theirs at the top of their voices, we can see what it's all about. This is Paris, Bob, and you and I are just a couple of GI Joes.

⚬⚬⚬

EXCEPT A PARISIAN immediately saw the resemblance and called Bob Langley "Lindy," which led another to object that Charles Lindbergh had been a Nazi-lover and this GI standing before them was obviously a hero, and a good-natured fight broke out. The two Frenchmen ended up sitting the two Americans down at a sidewalk café and toasting them with wine. Friends of the Frenchmen happened by and with them came women. One of the Frenchmen spoke some English and Wally Keaver had a little French, but with a common enemy vanquished and seemingly no limit to the wine, words were the least of it. Keaver had a sweetheart, a woman as studious as he, but he had not married and wouldn't until the war was over and its horrors had receded and an accustomed life could resume—which would include a wife and children, all of which he would eventually have. But the women who sat at those sidewalk tables and feasted on his friend Bob Langley were creatures unlike any he had seen. They might be dressed in clothing grown threadbare over the course of a war, and for four years they might have been living on the emotional equivalent of bread and water, but in Bob Langley's presence they seemed to experience a full-bodied eruption. Their eyes and teeth flashed, even though their teeth were sometimes bad. They threw back their heads, which allowed you to see the blood pulsing in their throats. They had warm, throaty laughs and long, elegant noses, and in their presence Wally Keaver found himself loosening his collar even though the weather had quickly begun to cool. Bob Langley had told him about his wife, but Bob had also told him that in order to enlist he'd had to defy her, and Keaver came to understand that for the duration of the war Bob's wife was on the sidelines, except for a promise she'd extracted from him, which was the last thing Bob had told his friend. She had gotten him to promise that if the war were almost over he wouldn't put himself in a position to be killed. She'd assumed that was a decision her husband would be able to make. Whereas these French women assumed the war was already over, and since they had to have a hero, perhaps a different one each day, they unabashedly singled out Wally Keaver's friend, who did indeed look like Charles

Lindbergh when he'd first landed his Spirit of Saint Louis at the Parisian airfield of Le Bourget and become Lindy to the world.

Portions of the 107th were being held in reserve and quartered in barracks just up the river. Patton had brought his army up from the south and was now located in Allied headquarters in Verdun. Montgomery was pushing down from the north. Ike had his combined forces moving inexorably eastward across a hundred mile front, thinnest in the Ardennes, but that was a forested area of narrow valleys through which a military operation of any size would be the act of a desperate man. The Allied forces had crossed the Meuse into Belgium and were closing on the Rhine. The German city of Aachen had already been taken. Churchill was indeed expected in Paris, after which he would confer with Ike. Held in reserve for what?

Ike was known as a shrewd card player and a very frugal man; victory by Christmas now seemed like a conservative bet.

Bob Langley, Wally Keaver, and their friends drilled and did some token training and kept their weapons and vehicles in high operating order, but there was time, time like they'd never had since they'd enlisted, and since they would know where to look, they could always find a jeep. There was much to see, Keaver insisted, and as long as the liberation party continued almost no door was closed. The party would continue until a darkness fell in December, and with it numbing snow, at which point even the outdoor cafes with their terrace-warming stoves would close. But until then Keaver continued his mindful whisper in his friend's ear—there were palaces and churches and theaters and museums. There was the largest museum in the world, the Louvre, which was closed but that was only because at the outbreak of the war the French had dispersed its treasures into chateaux in the western half of the country, hidden so well that even master culture thieves like the Germans couldn't find them. But Keaver had Bob Langley stand before the Louvre with its two enormous outreaching wings and asked him to imagine. Neither of them had ever seen a building that majestic and that big, and to imagine it full of great works of art, art for which wars might be fought, exceeded their powers.

The Eiffel Tower was size of another sort, and since the Americans had taken over its second deck as a center of communications with channel ports and Eisenhower's forces, it was possible for GIs with the stamina and leg strength to climb to the top. From there on a clear day you might see the Germans hurrying over the horizon, as if they really believed there was some place they could hide. Bob Langley, the strongest of the four friends and clearly the one with the most leg strength, remained on the ground. His eyes followed the others up the staircase until they reached the last level, where Randy Majors did a Horatio Hornblower imitation, scanning the sea for the enemy fleet, and Wally Keaver waved and Peter Brockbauer stood quietly at the rail with the sun on his face, all of which Bob with his excellent eyesight could see. He didn't much like the Eiffel tower—not even as an engineering feat—but that was not the reason he'd stayed on the ground. He didn't know the reason. He sensed he was not where he was supposed to be, and high on that tower he would be even farther away, further removed. From what? Had he not liked the attention the French men and the especially the women had shown him? He could feel the warmth of a woman's breath on his neck, at his ear, even though she might be seated on the other side of a table. In the cool breezes that blew on those café terraces he had a special sense for that warmth. Which he distrusted? The Frenchmen, in their ceremonial style, bowing down before him, their hands performing all sorts of flourishes before coming to rest on his shoulder. Which he resisted? His friend Wallace Keaver, that quiet civilized voice in his ear, saying, Bob, thank God this war has run its course. The world has taken a beating, and we've seen some horrible sights, but what was taken from us will be given back again, you'll see. Keep the faith, Bob. Which he'd heard enough of? Was that why he hadn't climbed the tower, which looked out on the oldest and most venerable part of the western world? He didn't know. He felt the need to remain on the ground. Nothing had been decided yet. His moment had yet to come. He saw his three army buddies up there, all impersonating, whether they knew it or not, conquering heroes of some sort, and he turned away.

He began to explore Paris by himself. And, very quickly, the weather turned. He saw Paris in a cold misting rain, behind a veil of November gray. He entered the cafes and drank his *café au lait* as the Frenchmen did, with a shot of cognac, and nursing an ember-like warmth in the pit of his stomach, stepped back outside into a city which he'd been led to believe was civilization made concrete, the possession of which could lead nations into war. The brightest things he saw were the river Seine, whose green was glossy, like crumpled velvet, and the gray of the slate on the mansard roofs. The buildings themselves were of a stone so institutional-looking and so heavily sunken they might have all been government ministries, or monuments, or even a succession of Bastilles, which he knew they weren't. Really, what they reminded him of were mausoleums. Except when he raised his eyes to the roofs and saw that gleaming gray slate and sometimes as many as three attic windows, one mounted of top of the other, and a profusion of chimney pots, he came to understand that the life of the city was all up there, that down below there was a Paris entombed within itself and above it a Paris of smaller, less grandiose spaces where the flame of life would be kept flickering during these cold November days.

If he walked out into the gardens he saw more of the same. The leaves might be rusted on the trees and the paths unraked and rutted in spots, but the formal geometry of the gardens of Paris was unmistakable. The statues were located at measured intervals and so bound to where they belonged in the scheme of things that even the Germans had not been able to take them away. But, considered individually, the statues were full of life. Most were of naked men and women, or of a centaur who had a naked woman thrown over his shoulder as he carted her away. Their nakedness fascinated him, made him uneasy, and caused him to look more closely. There was a young girl, a nymph, slightly folded in on herself, as if shivering in the cold. There was a statue of Cain, who was clenched in on himself in another way, as if eternally ashamed of the crime he'd committed. They all had their personal dramas, and they all played their parts in some impersonal, formal drama, too. Paris's drama, he supposed. Or maybe Europe's. They were local and Paris was…what? Universal? And you don't destroy a universal thing—how could you? For that reason the city had never been bombed. Universal rubble made no sense. It was as if from one point of view the city was an idea in somebody's head, then from another a colorful succession of streets, squares, and *cul-de-sacs* vibrant with life. If Bob Langley had had Wallace Keaver at his side, his army buddy might have come up with an explanation for this doubleness of things. If Bob had had a gift for introspection, he might have come up with an explanation on his own. For he, too, participated in a scheme of things; surely, there were those who felt his stature as a star far exceeded any particular feat he might accomplish on a playing field. He had a fleeting sense of this, moments when he felt he did not quite occupy his own skin. Perhaps that had been the real reason he had not gone up on that most famous of towers with his friends. Up there, at that rarefied height, on that highest of stages, he might have thinned out, he might have dissolved.

He stood overlooking the Seine. One bridge gave way to the next, like an optical illusion in a formal regression into infinity. Between the bridges he saw fishermen, some in their boats, some on the banks, in this time of scarcity taking what they could get. He fixed on one, an old gray man fishing the green water with a long cane pole. The fisherman let the current take his bait then lifted it out and swung it back to where he'd begun. The bait was a chunk of something Bob couldn't make out. Under his beret the fisherman was bundled in rags, and Bob Langley knew he could walk down by the river and... unbundle the old man. The old man might become a young old man, who would give off a smell of fish, if he'd been lucky, or of the bait he'd been fishing with if nothing had yet to bite. A toothless mouth or a mouth in which the teeth could be counted. A name. Not just any Jacque or Emil. Bob Langley would probably be "Leen-dee" for a while, then a Langley, one of the Langleys, one of them.

In his excursions, the day came when he stood before the cathedral of Notre Dame. In the arches around the doors, in every available niche across the front façade, he saw statues of gowned men and women, some churchmen, some, judging from their crowns, royalty, but all cast from the same mold and so crowded together head to toe that there was no use in trying to tell them apart. He opened the door and stepped into the cathedral itself. Except for certain gymnasiums or field houses, his experience with big buildings had been limited to one. The bomber plant where he'd worked as Charley Moody's stooge was unimaginably long and wide enough to contain two rows of assembled B-29's and just high enough so that the tails didn't scrape the overhead rails. Inside the Notre Dame, he was lifted out of his body and sent soaring straight up on a very narrow ascent. The stone of the columns around him and the vaulted ceiling overhead was so gray it was black, but for one panicky instant he was performing a breathless ascent, and the only thing he had to compare it to was one of his pole vaults when everything worked and he seemingly defied gravity, even though he knew, absolutely knew, that that was nothing compared to this. The panic passed and he waited for his breath to come back. When it did he took measured steps up the central nave to the transept, where the light entered from the stained glass to his right and left, but where that vertical narrowness was somehow compounded, and he understood that he was too broad-shouldered and multi-purposed to fit inside such a space. Standing before the altar he felt as constrained as one of those statues wedged into its niche, and before he'd made his way back outside he'd had a bodily sense of what the spiritual life was like. It was straight and it was narrow and it was enclosed in stone. There was no trace of a war, no trace of a world. Outside, he took a deep, audible breath.

But instead of walking away, he found himself moving down a street beside the cathedral, as though to leave without looking out back would be an act of cowardice. Something—perhaps the act of being looked at himself—caused him to glance up, and that was when he saw the gargoyles. They had the folded wings of bats and the faces of bulldogs and they seemed to be erupting from the stone, as though frantic to escape. They were everywhere up there, at every jutting angle, and the air should have been full of their fiendish cries. He had no idea what all that meant. Outside, the cathedral was erupting with demonic creatures while inside it was a sheer spiritual ascent, and around back he discovered it was a park, formal as all French parks were, but neighborly in size. Some GI's were out there, pointing up at the back portion of the cathedral, which was rounded and not so high and supported by graceful, free-standing buttresses. He might have asked these GI's to explain it to him for they seemed to be conversing knowledgeably and they seemed pleased. They seemed proud. If he could read their expressions at all, they were saying, We drove the Germans away and saved Notre Dame for the world. Let's hear a round of applause.

A woman was standing beside him, not like the adventurous women he'd seen in the cafes. A girl of about five stood beside her, and in the way the girl looked at him she seemed a small faithful replica of her mother. GI's had been issued Hershey bars and Baby Ruths for such occasions, and he offered one of each to the little girl, who took them without taking her eyes off of his. The woman looked at him steadily, too, but her eyes did not gleam in that hungrily awakened way the women's eyes in the cafes did. Her breath, he believed, if he were to feel it on his neck, would be cold. She didn't hold her hand out for money. He remembered the word. "*Jolie,*" he said, referring to the cathedral, which he knew was absurd. "Pretty" was the last thing the cathedral was. The woman might have smiled, for his pronunciation, for his misuse of a word, but it was only a flicker and there was no way to be sure. The little girl, who had a ragged, moth-eaten scarf around her neck, had both candy bars clutched in her hand. He took the Baby Ruth back, unwrapped one end, and tried to feed it to her. She glanced up at her mother, who must have made a sign, for the little girl took one bite and made one chewing motion, and then stopped. Bob knew another word, "*Bon.*" But he didn't insist. He placed the partially unwrapped Baby Ruth back in the little girl's hand, then looked back up at her mother, who had a quietly vigilant expression on her face. Her eyes were the gray of the day, of some of the stone, and their luster was as dim as November. It came to him. A woman with a daughter born perhaps at the start of the war. The husband and father killed. A monument to grief and survival and the sort of doubleness Paris was all about. He wanted to shake her. Her little girl, too. Instead, he pointed to himself and said, "Bob." He thumped his chest with the point of his index finger. "Bob! Bob! Bob!" Then he looked directly at her and said the name he had available to him. "Fran." And so that her daughter would not go without, he looked at her and said, "Judy."

Had he expected them to thank him for giving them their names? He didn't know what he expected. Although those other GI's were within hailing distance, he felt utterly alone and on foreign soil. All he could do was wait them out, which he did. There came a moment, signaled by nothing he could see, when they simply turned around, mother and daughter, and walked away hand in hand, large and small, although the little girl did carry in her other hand those candy bars of his. Curiously, he both felt he'd been abandoned and felt he'd been freed. Cast out and included in a scheme for which a name like "Bob" won you neither praise nor blame.

But it was true, when Winston Churchill and Charles de Gaulle drove up the *Champs-Élysées* to lay their wreaths beside that nameless tomb, he was back at Wallace Keaver's side. The *Champs-Élysées* was a wide boulevard that ran, with a kind of destined directness, from the *Place de la Concord*, to the *Arc de Triomphe*. The trees that hung over it were sycamores, with their peeling trunks and little bomb-loads of seeds, no different from the ones that grew in their towns back home. The crowd gathered on that day was enormous. But Bob Langley didn't have to climb a tree, as some had, or hang out of an upper story window, to see what he wanted to see. Churchill was dressed in the navy blue of the British Admiralty and de Gaulle in what looked like the wheat-colored uniform of the French Foreign Legion, with the round-crowned kepi cap. The day was grayer and colder than usual, and the flower colors of the wreaths were muted. What shone through was the orange-lapping flame at the tomb of the unknown soldier itself, that and the gleam off the headlights and the fenders of the limousine that would eventually drive the two leaders back down the boulevard to the thunderous acclaim of the crowds. Churchill had a gruff and rugged grin on his face, but de Gaulle looked as stern as if he were surrounded by Nazis still. Once in the limousine and rolling down the *Champs-Élysées* Churchill couldn't keep the satisfaction off his face and the grin broadened. De Gaulle, august in his self-regard, didn't have a grin to spare. Churchill looked as if he'd held a losing hand but had won on a masterful bluff, de Gaulle as if he'd never played a game of chance in his life.

"There you have them," Wallace Keaver said. "If you didn't know better you'd think they were some comedy team. All of Europe, the free world, and I'm thinking of Abbott and Costello. But this is history, Bob. When your grandchildren ask you, you can tell them we went over there and straightened matters out so that Churchill and de Gaulle could do their comedy routine all the way down the *Champs-Élysées.*"

But the crowd was festive and Wallace Keaver himself was in a very good mood. Who's on first, Bob? You can see them better than I can. Any chance you can pick one of them off?

Bob Langley looked down the avenue of applauding throngs and saw the end. The war was over, and he'd been transported halfway around the world just so that he could be witness to the victory parade. The *Arc de Triomphe* was a massive structure with battle scenes in relief and the names of France's heroes carved in its walls. German armies had passed beside it when they'd taken Paris, and now the unknown soldier's death had been redeemed and Paris had been taken back. Over. Done. That wound that Raymond Langley carried in his shoulder, that little puckered, about-to-spit mouth, had been avenged.

Bob Langley could turn around and go home. Charles Moody and Jolly Cholly Moody and four-eyed Ed Middleton would give him a good-natured, no-hard-feelings slap on the back when he returned and expedited a few more bombers until the Japanese gave up. What did he see up there, a head higher than the undernourished French?

Wallace Keaver worried about his friend. His friendliness was real, Keaver didn't doubt it for a minute. Bob was one of those people who let just enough of themselves show so that you could never doubt a wealth of self lay just out of sight, not so much like the tip of an iceberg and the massiveness underneath as a vein of gold, which if followed faithfully would lead you to the mother lode. For that reason, people wanted to keep Bob Langley in view. He was a public treasure; he was the kind of man you instinctively wanted to protect for future generations to know, which was ironic because just one look at him and you concluded here was a man who could take care of himself. A star athlete, who, Keaver sensed, needed his coach, and for those last few days, at least, Bob had gone off and played the game by himself. Keaver and his friends had commented on this. Peter Brockbauer pretty much blamed it on the army. You put that many men in quarters that close and sooner or later everyone needed to get off by themselves. It was the kind of behavior you could almost frame as a chemical formula. Randy Majors laughed it off. Bob Langley would need a lot more days than he'd been missing to take on the women who'd been throwing themselves at him. Greedy bastard, though, since he didn't want to pass them around. Wallace Keaver didn't discount the possibility of a woman, and none of them had entirely overcome the days they'd hung in their troopship hammocks one of top of the other like sausages slung up in rows. Not even in Paris where they'd taken over the ample accommodations the Germans had left. But there was something more. All of them had come to the war to defeat the Nazis, and each of them would have a picture in his mind of how he could best accomplish that. Keaver had read accounts of how the Germans in the First World War had come out of their trenches at Christmas time with their portion of a feast, and that was the picture that had stayed in his mind, Germans surrendering not with their hands raised but with their arms full of peace offerings, a meal they could all share. Hitler and his SS thugs would be excluded, of course. They would simply be driven off the field.

How had Bob Langley envisioned the end of the war? What was that final picture he carried in his head? Wallace Keaver could look up at his friend, as Bob looked out over the *Champs-Élysées*, and convince himself it all came down to that. Like the rest of them, Bob had a vision of how it would end and of the part he would play in it, and it wasn't of a man of his stature and command craning his neck to see Churchill and de Gaulle driving by, of that Keaver was sure. There was something far-seeing in Bob's expression and something puzzled and pained, as if his friend couldn't quite see far enough. Only far enough to know that it wouldn't end like this. Not with these two clowns driving by. Not Abbott and Costello to end the war that ended the war that had been fought to end them all. A modest man when it came to reading the minds of others, Wallace Keaver knew to a certainty that was not the picture Bob Langley carried up there.

December, Christmas season, a numbing cold and a gray-tinged snow, and the end of the war put on hold as Hitler counterattacked where only a desperate man would, through the wooded valleys known as the Ardennes. With his Panzer divisions and what was left of the Luftwaffe and a Wehrmacht reinforced by middle-aged men scraped off of the streets and boys of sixteen taken out of schools, Hitler disregarded the advice of his generals and under an artillery barrage drove into the Ardennes as the phone in my father's study began to ring. Hitler's objective was to open a breach between the British forces in the north and the Americans in the south, cross the Meuse and take as many channel ports as he could, with Antwerp being the prize, and my father's phone never ceased to sound the alarm. Towns in the Belgian Ardennes began to fall, and the vital crossroads town of Bastogne, commanded by Brigadier General Anthony McCauliffe, came under siege. In Verdun, where during the First World War three battles had been fought for a negligible stretch of land and a million had died, Patton assembled his Third Army and began a three day march to McCauliffe's relief, while in Paris the 107th made ready to relieve Patton once the siege had been lifted, and Christmas came with its bells in the most beautiful city in the world and the alarm continued to sound.

"I'm here. Where are you?" my sister said.

Where I'd been, I said.

I heard airport loudspeakers and crowds of herded people, and she heard a crowded quiet and a thunderous silence of guns.

"I thought you'd be here, Jay. I'm the only family you've got. I talked myself into believing you'd come pick me up."

No, I said. I wasn't sure she was coming.

"I told you I was. We made a deal."

And I hadn't reneged, I told her. I'd never stopped holding on.

"You don't know how badly you need to get out of that house and into your car. If you did know, I wouldn't have to be here. You don't know, Jay."

No, I said.

"What do you mean, no? Jay, don't do this to me, please. Meet me halfway. Are you coming or not?"

Not now.

"Not now? And what is that supposed to mean? When? I'm alone here, you know. This is one of the biggest airports in the world, and I don't recognize a soul."

I told my sister she'd been gone too long.

"I'm here now."

Her voice sounded weak, petulant, little girlish, stripped bare. She sounded as if she had no resources left and was running on past grievances, as when a family had been out to thwart her, except she no longer believed it, so finally she just sounded lost. In an airport so colossally outsized there was no way pitted against it she could survive.

All I had to do was step outside, I told her, and a familiar face would drive by. Donnie Abbott had asked about her. Did she remember him?

"Jay! Donnie Abbott? No," she confessed, a peeved sigh. "Who is he?"

Worked for our Uncle Raymond. Then bought the store from him? She might remember him as just one more young man who had idolized our father.

I heard what sounded like the start of a groan, something she bit back on. Then she surprised me. She won my attention. She said, "How is our father? Where is he now? Where have the two of you gone?"

Paris, I said.

"Paris?" she said. "Paris, France? Our father was there? Are you sure?"

Positive, I said.

"But he's not there now," she said.

I said he was leaving.

"Leaving? Jay, are you coming to get me or not?"

I said he was leaving in the coldest winter on record in years—

She actually interrupted me. "Isn't that what they always say, 'the coldest winter on record in years?'"

In this case it was true. In the coldest winter on record in years he was marching to a field in the Ardennes.

"With his army buddy," she said, without mocking me. I made sure. Then she said, "I've forgotten his name."

Wallace Keaver. Or Walter. There was some debate about that.

"Who's debating?"

I meant it was still up in the air.

"Jay," she said, "are you coming or not?"

I told her she'd caught me at the worst possible time. I mentioned the name of Patton, and then she did groan and asked me to stop. She was my sister, we'd grown up side by side. She wasn't even sure if Patton was a real figure or someone she'd seen a movie about. I heard flights being announced, and then it occurred to me, perhaps at the same moment it occurred to her: she could get on the next one and go back. In one sense we had almost nothing in common, but in another I knew my sister and I thought exactly alike.

"Jay..." she said, allowing a space to grow after my name.

I told her where she could rent a car. I told her the corridors and escalators she would need to take to get to the car rental counters, and then I told her the numbers of the expressways that would take her to the belt that circled the city. I got her to write it all down. The numbers and the names.

Then I stressed that she was not to take the expressway here. It wouldn't work that way. She should get off the belt onto 51 north and drive down along the old train tracks. I named the little whistle stop towns she would pass on her left. I told her if she kept her eyes open on her right she would see the remains of some old lumber mills and poultry huts. If she turned off the AC and let down a window she might be able to pick up a lingering trace of their scent. That would lead her back to a time when the scent was real and pretty rank and nothing had been decided yet. Not definitively, not for good. Meanwhile, I said. But I didn't continue.

"Meanwhile what?" she said.

Meanwhile I would be here, I answered.

"In the coldest winter in years?"

Just when they'd thought the war was over.

"Isn't that the way it always is? You start to celebrate and the nightmare begins again."

I didn't answer her. She was talking about her own life. Long before the rest of us had, she'd buried the man, gone to her river, stepped free from all that oppressed her, and entered its flow. Then her nightmare had found her again.

"Jay," she said, "on second thought, I don't think I will rent a car. I think I'll call Karen Ambrose instead. She doesn't live far from here. She'll be happy to come get me, and together we can come find you. All right, Jay? Is that what you prefer? Tell me, Jay."

I told her the nightmare was never over. That didn't mean that sooner or later you couldn't win.

"What was that place you said?"

Place? Paris?

"No, not Paris."

She meant the Ardennes.

"Yes. If that's where you're going, be back when we get there," she said. She issued her command. "Otherwise…"

I waited. I waited longer than I should have, and the tanks and trucks began to rumble past the column of marching men on a road open to the weather and a gusting wind. There was a battle up ahead. Artillery mixed with the stuttering clatter of machine gun fire and the compressed thud of mortars. The marching men made no sound. Bob Langley, Wallace Keaver, Randy Majors and Peter Brockbauer were soldiers now, in the business of transporting themselves. The snow was up to their knees.

Otherwise? I finally said into a dead phone.

My sister had begun her approach.

And the battle the 107th marched to continued to recede. Patton's army had relieved the besieged forces at Bastogne. It was as if the sound of their battle had been left in the air, as if the closer the 107th got the farther they had to travel to reach a battle that had already been won. The land they marched over in the blowing snow was invisible to them, but until they passed Reims it was as broad and flat as the American Midwest. They were dressed in all the clothing they could find. Field jackets and full-length wool overcoats. Wool knit caps under their helmets, two pair—American wool and German leather—of gloves. Double socks. Galoshes, stuffed with scraps of cloth and newspaper, over their boots. For warmth—and a sense of direction, a sense of purpose—they tried to fall in behind the tanks, but all too often they were left to follow the man in front of them, who followed the man in front of him. It was like a buddy system when they were kids. Going into battle they were loaded down with ammo for their M-1's and their Smith and Wesson's, and hand grenades hung heavy from their cartridge belts, but children will plow doggedly ahead if they can be made to believe that a grand time awaits them in the winter wonderland just over the hill.

Hills had begun to appear and patches of forest. When the wind fell and the snow abated they saw that they were now marching up valleys. The battle sounds were out there, swelling and subsiding, it seemed, on the strength of the wind, but the snow was too deep and their progress too slow to allow them to catch up. All they knew was that General Patton awaited them in Bastogne, where they would offer relief to the most famous fast-marcher in American military history since Stonewall Jackson. To a man—Bob Langley foremost among them—they pictured Patton striking an embattled stance in the North African desert, his ivory-handled revolvers on prominent display. Patton knee-deep in snow belonged to a surreal world.

In the towns they passed the houses were made of brown stone and red brick. Some were blasted to their foundations, many were smoke-blackened shells. They found cellars to sleep in, and in those cellars, if they were lucky, they found caches of cognac and champagne. They drank—Bob Langley among them—to keep warm. Internal combustion, Randy Majors, their erstwhile mechanic, remarked, raising his bottle again and again. In the fields there was no shortage of frozen cattle. There were butchers among the soldiers, too, and butchers' knives appeared. Steak and champagne, and that voice Bob Langley carried inside him resumed its heckling. Too soft, too soft. The German you're bound to meet up with will be in better battle-trim.

They came to the French town of Sedan, located on the river Meuse, dominated by the biggest fortress any of them had ever seen. The Germans had been gone for days, but the fires still burned with a wintry sort of flame that gave off little heat. They crossed over into Belgium, where the snow was heavier still, and entered the forests the region was known for. They saw signs where in years past lumbering had taken place, but mostly they saw the gashes left by the artillery barrages. Bob Langley recognized beech trees by the silver of their trunks and the straight-standing firs by the feathery fineness of their needles; they had been snapped like so many twigs. Shell craters and foxholes appeared. Burned-out half-tracks and tanks. Both Americans and the Germans had advanced and retreated through this forest, and the men of the 107th began to see the dead. Arms and legs stuck out of a snowdrift, the round of a shoulder, the bearded, ice-grayed side of a head. Those who had crawled from the burning tanks lay black as charred timber against the white of the snow. Of the bodies sprawled out in the open, it was frequently impossible to tell GI's and Germans apart. The Graves Registration units, responsible for retrieving the remains of dead, were reputed to be among the most efficient the Army had, but many of these bodies had had their uniforms stripped off by soldiers seeking further protection against the cold, and once down to the frozen flesh Americans and Germans looked pretty much the same. As an identifying measure, a M-1 with its bayonet stuck in the snow and a helmet balanced on top seemed almost quaint.

A dead soldier sat in the roadside ditch with half-closed, iced-over eyes watching them pass. This man they were sure was a GI since his dog tag had been stuck in his mouth. But there was a good chance a body positioned like that with the dog tag stuck there like a lollipop had been booby-trapped, and they were warned not to touch him. A dog tag in the mouth was standard operating procedure, but they had begun to notice that many of the dead soldiers they thought were GI's no longer had theirs, which probably meant the Germans did. A dog tag left invitingly in place should have set off an alarm. But they were exhausted and half-frozen. They were inexperienced. They had not seen war-dead before, and a man sitting beside a road the way men back home sat on their porches to watch the world pass by spoke to them. It made them want to reach out. They touched their own dog tags instead and averted their eyes.

They continued to hear the remains of battles up ahead. Isolated bursts of machine gun and small arms fire. Muffled rounds of artillery. Overhead, bombers passed, but with the cloud cover so dense they didn't expect to hear bombs, even though they would convince themselves they did. Once they heard what they were sure was a Hitler buzz bomb headed for Antwerp or Calais that had gone off course. Its buzz was an icy-high whistle, and they waited for it to suddenly cease, which would mean it had begun its descent. In reality, any sound they couldn't identify they attributed to one of the many secret weapons Hitler was said to possess, any of which could come down on them.

They emerged from the forest into a narrow Belgian valley where they came to a town. This town had escaped bombing, and its houses and its church were faced with rhomboidal cuts of slate. In spite of the armies that had marched through it, the town still smelled of cows. The Americans were welcomed and immediately treated to stories of German atrocities. The town might have still been standing but many of its inhabitants weren't, and the GI's were shown the graves in the churchyard where twelve of the town's elders lay, freshly slaughtered by Germans, retaliated against in advance for the welcome they were sure to give the Americans. This had been German practice in town after town. A pregnant woman had had her belly ripped open and her unborn child brought out on the point of a bayonet. When Hitler's forces had broken through at the onset of their attack, they had taken eighty-one American prisoners in the town of Malmedy and executed them all. Whatever the Americans wanted the Belgians were happy to provide, as long as the GI's would drive the Germans back beyond the Rhine and keep them there.

Randy Majors wanted to know what they were doing stopping there. Patton was the man to drive the Germans back into their bunkers, and the sooner they joined him the sooner he could get the job done. Peter Brockbauer had to agree. There was a time for a measured response, but that time had passed, and once they reached Bastogne their best course lay in linking up with Patton's army, driving into Germany, and in effect saving the Germans from themselves. Wallace Keaver sighed heavily and closed his eyes. Nothing in him thrilled to the display General George Patton so boastingly made of himself, but in this frozen ground these were freshly dug graves, and somehow it all had to stop. Hitler was beaten, but a half-dead man could continue to kill if he had the means and lacked the...what? The humanity? That was the problem. Hitler was human, just as Churchill and de Gaulle were. It did no good to call him evil incarnate and fail to recognize the sort of human he was. Patton, with his six-shooters on his hip, was another sort of human. Wallace Keaver looked at his friend Bob Langley.

Bob Langley looked away. Yes, he had made that promise to his wife. He had made it at the train station. As they had once put a young man named Steve Mitchell—hardly a man, more of a boy—on the train, so they had now gone to see Bob himself off. Judy had been in her mother's arms, and his sister Louise had come too. At the last minute, as the whistle blew, Fran Langley passed Judy on to her aunt and took Bob aside. She placed her hands on both sides of his head and, seemingly at his height, looked directly into his eyes. Straggling men were hurrying to get on board, but Fran established a no-go zone around her and regarded her husband for what might have been minutes, might have been hours, there was no way to say. Then she told him who he was. With more authority than any officer would ever address her husband, and with the warmth of her hands flush on his face, she told him he had a family back here and here was where he belonged. She did not say he had left a part of himself growing in her womb—she didn't need to because he would have known she spoke for them all. Then she extracted his promise, which was the same as having him repeat, I am Bob Langley and I will continue to be Bob Langley till the end of time. His sister Louise was standing there, in case there was any doubt. Bob Langley will not put himself in harm's way. Bob Langley will return. Bob Langley will go on and on. Bob Langley will not be the last man killed in any man's war.

This Belgian valley was snowed in. There was the blurred suggestion of upland pastures, and the ashy grayness and the darkened green of forests on the slopes. Down the valley ran a frozen stream. American war machinery came and went with a succession of snorts and snow-crunching growls. How did Bob Langley feel about linking up with General Patton, driving into Germany, avenging the Belgians, the Jews, the Brits who had withstood the blitz, the Russians who had been so foully double-crossed, any number of little countries that had been sucked into the German maw? Avenging his brother Raymond and maybe the smallest wound he had ever seen, a little whirlpool of flesh that traced the descent of a German bullet until it squeezed shut and never ceased to speak?

How did he feel about that?

He shouldered his pack, shouldered his weapon, and fell into line.

They crossed a river named the Semois, on a pontoon bridge the engineers had laid down. Whether in the haste of an American retreat or a German one, half-tracks and tanks had gone partially under, leaving jagged rifts in the ice. He was reminded of Omaha beach, the ebb and flow of the rubble there, the waste.

Fresh snow fell heavily, and they all knew those humped shapes they saw in the fields or in the ditches or in the woods, and which on other occasions might have been taken for bales of hay or piles of manure or the decaying trunks of trees, were bodies. Back in the fir forests the snow piled up on the overhead limbs and created tunnels, which they trudged through the way anybody passes through a tunnel, awaiting a blossoming of light and release at the end. There was no release and the light failed to bloom. They heard those distant thuds and a stuttering of gunfire, they did and they didn't, and a truck was always stuck in the snow, and, with a clanking of treads, a tank was always climbing a hill. There was a string of muttered curses back and forth in line, then a silent laboring of muffed footfalls and shuddering breaths. The cold sharpened their senses, then numbed them, and their salvation lay not in Patton awaiting them in Bastogne but in a moving line, a body of troops going somewhere, for once they stopped the cold with its silent stealth took possession of them and cut off any avenue of retreat. It was as if a little ice age had fallen on them there in the Ardennes. It was as if a glacier were moving down the road to meet them and the war was between forces of nature and not men.

They entered the town of Bellevaux, clustered in the bowl of a valley. The name of the town meant "beautiful valley," which they would have to take on trust. Some of the slate-fronted houses had been hit, but the church, with its adjoining graveyard, still stood. Snow was mounded over fresh graves. They would hear the horror stories and then they would be invited to occupy cellars and barns and to help themselves to strong Belgian beer. They smelled cows and took heat off the cows, and during the night a young Belgian girl entered the barn where Bob Langley and his three friends slept and slipped in among them and slept in their heat. She'd been terrified by the Germans. As best as Wallace Keaver could understand, she reasoned if the Americans allowed her to sleep in their midst they wouldn't kill her. She had a thin face and a cold bony chin, and no sooner had her life started than she had nothing left to lose. They gave her candy and sticks of gum.

Before they left Bellevaux they were warned by Americans in a field hospital there that on the road to Bastogne they might encounter some resistance. Disoriented Germans might still be wandering through the forests up there. With the weather as bad as it had been, no one had been able to distinguish the terrain they were taking from terrain they were giving up. The logging roads in those forests went in circles, and if you took a wrong turn you could end up mounting a rear guard attack on yourself. Germans had been dressing as GI's; they had dog tags, they had names. Some of them knew how many home runs Babe Ruth had hit in 1927, or how many bases Ty Cobb had stolen in 1915. But not many knew who Betty Grable's husband was, or Jane Russell's. They should have a question ready. A question they could answer themselves. This battle had been as close to chaos as they'd come during the entire war, and if they knew one thing for a certainty they should cling to that.

Wallace Keaver did not know who Betty Grable's husband was, although Jane Russell's he did. With Peter Brockbauer it was the reverse. That morning they marched off on the road to a town called Neufchateau with images of Betty Grable's or Jane Russell's legs flashing before their eyes, in effect taking their not entirely remembered husbands' places.

Bob Langley began to think of a question.

The snow was not quite as heavy as the day before. The battle sounds seemed routine, a muffled explosion, a muttered response of small arms fire, and then a workaday silence in which they could hear the rise and fall of the wind, also not as willful and punishing as it had been. They emerged from a forest and crested a hill and fell out beside the road for a K-ration lunch of dog biscuits and cheese flecked with ham. They did not sit. They stood and smoked and stamped their feet. Before they started up again a wind had risen and with it snow, blowing in near-horizontal sheets.

Who was Blondie's husband, and who made for himself a sandwich as tall as the Empire State building?

They marched on in the snow, as blindly as sheep, trusting their leaders that this was the road to Bastogne and the first leg of their advance on Germany, where they would make good on every just grievance, and certain doubters and naysayers and string-pulling daddies would be hooted off the stage.

Who climbed the Empire State Building holding a blonde in one hand and shaking his free fist at the world?

Briefly, they were in a forest again, in as tight a passage as they'd negotiated the whole march. When they came out, the ordnance and supply trucks stuck to the road as, on one side of a hedgerow, it worked its way down a hill. On the other side the men, Bob Langley among them, fanned out over a field as if to stretch their legs and take one long, unconstrained breath. They were in a cow pasture, many times larger than those in Normandy. Hard to their right was a beech forest, diagonally past that a forest of firs, a dark clouded green in the blowing sheets of snow. Down the slope directly ahead there appeared to be an opening in a hedge where cattle might wander in their leisure from one pasture to another and through which a company of soldiers might pass. At the limit of hearing Bob Langley heard a patter of shooting, such a domesticated sound it reminded him of his mother stitching away on her foot-pedal Singer with her mind somewhere else. The memory came to him unbidden, and a smile of fair boding formed on his mouth.

"Hen-reeeee! Hen-ree Al-drich?" Every Thursday evening, who said that?

Huey, Dewey, and Louie Duck had a mother. What was her name?

In the coldest winter on record for years, they were all near to numb. For that reason, any stinging show of life, though painful, was taken as a gift, so that when Bob Langley felt such a life-affirming pain in his left calf it brought to his mouth another smile. Somehow, it took its place in the picture he retained of his mother at her machine, her foot pumping heel to toe for each piece of stitching she wanted done, and he could imagine her needle entering his flesh but only as she might shake him back to life in the mornings, saying, Bobby, time to get up. Don't want to be late for school.

Then it occurred to him he might have been shot, and only then did he remember in the midst of all the motor noise coming from behind the hedgerow to his left a quiet cracking sound from the fir forest diagonally down to his right, a sound so incidental and remote it didn't seem possible he could have heard it or that it could have resulted in a bullet traveling from there to here and burying itself in his leg. At such a distance and in such sight-obscuring snow, it seemed like a miracle of some sort, an act of marksmanship that had one chance in a million to succeed.

In that first moment it didn't occur to him to take cover. It was more the opposite. He stood there wondering what the chances were it could be done again.

Then, as he watched his friends and comrades in war trudging on through the snow and down the slope, he laughed at himself. Of course, he hadn't been shot. The war was out there, somewhere beyond the last field, and he had been singled out to receive a projectile of some other sort, some strange European out-of-season insect had stung him, or perhaps something meteorological, a tiny little meteorite itself had found its way down to earth and entered his flesh. It took him a moment before he actually removed his gloves and with his right hand felt under his overcoat and field jacket to the hole in his pants legs the bullet had made. He wore two pair of pants and there were two holes, and he worked his finger through both. The wound was there, a rawness that was not yet bloody and hadn't really begun to throb. He didn't need to uncover it to know what it would look like. The rawness would soon be converted into a little cartilaginous whorl, and he too would have another mouth through which he could speak. He removed his finger and covered the wound back up. He looked up and found himself smiling in the blowing snow in the direction of the fir forest.

Only then did it become clear to him. He'd been shot by a sniper stationed in that fir forest, and if he continued to stand there, in a wide-open field, he'd be shot again. It was his wife's voice he heard then. Get down, Bob! Not everybody loves you! Somebody's trying to kill you out there!

He dropped out of sight, face down into the snow. He found a little cavity in which to breathe and lay like that considering his options until his wound finally did begin to throb. Packed in snow, he believed, it was unlikely to bleed heavily, and the throbbing was like an SOS he was sending to himself. He raised his head out of the snow, just enough to see the last members of his company passing through that breach in the hedgerow, exactly the way cattle, heavy-coated and plodding, returned to their barn at night. One of his options was to try to cross that field and join his company. Another was to somehow crawl back to the road and put himself into the hands of a medic. A third was to lie there and play dead in hopes of luring that sniper into closer range. There was a fourth. He could turn and bellycrawl his way under the cover of the snow back to that forest of beech trees, where he could sit with his back to a trunk and give himself perfect field position. He could wait for the German to emerge from that fir forest. A hunter's code was in effect here. If you killed your prey you retrieved it. Whatever you wounded you put out of its misery. You didn't leave duck, quail, rabbits, possum, or deer to bleed to death in a slow agony. You emerged from your blind or your perch in a tree and finished what you started. If his German did that, Bob Langley further reasoned, the two of them would be like-minded enough to conclude a pact. Why should this war go on with all its senseless brutality and destruction when two men could settle it right here? The world could be reduced to rubble, or two men fighting a single combat in a cow pasture in Belgium could find a cleaner, less wasteful way. He lay wounded in the snow considering his options, and the one he liked best was this last, two men coming together on the field of battle to settle the world's differences between them.

Bob Langley reasoned he could kill a single last German and end the war.

As he'd once bellycrawled under barbed wire with machine gun fire passing thirty inches above his head, he turned in the snow and like a mole dug his way back up to that forest of beech trees, where he pulled himself up behind a trunk and waited for his German to emerge. He was not sure of the time of day—sometime in the afternoon because they'd stopped to eat lunch. The wind rose and fell and with it his visibility over that field. The men from his company had long since gone, which included Wallace Keaver, Randy Majors, and Peter Brockbauer, but other men from his regiment were wandering through and Bob Langley sat against his tree with his M-1 laid over his lap and, when the snow permitted, watched them pass. Of course, he was reminded of the dead GI sitting beside the road with the iced-over eyes and the dog tag stuck in his mouth, but there was all the difference in the world. That GI was content to watch the world ebb and flow before him; Patton could give way to Churchill and de Gaulle, Hitler to Ike, and he would not have blinked. In his icy indifference that GI was a trap. Whereas Bob Langley was clearly annoyed with these straggling members of the 107th, whose desultory movement across that field was worse than cattle. Cattle had a barn to return to at night, while these soldiers in their aimlessness simply cluttered up the field.

Like his German in the fir forest, he waited for them to pass. A true sportsman would wait. A less than true sportsman might have given in to his boredom and impatience and taken a shot at one of these remaining members of the 107th, but that was not the German Bob Langley had across from him in that fir forest. Bob had his counterpart, whose name, until he knew better, he decided would be Hans. Like Bob Langley, Hans came from a small German town and was used to performing on center stage, and like Bob Langley, Hans in that moment was telling himself to let the stage clear. Both these men had been used to preliminaries; before the varsity match the jayvees had to play. The jayvees' clumsiness only whetted the fans' appetite for sportsmen who wasted no motion and whose skills on the field of play came as naturally as buds to the trees. For sportsmen like Bob and Hans, there was no such thing as a stray bullet in the air. True sportsmen were not hit by stray bullets in the air; nor did they stumble and shoot themselves. They were only hit by bullets for which they had been singled out.

Bob reminded himself that not all Germans were honorable men. In starting a second war soon after losing the first, they had not behaved honorably. He didn't doubt it. But he had not been hit by one of them. There was a keenness to the pain he felt; in the little heartbeat of its throb, there was an intimacy that didn't allow him to doubt that the man who had inflicted it on him would do the honorable right thing.

Hans, who confessed to chopping down an innocent little cherry tree? Who walked three miles in the snow to return a single penny to an overcharged customer?

Hans, who said, Why doncha come up and see me sometime?

He smiled. Although he didn't need to, he checked his M-1 to make sure it had a full clip of ammunition, his Smith and Wesson to make sure it contained six bullets. His bayonet was fixed. He felt for his trench knife on his hip. With his extraordinary throwing arm the weapon that would have given him a decided advantage were his hand grenades, but perhaps for that reason he resisted them. Or perhaps because when he threw a baseball or a football or anything else up into the sky there was something about its long vanishing arc that went beyond playing fields and scorekeeping and gave him a moment's pause. What if the ball hadn't been caught and the winning touchdown, say, hadn't been scored, would he have walked away an unhappy man? What if he lost a game but the ball he'd thrown had sailed out of sight? A bomb blast at the conclusion of something he'd hurled into the air was sickening to think about and out of the question, of course. He left his hand grenades on his belt.

He would shoot Hans, instead. That was the weapon his opponent had selected, and he would honor the choice.

He picked up his rifle and sighted it along the mole-like path he'd dug in the snow. He came to where he'd been hit and where he'd fallen to the ground. Men had trampled through the field since then and snow had continued to fall, but Hans would know the spot and before the day was over would come to it. He would examine the ground carefully, perhaps detect drops of blood, and then as any hunter must, he would follow the trail his wounded prey had left up to the beech forest. And once he was close enough to be looked in the eye, Bob Langley would emerge from behind his tree trunk and shoot him.

He waited all afternoon, until the light withdrew back into the forests and the snow itself turned a ghostly black. Contrary to what certain people would come to believe, he did not pass out. Nor did the army desert him. Trucks and tanks continued to pass going down the hill beyond the hedgerow, and when they no longer did it wasn't because they were turning their backs on Bob Langley or giving him up for lost. They were refueling to continue the advance. A soldier in Bob's company had gone AWOL in France. It turned out he'd had family on the outskirts of Paris and had overstayed a visit and was teetering on the brink of becoming somebody else, and the army had gone out and claimed him. The army brought back its own. Only someone sitting at his side and aware of his thoughts could know how little Bob Langley blamed the army for anything. On the contrary, the army had brought him here and set him against this beech tree and provided him with the sort of wound that spoke clearly and unfalteringly on a three throb beat: End the war. End the war. Even at the darkest moment of the night when the wind itself seemed to freeze and nothing moved—not the loose snow fallen on the trampled field, not a frozen twig in the limbs overhead—Bob Langley had nothing but positive thoughts about the army. The army had given him this chance. The army had not trained him for this singular occasion because there was no way to train a natural. But the army had chosen the right man.

Hans, his German counterpart, of course, failed to appear. But not until dawn did Bob Langley's thoughts turn dark. Until then, if he harbored in his innermost thoughts a killing, he was nonetheless the Bob Langley that everyone admired and he'd sworn to his wife he would remain. Without putting it in so many words, he understood that all the baskets and touchdowns and runs he'd scored were in preparation for this moment. That he'd been deceived by Charles Moody and his underlings and held back until now also played. That his wife had extracted from him that promise, just as she'd extracted his seed, only meant that in ways she might never understand she remained at his side. He talked to her. Argued, good-naturedly, a bit. When she suggested they give up the vigil, he wondered where her spirit of adventure had gone, and she immediately gave in. They might have been sitting with their heads tilted together, bundled up for winter on a day bright with spring, so like-featured they could have been mistaken for twins. They looked into the future—all clear. If they saw a war out there they also saw the war's end. If they saw a dark night, they saw a radiant dawn. If they saw a frozen field on which blood would be spilled, they saw the abundance which the field could be expected to yield, which would sustain generations to come. Children begetting children and family reunions growing exponentially on cow pastures around the world. They saw their daughter coaxed out of all future foul humor by the cardinals at her window and the soothing depth in her father's voice. They saw their son, not as if he stood on the other side of a widening divide, but at their side, privy to their every thought, their unspoken desires, their secret deeds, about which authoritative versions could now be told. Bob Langley spent the last night of his life as the Bob Langley everyone knew in the company of his wife, just as Hans in his fir forest spent his last night in the company of his wife, whose name almost certainly was Hanna.

Hans, who is Bob Langley married to?

Hans, who's the luckiest guy in the world to have Fran Langley as his bride?

But just before dawn, Hans reconsidered his options and rather than step out onto that field decided to go back and die in the rubble of his country in the company of his Hanna, and Bob's wound flared up in protest. The pain that had kept numbness away now became the pain of a burning aggravation. He felt down his pants leg again and worked his finger through the double hole. He detected no slickness of fresh blood, but the area around the wound was too inflamed to touch. He pulled his finger back and began inching forward to see how close he could get and was a little alarmed but mostly angered when he discovered that too-sensitive-to-touch area had extended well up his leg. By shifting position he gave himself a moment's relief, but what had been a tolerable throb soon became a hammering. He blamed Hans, not for shooting him but for making him wait all night. For jilting him, really, for that was what it had come down to. He withdrew his hand and muttered with some affection, but with a mean streak, too, "Goddamn it, Hans, you fucking kraut!" Then as the darkness dimmed around him and a grayness breathed up out of the earth, he closed his eyes and gave himself five minutes sleep.

When he woke he heard truck and tank traffic moving down the road. The day had dawned clear and up through the empty beech branches he could see pale blue glimmers of sky. It was the first clear day they'd had in he couldn't remember how long. But the blue of the sky did not look fresh born. It had a pallor to it, an Old World cast, so to say that the dawn had broken clear was to exaggerate. He could only say, it was no longer snowing, visibility was available, what passed for blue was in the sky. He pulled himself around and looked out at the field. He'd made a mess out there where he'd fallen in the snow, burrowing down, then frantically turning so that he could crawl flat on his belly to where he now sat. A cow might have flopped down there and rolled over. A cow might have fallen there, felled by a mine, and flailed around before coming to rest. Twisting to his right, he looked at the fir forest and saw a wall of straight-standing trees, without a gap or gash, a series of regularly spaced trunks against any one of which a sniper could have steadied his rifle and drawn his bead. Why hadn't Hans fired a second time, or a third? Bob Langley had a memory of standing out in that field like a bumpkin, wondering what it could have been that had ploughed into his leg, in a theater of war trying to decide what would be flying through the air at that kind of speed. Could it have been a bullet? Could he, Bob Langley, have been shot?

Hans, who said, There's a sucker born every minute?

Whether he knew it or not, right then, not when he'd been wounded and not during the night he'd spent waiting for his assailant to appear, was the crucial moment of his life. Had an American soldier or a Belgian farmer or even a disoriented German seeking a separate peace appeared and said, Here, let me give you a hand, Bob Langley might have leaned his wounded weight against that other and remained the Bob Langley his wife had seen off in the Russellville train station. Had Bob Langley had a gift for introspection and been able to talk to some part of himself that was not the part whose Daa-dee had dealt him so low a blow, then the Bob Langley that Hugh Langley knew and revered might have survived. Had Wallace or Walter Keaver, who had already gone into mourning over the loss of his friend, been able to retrace his steps through the snow and, instead of an enemy marksman or a hunter tracking his prey, approached the man seated with his back to a beech tree, and said, You see, Bob, not everyone's out to kill you, then it would have all been different, meaning Bob Langley might have continued the same. Or if Bob Langley had heard that distant stutter of gunfire and thought of his mother at her sewing machine again. Anything. If he'd thought of me, well along by then, ten fingers, ten toes, and all my faculties in the making, growing inside his dear wife's womb. If he'd thought of his wife, nothing else, just her, her eyes, her hands, the warmth she reserved for him at her heart's core. Anything. His daughter and the gurgling song she sang when the flutter of cardinals brought him into her room.

But he didn't. He saw the mess he'd made in the snow, he felt the mess of his wound as it spread up his leg, he admitted the mess his life had come to and the fool he'd been, and he knew he had a decision to make. He could stay where he sat. He could make it easy for the army and place his dog tag in his own mouth. He supposed with a hand grenade he could figure out some way to booby trap himself.

He could become the standing example of who not to be like, a sort of Babe Ruth to the army's concept of how a sensible soldier should behave. Or he could get to his feet and using his M-1 as a crutch hobble back to the road and let the army medics fix him up. He could tell them a story of how he'd spent the night waiting to gun down the German who'd taken that dastardly shot at him, and had withdrawn only when the 107th had safely passed through and he was assured the field was his. He could tell the story they'd all want to hear and make of himself a hero. Or he could shut up. He could let somebody else tell the story if anybody was that big a fool. There was no shortage of storytellers and no shortage of fools. Meanwhile, he would drag himself back to the army and, once they'd fixed him up, dedicate his life to living with eyes in the back of his head, a colder, shrewder, keener-sighted Bob Langley.

Which was what he did. With his rifle as a crutch, he hobbled out onto the field just as two things happened: a squadron of B-17's flew by overhead scattering shining pieces of silver foil in their wake to confound the German radar. The sky filled with that deep-bellied drone and infinitesimal, sun-struck specks. The second thing that happened was that Karen Ambrose and my sister drove up and parked out front, which I heard on an entirely different frequency, one reserved for a dailiness of things. Their car door opened and closed, their footsteps sounded on the walk, and the house door was next. Their voices were muted and matter-of-fact, not yet alarmed, as though they had yet to conclude one topic of conversation before they took up another. Then a third thing happened: his bayonet stuck in the frozen earth like the foot of a compass, my father turned back over his shoulder and with a head motion quick and curt, intemperate really, beckoned to me to join him. By all accounts, there was once a Bob Langley who had never been quick or curt and whose temperance had fallen like shining silver out of the sky onto a field of upturned faces. But that was not the Bob Langley I knew. My father extended his invitations once, and you either joined him or you didn't. Not many did, but I hurried to catch up.

I owe a lot to Marc Estrin and Donna Bister for extending themselves the way they have in the cause of "literary fiction," a near-extinct genre. Their Fomite Press is an invaluable, unaggrandizing labor of love. And to Fred Ramey of Unbridled Books for putting me on to them.

Fomite

A fomite is a medium capable of transmitting infectious organisms from one individual to another.

"The activity of art is based on the capacity of people to be infected by the feelings of others." Tolstoy, What Is Art?

Writing a review on Amazon, Good Reads, Shelfari, Library Thing or other social media sites for readers will help the progress of independent publishing. To submit a review, go to the book page on any of the sites and follow the links for reviews. Books from independent presses rely on reader to reader communications.

For more information or to order any of our books, visit
http://www.fomitepress.com/FOMITE/Our_Books.html

Nothing Beside Remains
Jaysinh Birjépatil

*The Way None
of This Happened*
Mike Breiner

*Summer on the
Cold War Planet*
Paula Closson Buck

*Foreign Tales of
Exemplum and Woe*
J. C. Ellefson

Free Fall/Caída libre
Tina Escaja

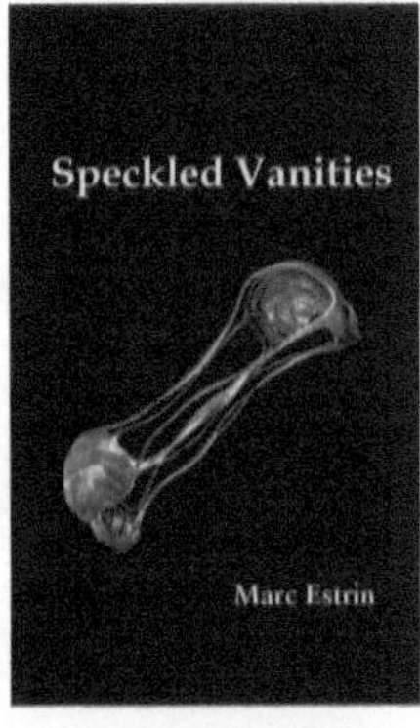

Speckled Vanities
Marc Estrin

Fomite

Off to the Next Wherever
John Michael Flynn

Derail This Train Wreck
Daniel Forbes

Semitones
Derek Furr

Where There Are Two or More
Elizabeth Genovise

The Three Lives of Jonathan Force
Richard Hawley

In A Family Way
Zeke Jarvis

A Rising Tide of People Swept Away
Scott Archer Jones

A Free, Unsullied Land
Maggie Kast

Shadowboxing With Bukowski
Darrell Kastin

Fomite

Feminist on Fire
Coleen Kearon

Thicker Than Blood
Jan English Leary

*A Guide
to the Western Slopes*
Roger Lebovitz

Confessions of a Carnivore
Diane Lefer

Born Speaking Lies
Rob Lenihan

*Unborn Children of
America*
Michele Markarian

Interrogations
Martin Ott

*Connecting the Dots
to Shangrila*
Joseph D. Reich

Shirtwaist
Delia Bell Robinson

Fomite

Isles of the Blind
Robert Rosenberg

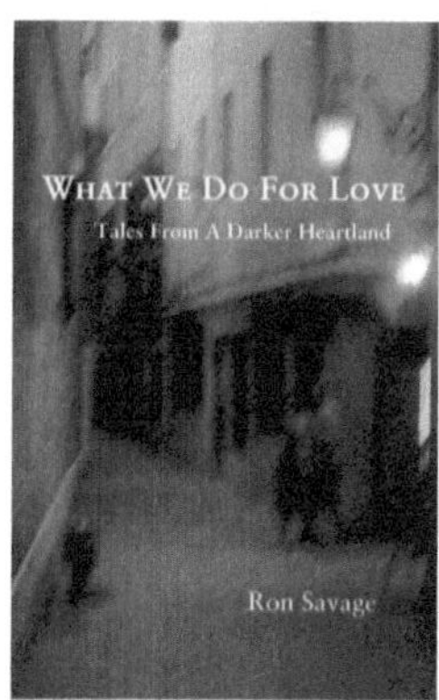

What We Do For Love
Ron Savage

Bread & Sentences
Peter Schumann

Principles of Navigation
Lynn Sloan

A Great Fullness
Bob Sommer

Industrial Oz
Scott T. Starbuck

Among Angelic Orders
Susan Thomas

A Day in the Life
Tom Walker

*The Inconveniece
of the Wings*
Silas Dent Zobal

Fomite

Ron Jacobs — All the Sinners Saints

Ron Jacobs — Short Order Frame Up

Ron Jacobs — The Co-conspirator's Tale

Kate MaGill — Roadworthy Creature, Roadworthy Craft

Tony Magistrale — Entanglements

Gary Miller — Museum of the Americas

Ilan Mochari — Zinsky the Obscure

Jennifer Anne Moses — Visiting Hours

Sherry Olson — Four-Way Stop

Andy Potok — My Father's Keeper

Janice Miller Potter — Meanwell

Jack Pulaski — Love's Labours

Charles Rafferty — Saturday Night at Magellan's

Joseph D. Reich — The Hole That Runs Through Utopia

Joseph D. Reich — The Housing Market

Joseph D. Reich — The Derivation of Cowboys and Indians

Kathryn Roberts — Companion Plants

David Schein — My Murder and Other Local News

Peter Schumann — Planet Kasper, Volumes One and Two

Fred Skolnik — Rafi's World

Lynn Sloan — Principles of Navigation

L.E. Smith — The Consequence of Gesture

L.E. Smith — Views Cost Extra

L.E. Smith — Travers' Inferno

Susan Thomas — The Empty Notebook Interrogates Itself

Tom Walker — Signed Confessions

Fomite

Sharon Webster — Everyone Lives Here

Susan V. Weiss —My God, What Have We Done?

Tony Whedon — The Tres Riches Heures

Tony Whedon — The Falkland Quartet

Peter M. Wheelwright — As It Is On Earth

Suzie Wizowaty —The Return of Jason Green

www.ingramcontent.com/pod-product-compliance
Lightning Source LLC
Chambersburg PA
CBHW032114180726
48284CB00002B/560